The Dog That Saved Stewart Coolidge

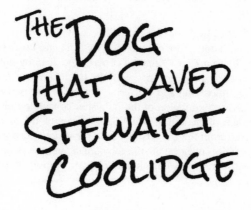

THE DOG THAT SAVED STEWART COOLIDGE

a novel

JIM KRAUS

New York Boston Nashville

Copyright © 2015 by Jim Kraus
Reading Group Guide copyright © 2015 by Hachette Book Group, Inc.
Preview of *The Dog That Whispered* copyright © 2015 by Jim Kraus
All rights reserved. In accordance with the U.S. Copyright Act of 1976, the scanning, uploading, and electronic sharing of any part of this book without the permission of the publisher constitute unlawful piracy and theft of the author's intellectual property. If you would like to use material from the book (other than for review purposes), prior written permission must be obtained by contacting the publisher at permissions@hbgusa.com. Thank you for your support of the author's rights.

FaithWords
Hachette Book Group
1290 Avenue of the Americas
New York, NY 10104

www.faithwords.com

Printed in the United States of America

RRD-C

First Edition: October 2015
10 9 8 7 6 5 4 3 2 1

FaithWords is a division of Hachette Book Group, Inc.
The FaithWords name and logo are trademarks of Hachette Book Group, Inc.

The Hachette Speakers Bureau provides a wide range of authors for speaking events. To find out more, go to www.hachettespeakersbureau.com or call (866) 376-6591.

The publisher is not responsible for websites (or their content) that are not owned by the publisher.

LCCN: 2015946134

ISBN: 978-1-4555-6254-1

To good dogs everywhere and to the humans that love them.

THE DOG THAT SAVED STEWART COOLIDGE

Chapter One

T HE DOG, who did not yet possess a name, stood no more than twenty feet from the twin automatic doors of the Tops Super Market in Wellsboro, Pennsylvania, trying not to be conspicuous. If anyone noticed him, they would think nothing was out of the ordinary, at least in Wellsboro, that is. Dogs, outside dogs, were not an uncommon sight.

This one particular dog, a sturdy animal, solid, with no pampered excess weight, perhaps even edging toward skinny, was of middling height and mostly black with white paws, muzzle, and chest, and a pencil-thin white stripe of fur running from nose to forehead. His deep-set, wide eyes glistened with intensity and showed a focused, steady gaze. He had arrived in Wellsboro that morning. He did not remember how far he'd walked. He did know that he was hungry.

And he knew that food came from buildings just like the one he stood in front of. He looked up at the sign above the door. It was not a sign that appeared familiar. He knew food came from other places, but he also knew that those places would not offer what this place did.

This dog possessed a keen intellect, and he appeared to be more aware of his surroundings than most people—as if he knew and sensed and felt everything that was occurring within a large radius, and nothing occurred within that circle that escaped his notice. He assumed all dogs, well, most dogs, dogs who spent time outside, possessed these abilities. And he considered some humans to be so aware, as well. But not many humans. Of that, he was certain.

The dog sat down and sniffed, his nose in the air, just slightly, opening wide to draw in one particular scent.

From beyond the whooshing doors came scents that he recognized. One, in particular, he took notice of. And when he was certain that it came from inside, he stood up and walked closer to the doors, then sat again, to the side, out of the way of customers, as if he had been told to sit there by some person.

And, in fact, a few people stopped, on their way out of the store, either carrying bags or pushing a cart. He could tell which people were dog people and which were not—and which were cat people, but they were of a different breed altogether.

The dog people had the scent of dog on them. That was an easy thing to discern. He could almost tell what sort of dog it was—small or large, male or female, young or old. Most of the time, anyhow. And a few of the dog people stopped and chatted with him.

"You're such a good dog," one lady said. "Your owner must be very confident."

Another woman, an older woman by the scent of things, stopped and patted him on the head. He looked up and smiled. He knew humans felt a special kinship when a dog smiled.

"Good dog," she said, her voice like wrinkled linen.

The dog waited until an older man walked up to the door. He did not stop to chat. He was not a dog person, but he moved slower than most. When the automatic door swished open, the dog stood and followed the old man, only a few steps back, but not close enough that he would be aware of being followed. The dog was convinced that the old man would not be observant enough, nor hear well enough, to hear the muted, quiet chatter of a dog's nails on the rubber mat.

When the second door opened, the dog smiled, just a little, more to himself than to anyone. He sniffed again. The scent was oh-so-obvious. There were scents of meat and fish and chicken and chemical smells and the scent of fresh-cut green things, but none of those mattered, not this morning.

The dog walked, with canine confidence, along the row of checkout counters, mostly unoccupied at the moment. After all, it was not that many hours since sunrise. Without hesitation, the dog turned and headed straight down the fifth aisle, not that he could count. It was the scent. Halfway down that aisle, amid the paper and kibble smells of long rows of bags of food, was what he had sought. He saw it and then he did smile fully—a bin of rawhide bones, at floor level, large rawhide bones. Smaller ones were kept higher up. Those he did not want.

The dog walked to the floor-level display and calmly grabbed the largest and the closest one to him in his mouth. He made sure he had a good grasp on it, turned around, and headed to the front of the store again.

If people saw him, they paid no notice.

That was unusual. In the past, someone, from somewhere, would get excited and call out.

Not today.

The dog walked slowly toward the doors again, watching carefully. A young woman, carrying a small person in one arm and a bag in the other, made her way to the rubber mat that would cause the door to whoosh open. The dog matched his pace to hers, and as she walked out, he accompanied her.

It was at that moment that the dog heard the shout.

He had heard such shouts before. They were usually too late to stop him, and this morning, he was already outside.

"Stop that dog!" a man shouted, his voice rising in intensity. "He didn't pay for that bone!"

The dog took off down Main Street at a trot. He was not certain where he would go, but soon enough, a quiet place would be evident, a safe, quiet spot, out of the way, almost hidden, where he could nibble off the plastic wrapper and begin gnawing on his breakfast, the first food he had had in a few days.

$\leftarrow$

Mr. Ralph Arden stood in the front of the Tops Super Market in Wellsboro, Pennsylvania, flapping his arms, looking much like a perturbed bird, or perhaps more accurately a perturbed, wet rooster, his white smock designating him as the store manager flapping along with him, the overstarched fabric creaking as it inhaled and exhaled, as it were.

When upset, Mr. Arden's voice rose in pitch, so his shouts of excitement sounded like the screech of a twelve-year-old boy. Or a twelve-year-old girl, depending on the severity of the situation.

This event had evoked his highest pitch.

"That dog stole from my store!" he shouted, glaring at the

two bag boys who were on duty that morning. "And you let him go!"

Mr. Arden tried to glare, did not do glaring well, and then pointed at the bag boy closest to the door. "You. What's-your-name. Go get him. That's one hundred percent organic gourmet rawhide and I want it back."

Stewart Coolidge pointed at himself in a puzzled manner.

"Me?"

"Yes. You. Go. Before he gets away."

Stewart shrugged as if this sort of activity was an everyday occurrence at the Tops Super Market in Wellsboro, which it wasn't, but Stewart did not feel up to discussing this aberration of employee responsibilities with his employer. So he took off, after waiting for Mrs. Grace Thickens, who stood, puzzled by the commotion, in between the two automatic doors.

By the time Stewart got to the street, all traces of the dog were gone.

If Stewart had had a dog with him, perhaps a bloodhound of some sort, he could have given chase, but he did not. So instead of running aimlessly, he set off with quick steps toward the west side of downtown, figuring he would search Main Street until he got to the Wired Rooster Coffee Shop, where he might catch a glimpse of Lisa Goodly, his downstairs neighbor.

No sense in wasting a break and having it end too soon. And the weather this morning is really . . . nice.

As Stewart walked, he felt something twinge, an unusual twinge, somewhere inside himself, as if this moment would be a moment he would look back upon and tell himself, *That's when it all started. Right there. On Main Street. In the spring. Chasing a dog.*

Chapter Two

STEWART RETURNED to the Tops Super Market empty-handed.

"Did you catch him?" Mr. Arden demanded. He must have remained on vigil, at the front of the store, waiting for a firsthand report on the chase and hopeful of apprehension of the thieving dog. Stewart imagined his level of success, or failure, was obvious, since he had returned without a dog or a rawhide chew.

"Nope," Stewart said. "I looked all over. But there wasn't any trace of him anywhere."

Mr. Arden drew his eyes nearly shut, puckering his lips in apparent disgust, but he held his tongue.

"Well, from now on," he said, his words clipped, "you will be responsible for making sure this . . . does . . . not . . . happen . . . again."

When Stewart had applied for this job a few months after his graduation from Penn State, he'd assumed it would only be temporary, until something better came along. He had never once imagined that his duties would include being placed on permanent dog patrol.

"Okay." Stewart had read somewhere that a worker should accept challenges without hesitation. *What's the worst that can happen?*

"I know dogs," Mr. Arden explained, "and I know criminals. Criminals return to the scene of the crime. That's a well-known fact. And so do dogs. That one, I could tell, he'll be back. A criminal dog, to be sure."

He stared at Stewart's name tag, which sat a few degrees off horizontal above his left pocket.

"And... Stewart, you'll be ready next time. Correct? Ready, right?"

Stewart nodded, feigning enthusiasm, then added, "You bet. I'll be ready."

But, as the tale unfolded, Stewart was not ready.

It was as if the dog had overheard the conversation and cleverly adjusted his modus operandi.

꘠

Stewart's shift ended at two in the afternoon, and he walked home, enjoying the pleasant weather. He walked because his 1997 Nissan had given up the ghost during the winter and Stewart spent hours debating with himself over the merits of spending good money on a very old car, or saving up slowly and buying a different car, but newer. Delaying his decision was the fact that springtime in Wellsboro, and perhaps everywhere in mid-central Pennsylvania, was a most pleasant season—sharp, crisp air, not cold, with the hint of warmer days to come, when the mornings were marked with an orchestra of birdcalls, and the scent of new greenings enveloped the area.

Stewart liked walking. It gave him time to think. And he had only a few places to go, and those didn't absolutely require a car.

Stewart thought he should be happier than he was, but he wasn't.

As he walked, he used his phone to check e-mails. There

was a spate of junk e-mail that he immediately deleted. There were a few Facebook postings from friends, nothing important. There were no e-mails from any corporation or business where Stewart had applied for open positions. Over the past months, Stewart had sent out dozens of e-mail applications and letters of inquiry, and had posted his résumé, scant as it was, on several job sites—all promising to deliver some sort of job.

"Nothing."

He turned off Main Street and walked down King Street and on to Rectory Lane, where he lived.

"Rats."

There might be a rectory on Rectory Lane, or had been one once, Stewart thought, but he had never seen any signs pointing to a rectory, nor were there any structures that looked like a rectory, although Stewart wasn't sure what your standard rectory was supposed to look like.

Maybe they don't want to advertise where they live. Priests, I mean.

Then he thought for a moment longer.

And I'm not sure just what a rectory is. Priests live in them, right?

Not being Catholic, or a functioning religious person in any denomination, Stewart had only a faint understanding of such things.

Midway down the block stood an old, hulking, nearly ramshackle, three-story Victorian house. Overgrown evergreen shrubs crowded the front, while gray paint peeled on the east side. The front porch listed, but the turret didn't, and most of the original decorative woodwork was still in place. Stewart occupied the entire top floor, which sounded large, but it was not. He stopped at the mailboxes on the front porch and pulled out a thicket of mail, the bulk of it made up of the weekly Tops Super Market flyer, which, of course, he had already seen, a large, glossy postcard from a local car dealer offering "Dyn-o-mite Deals," and a few credit card solicitations. There were no bills and no personal letters.

When was the last time I got a real letter in the mail? Must have been my birthday when my grandmother sent me a birthday card. Do birthday cards count as real mail?

He tossed all the mail into the blue recycling bin behind the house.

I think they do.

As he approached the back staircase, he noticed, just at the far corner of his vision, a slight blur, a black-and-white sort of blur. He spun around.

It's that dog.

But when he looked, there was nothing. The backyard had always been relatively unkempt, and the copse of bushes along the rear of the property line was more unkempt this year than last. If it had been a dog, it could have easily disappeared into the jungle of a new growth of weeds and vines and brush.

Maybe it followed me?

As he stood and looked, and listened, he told himself that it probably wasn't a dog, or, more specifically, that dog, and more likely a squirrel or a couple of squirrels giving chase.

After all, this is springtime and all that.

He walked up the two narrow and long flights of stairs, thinking about what he might have for lunch and wondering, for the hundredth time that week, about his decision to major in political science at Penn State and not something useful, and eminently employable, like nursing or computer repair, where he would be assured of a job at this moment.

No one could tell me anything back then, could they?

He stood in the middle of his small kitchen and looked out the eyebrow window, catching the first shafts of the afternoon sun. He wished things were different. He wished that the lost feeling inside his chest would dissipate, would lessen. But instead of growing smaller, the lost and alone and abandoned feelings grew.

Something has to change. Something has to be better than this. Life, I mean. Something better.

⤝

Stewart's late lunch consisted of macaroni and cheese—the Tops private label brand, which was on sale when Stewart bought ten boxes of it—and a banana.

I should probably eat better. Or more healthy. Healthier. Or something.

He read through this week's issue of the *Wellsboro Gazette.* The help-wanted section ran two full columns: bartender, road crew for asphalt repair, radio advertising sales, assistant track coach at Wellsboro Area High School, night custodian for the school district, part-time housekeeper, and kennel supervisor.

Stewart sighed and stared out the window of his tiny living room, situated in the house's turret, with two upholstered chairs and an ottoman taking up the majority of the floor space. The two oak trees out front had just started to green and he looked forward to the dappled sunshine they would allow once the leaves came in.

Maybe I could apply for that kennel position. I like dogs.

Then he remembered that he had never owned a dog growing up, only a cat, and that was just for two months, until his grandmother decided it was not a clean animal and sent it off to live with another relative.

They did say "supervisor." I'm not sure what a kennel supervisor does.

He tossed the paper to the floor.

I don't think I learned much about kennels in college. Or dogs.

From his perch he heard the familiar squeal of worn brake pads. He stood up and peered out the curved window that overlooked the street. He caught the flash of a faded red car. That would be Lisa coming home.

He checked his reflection in the small mirror by his front door and smoothed his short hair. He wished it were a more dramatic color than mousy brown, but that was what had come with him into adulthood. He always said that his hair matched the color of his eyes. He practiced a smile.

Not bad. Not Brad Pitt, but . . . okay. For Wellsboro.

He grabbed the small bag of trash he'd left by the steps and waited until he heard the downstairs door squeal open on its rusty hinges. Then he bolted out his door and hurried down the stairs.

He and Lisa met on the second-floor landing. Her apartment consisted of most of the west side of the second floor. It was a good deal larger than Stewart's, and he imagined that either the coffee shop paid better than Tops Market or her parents augmented her meager earnings with some sort of stipend or she was just wealthy on her own.

"Hi, Lisa," Stewart said as unrehearsed as he could.

Lisa smiled back at him as she fished her key out of her purse.

"Oh, hi, Stewart. You're off early."

"Morning shift this week," he replied, trying to be both blasé yet interested in conversation at the same time.

"Me, too. But I guess I don't start as early as you."

"I guess."

She inserted the skeleton key into the lock. Stewart imagined that any criminal with a bobby pin could pick all the locks in the house, but he also imagined them casing the residence and saying "Why bother," after looking at the general shabbiness of the place, and "What could be worth stealing in there?" Stewart's lock and key on his front door had been replaced when he'd moved in, and featured a contemporary latch/lever sort of mechanism, with a modern key, but was no more secure.

The lock clicked open and Lisa hesitated, just for a moment. Stewart managed to suppress his excitement.

"Anything happen at work today? I thought I saw you walking down Main Street this morning. Were you on your break or something? Do you get to leave the store on breaks? We don't."

A conversation starter, Stewart thought, almost rejoicing. For the past six months of being neighbors, he and Lisa had exchanged only a few dozen words—mostly "Hello"s and "Good morning"s. *Maybe she's coming around . . . or something.*

"No, we have to stay at the store, too. But this morning, well, I was out looking for a dog," he replied.

Lisa offered him the most curious—pert and curious and cute—glance.

"A dog?"

Stewart provided a review of the events of the morning, Lisa smiling and laughing at Stewart's imitation of Mr. Arden.

This is going great.

"So you never found the dog, right?"

"Nope. He vanished."

"He?"

"I assumed it was a he. Being a criminal and all."

Lisa offered a wry, mysterious smile.

"Well, maybe. I know some shes that are pretty shady."

Stewart tried to think of a witty reply, but nothing came to mind.

"Stewart, would you mind if I wrote about this? For the *Gazette*."

"You write for the *Gazette*?"

"Well, no, not exactly. But I did talk to the editor once and he said if I ever had a local story, maybe he would print it. You don't mind, do you?"

Think fast.

"No. I guess not. Just don't mention that I made fun of Mr. Arden. I think he's sort of sensitive."

"I wouldn't. I'll let you read it, if you want. I mean, before I send it in. I don't have to mention your name, if you don't want me to."

"Okay."

"And if I have any more questions, could I ask you later?"

"Sure."

"Thanks, Stewart. That's so nice of you."

"Okay. No problem."

Lisa flipped her longish blonde hair back over her shoulder and stepped inside her apartment.

Stewart took a breath and smelled lilacs. *Or some sort of flower. Floral.*

He sort of half-waved his good-bye and began to climb his steps back upstairs.

Before she shut the door, she stopped.

"Aren't you forgetting something?"

Stewart stopped cold.

Think fast.

And he didn't—think fast, that is.

"Your trash," Lisa said.

Stewart hoped he did not blush. He was not normally a blusher, but with Lisa, he wasn't sure.

"Oh, yeah. Trash."

"Well, bye," Lisa said, her smile almost a knowing one, as if she was aware of the effect she had on him. But Stewart was pretty sure she wasn't, or didn't know. The door closed with a ratchety, hesitant Victorian click.

And Stewart slowly descended the steps to the outside trash bins, all the while smiling broadly to himself.

Chapter Three

STEWART THOUGHT about going out that evening, but didn't. There were several bars in town within easy walking distance, but he never really felt comfortable going to bars. Perhaps he kept hearing his grandmother: *All rum is demon rum, all bars are the devil's playground, all women in bars are not the sort of women you would bring home to meet your family. Is some bar floozy the sort of woman you want to meet? I think not.* His grandmother, who had been the person most responsible for raising Stewart as a child, had grown more strident and brittle in the past few years, as if trying to make up for time wasted just being normal and not sort of church crazy.

And he did not like having to shout to carry on a conversation, which always happened in bars.

He wondered if Lisa went to bars. He saw her leave the house on occasion, always by herself, and return home at a relatively early hour.

He mentally replayed their conversation this afternoon.

She's probably not interested in a relationship. Probably not. And not with me, at any rate. I mean, let's be realistic here, Stewart.

He grabbed the TV remote and flipped through the channels.

I'm a bag boy at the Tops Market. Not exactly a position that attracts women. Not much of a future there.

He got up from the couch and walked the four steps into the small kitchen. He stared at the counter for a moment, weighing his options.

Maybe a cup of coffee.

He filled the electric kettle with water and set it to boil while he measured out the instant coffee and instant, powdered cream.

I could go down to the coffee shop where Lisa works and get a real coffee...but that's a ten-minute walk. And four dollars that I don't need to spend.

He waited for the kettle to reach temperature. On the one end of the counter was the Verse-a-Day calendar that his grandmother had sent him for Christmas. The top sheet still showed January 6: *Let your conversation be without covetousness; and be content with such things as ye have: for he hath said, I will never leave thee, nor forsake thee. Hebrews 13:5*

Stewart had read that same verse for four months.

I don't like to be reminded of what I'm not doing right. That is why she sent it. And I don't think I am being covetous...even though I'm not exactly sure what it means.

He had toyed with the idea of simply throwing the calendar away but worried that his grandmother, if she ever visited, which was highly unlikely, would look for it. And then what would he say?

Maybe I should start going to church, like she keeps telling me. "That's where you'll meet a nice girl," she says. "A girl you won't be ashamed of."

He poured the hot water in the cup and stirred it into a mud-colored mixture.

But wouldn't they know I'm there just to try and meet women? Hardly seems like a religious thing to do.

He walked back to his couch and set the cup on the small end table.

He stabbed at the remote again.

He got only a few network channels, sports channels, and that one that showed old TV shows, so there wasn't much to choose from.

Today, two college basketball teams were playing, neither of which he had any real interest in, but it was better than anything else he had come across.

Midway through the second quarter, the score at 35 to 39, Stewart sat bolt upright.

Was that a knock at my door?

He stood and waited. Then he heard the knock again, a polite, small knock, not demanding at all.

Not a Jehovah's Witness, I bet. Those guys are usually loud.

He hurried to the door, wiping his hands on the backside of his jeans.

In his doorway stood Lisa Goodly, with a small steno pad in her left hand and a pen in her right.

"Uhhh . . . hi."

"Hi, Stewart. I hope I'm not bothering you. Am I?"

"No. I was just watching some game. I'm not really sure who's playing, to be honest with you."

Lisa laughed.

I made her laugh. That's a good sign, isn't it?

"I had my doubts about guys and sports. You've just confirmed it," she said, her eyes sort of twinkling, Stewart thought. "Doesn't matter what it is, just as long as it's a sport."

Stewart grinned, hoping to match her amusement.

"And there wasn't anything else on I wanted to watch. Reruns of *The Andy Griffith Show* ran a close second."

"I love him," Lisa said. "And Floyd the barber is my favorite. Creepy, but funny."

Stewart nodded.

She can't be up here just to discuss my television habits. Can she?

"I wanted to ask you more about the dog. At the supermarket this morning."

It took Stewart a moment for the question to fully register.

"Oh, sure. Come on in. Sit down. Want coffee? All I have is instant. I have some tea, if you'd like."

Lisa demurred on refreshments. Instead she asked him if he knew the price of the rawhide bone—"Two seventy-eight, plus tax." And if he could give her a better description of the dog—"Not really. Black and white, but mostly black. Medium. Sort of longer hair, or fur, or whatever. You know, sturdy-looking. But I didn't get a long look at him."

At the end of the questions, Lisa closed her steno pad and sighed, loudly, for effect.

"Do you think he'll be back? The dog, I mean."

"Mr. Arden claimed it would. Maybe. Maybe it's hungry. It didn't have a collar. At least I didn't see one."

Lisa brightened, flipped open the steno pad, and scribbled that detail down.

It looks like she has good penmanship—even when she's writing fast.

"Stewart, this is such a cute story . . . but it just isn't long enough yet. If he comes back, will you tell me right away? And will you try and remember the details? Assuming you don't catch him, that is."

"Sure."

One reason not to catch him.

"I don't know if you knew that I majored in communications and journalism at Pitt."

"In Pittsburgh? I mean, at the Pittsburgh campus? That looked like a fun school. I had a friend who went there."

"No. The Johnstown campus. It was easier to get in and a lot cheaper since I could live at home."

"Sure."

"But I want to write. Or maybe be on TV. On the news. I thought that if I can start writing for the *Gazette* . . . it would look good on my résumé."

"Sure. Well, if the dog comes back, I'll let you know right away. Maybe I could take a picture. If I have time. And if Mr. Arden doesn't see me doing it. "

"Oh, Stewart, that would be just great. You are such a sweetie."

And with that Lisa gathered up her pad and pencil and departed, leaving Stewart sitting, smiling, with a cup of coffee that slowly grew colder and colder.

⌐

Stewart sat, for a long time, with the basketball game and the flickering blue light of the TV in the background, the sound muted, and stared out the window of the turret. He had cracked the window slightly. The third floor seemed to gather up all the heat in the house. It was great in the winter, not so great in the summer.

As he listened, he thought he heard the bark of a dog, down by the front porch. He tried to look out but the window would not budge open more than three inches.

Maybe it's that dog. And maybe . . . this is the start of something in my life. Wouldn't that be great?

Chapter Four

TWO DAYS PASSED.

There was no dog thievery at the Tops Market. And Stewart began to despair. And grow more and more disappointed.

So did Lisa—but she was disappointed for different reasons than Stewart.

At least we're talking every day, Stewart thought. *That's something. Even if it's only to ask about the dog.*

On the third day, the dog reappeared, and, as Mr. Arden would say, "the criminal returned to the scene of the crime."

Stewart saw him as he stood outside the automatic doors. But he did not say a word, or sound the alarm as Mr. Arden had requested.

I can't be totally sure it's the same dog. Maybe a customer left him out there. I don't want to upset a good customer just because of a case of mistaken identity.

Stewart kept to his work, and watched, just out of the corner of his eye. He also did not want to alert the proper authorities, at least not yet.

The next time Stewart looked over, the dog had disappeared.

Must have been a customer's dog.

But he also heard a commotion—a sort of small commotion in aisle five.

That's the pet food aisle.

Stewart grabbed his phone from his pocket and switched it to camera mode. He held it up, and from around the corner came the black-and-white dog, holding a large rawhide chew in its mouth, trotting, as casual as could be, through an open gap offered by an empty register, which had been secured with a small chain, hung at waist level, holding a sign that read CLOSED.

Stewart snapped three pictures.

Then he heard the clumping of a large man rapidly and clumsily descending a flight of stairs. Mr. Arden's office was above the pharmacy department on the second floor, just by the employee break room.

Mr. Arden wheeled out into the store, trying to force his right arm into the sleeve of his manager's jacket, shouting and sputtering at the same time, "Get that dog! Get that dog!"

He spun around the corner, almost colliding with an end-cap display of Vernors ginger ale, waving his hands.

"You! Stewart. He's back. That dog. Get the dog!"

Stewart snapped a picture of Mr. Arden in full stride, white coat flapping behind him, his face nearly scarlet with anger and exertion. Then Stewart took off as well, running toward the door, a good fifteen steps behind the dog.

Whatever level of intelligence this dog possessed, Stewart thought he had a superb sense of timing. He made it to the exit doors at exactly the same time Mr. Rinners did, hardly breaking stride at all, and heading west down Main Street. Once outside, Stewart took off at a gallop.

He was nearly positive that Mr. Arden would not follow, nor leave the store unmanaged, even for a few minutes. Stewart saw the dog loping down Main Street.

And a curious thing occurred. The dog stopped, dropped the rawhide, and turned to stare at Stewart.

Stewart, not well versed in the ways of dogs, slowed as well.

"Good boy. It's okay, doggy. I won't hurt you. It's just that Mr. Arden wants that bone back. You didn't pay for it."

Then Stewart snapped another picture of the dog, full in frame and smiling.

That is a good-looking animal. Handsome for a dog. And he seems as if he knows it. Sort of posing, isn't he?

The dog tilted his head to the side, appearing to be memorizing Stewart's face. Then he bent down, took the bone in his mouth, and took off like a furry rocket on steroids.

Stewart plodded on a few more steps and realized that giving chase would be futile.

I ran track in high school, but even back then I wouldn't have been able to keep up.

The dog ran down to Walnut Street, then headed south.

As Stewart walked back to the Tops Market, he passed the Wired Rooster Coffee Shop. He looked inside. Lisa was behind the counter, offering a broad smile to a customer while handing him a cup of coffee.

Stewart took a deep breath and entered the store.

"Hi, Lisa."

"Stewart. What are you doing here? On a break?"

He leaned toward the counter and whispered.

"The dog came back. I have pictures. We can talk after work."

Lisa's smile beamed at a mega-kilowatt level.

"What time do you get off? Early, I hope."

"I'll be home at two thirty."

"I'll be up at three. And I'll bring coffee. You like lattes?"

Stewart did.

"Sure. I'll see you at three."

Today is going to be a good day.

‒

The dog ran three more blocks, then veered west. He slowed to a trot, hardly breathing fast, but a running dog drew suspicion and this dog did not want to draw more attention to himself than he already had.

The weather had grown warmer, and for that the animal was glad. God indeed designed most animals to live outside, and the dog had a good coat of fur, but during the cold winter nights, well, no animal is truly and totally comfortable—at least none that the dog knew.

But he made do, and he was grateful that whatever power created him, and cared for him, continued to do so, even in this time of being alone and lost.

Most animals simply endure the cold without complaint, because complaints would serve no purpose. None complained, especially not that lumbering black bear with a thickly layered coat of fur that the dog had encountered in the woods several months back, just as the cruelest part of winter had broken. The bear had sniffed and snorfed and growled in the dog's direction. The dog had considered growling or barking in rebuttal, but did not, thinking that this strange, shambling beast might take any harsh noise as a threat, even if the dog kept the bark informative and not threatening.

Instead, the dog had backed up several yards, putting a thicket of dry brush between the two of them, then turned, and, as noiselessly as he could, had taken off at a full run, away from the black, large, furry creature.

And now that the warm had come back into the air, at least during the day, the dog did not feel as precarious, or as threatened. There was open water about, and often some food. The rawhide bone he now carried was not filling, not exactly, but it softened the growling in his stomach and made sleep come easier at night.

He trotted on, down the sidewalk, doing his best to act like a normal dog. He sniffed and noted the familiar scent. He had found a secluded place, deep in the brush, between places where humans lived, with only squirrels and rabbits in the vicinity, and none of those posed any threats.

In the past—how long he did not know—he had encountered the scents of coyote and fox and porcupine and skunk in the woods—all creatures he did not want to encounter in the physical. He sniffed to determine which direction the scent came from and did his best to pass as far from them as possible. Skunks and foxes were not dangerous, he knew, but they smelled horribly, and the dog, while not in the company of humans, not just now, was a fastidious animal and did not want to have an awful odor clogging his nose for days on end.

Coyotes could be dangerous. He had heard them, many months earlier, attacking something, and did not care to test his mettle against a crew of them.

No, this place where he bedded down was quiet and far enough away from humans that they would not see him or even take notice of him being there. In the cove of a fallen tree, a small depression filled with dry leaves, was a spot that made a perfect bed—at least for now, the dog thought.

Perhaps that human on the street, the one that talked nicely to him this morning, perhaps that human might offer a better form of shelter. But not today. Today the dog would peel off the plastic wrapper and gnaw on the bone until it was finished.

That human, the one with the nice voice and the nice face, he lived around here. The dog noted his scent the day he took the first bone. It was a unique scent, as all humans had, but this one he remembered. And that scent was strong here.

Perhaps, the dog thought, that human lived near this place.

He chewed and smiled to himself, stopping every few minutes to listen closely, as if to say that he knew that there was a power that looked after nature and all the creatures within, and would continue to look after this one dog and that there will be just the right amount of time to find the solution to this one dog's problem. In good time, all in good time.

Chapter Five

S TEWART NEARLY ran the entire way home that day and did his best to complete a fifteen-minute cleaning regimen: dishes washed, bathroom cleaned, clothes stowed haphazardly behind a closed closet door, bed made, pillows fluffed. He lit a candle that he had bought at the market during the 50-percent-off-all-Christmas-merchandise sale in January.

It smelled of pine.

Pine is okay, isn't it? It doesn't have to be Christmas to light a pine candle, does it?

One or two minutes past three, Stewart heard the familiar, and welcome, squeal of brakes from the driveway below. He opened his door and left it open.

In another moment, Lisa rushed in, carrying a tray with two large cups wedged into the holes, and her steno pad.

"They're both lattes," she explained. "So it doesn't matter which one you pick. Full caffeine, if that's okay with you."

"Sure," Stewart said as he took the cup closer to him. "Let's sit down in the living room. It's more comfortable. I know it's small, but they don't build turrets like they used to."

At this, Lisa laughed.

Somewhere Stewart had read that a woman values a good sense of humor above nearly every other criteria when judging a man.

I'm off to a good start. I'm okay with funny. It's not like I can will myself handsome.

Stewart winced to himself.

As if being funny will really make a difference. I mean, come on, now.

"Show me the pictures," Lisa said, excited.

Stewart pulled out his phone and displayed the five pictures he'd taken.

"That is such a cute dog," she said, even more excited. "How did you get him to pose like that? With the bone and all?"

Stewart shrugged.

"Seemed like he knew what I was doing—or wanted."

Lisa asked him to recap every bit of the theft, which Stewart was happy to do. As he spoke, she scribbled notes down in the steno pad.

Do they still have stenographers?

"You don't have to mention me in the story, do you?"

Lisa smiled at him and stared back.

"I don't think so, Stewart. But if I get the Pulitzer Prize for this, they're going to want to know."

He mimed wiping sweat off his forehead.

"That's a relief. I mean...not that you couldn't win the award and all...but by that time I'm hoping that I won't be working at Tops anymore. Like I'll have a real job by then."

Lisa paused and looked down at her hands.

"It is hard, isn't it? Getting started. I thought by now I would be doing something important and not making lattes."

"Which are very good, by the way."

"Thanks."

She keeps smiling back at me. That's a good sign.

"Well, I think I have enough material now. Like I said, I'll call you if I think of anything else."

"Sure."

Lisa stood to go, then glanced at the kitchen counter.

"You know it's not January sixth anymore."

She was looking at his Verse-a-Day calendar.

"Oh, yeah, I've been meaning to get that up to date. It's on my to-do list."

Lisa laughed again.

She laughs easily. And it sounds pretty.

"I didn't know you—you know, went to church and all that. You know, faith. Jesus, and all that."

Stewart's thoughts raced as he tried to come up with a reply that might fit.

"Well, sure, I go. Not all the time. My grandmother sent that to me. But I like it."

Did that sound convincing?

"That's good," Lisa replied. "Nice to know that a neighbor feels the same way I do. Well, I'll get writing. And send me a copy of those pictures, okay?"

"Sure. I'll do that right away."

And she shut the door behind her.

Feels the same way I do? About what?

⟶

The next day, only minutes after the Tops Market opened, the bandit dog struck again. Mr. Arden was not there—he was attending a managers' meeting in Sunbury—and Stewart managed to take two more photos of the dog in action. As he tracked him from the store, he managed to get within a dozen feet of the dog, who, by this time, almost seemed to enjoy being near Stewart. Stewart would have sworn that the dog slowed down to let Stewart keep pace with him, at least for half a block.

Stewart stopped at the Wired Rooster and gave Lisa a heads-up.

"How did he sneak in this time? I thought the store would be at DEFCON Five by now."

"Managers' meeting. Our assistant manager was in the back signing for a truckload of frozen stuff. And the dog shadowed the bread guy as he wheeled his rack inside. They're supposed to come through the back, but he didn't. So the dog was hidden behind the bread and stuff until he was well inside. Then he took the bone and hightailed it back outside."

"Do you think he's reselling them somewhere?"

At this, Stewart laughed.

She's funny, too.

"Well, the *Gazette* doesn't publish until tomorrow night. I'll add this to the story and run it over there. Any new pictures?"

"Just two, inside the store. But they're kind of blurry."

Stewart leaned close and showed them to her.

He smelled lilacs. Again. Lilacs and coffee. It was a heady mixture.

Must be her shampoo or something.

"Send them to me. I'll let them pick one if they want it."

"Sure."

"You're so nice, Stewart. If they publish this, I'll treat you to dinner. Or cook dinner. Something."

Stewart was going to say that she didn't need to bother, but he did not.

I would really like to have dinner with her.

❧

The *Wellsboro Gazette*, printed just once a week, hit the streets early every Wednesday morning. Above the fold, as newspaper veterans would call it—the top story this week, just under the newspaper's logo—featured a very sharp, four-color picture of a smiling, black-and-white dog under the lurid headline CANINE CRIME CAPERS: DOG BANDIT STRIKES TOPS MARKET AGAIN AND AGAIN.

The byline at the beginning of the story read: "By Lisa Goodly, Special Assignment Reporter for the *Gazette.*"

Stewart's picture of the dog took up nearly a quarter of the front page. The credit line simply read: GAZETTE PHOTO. Stewart, surprised that the newspaper put the story on the front page, scanned through the piece quickly.

She didn't name me. That's good.

Then he read it more carefully.

She's a good writer. Why is she making coffee for a living? She should work for a magazine or a newspaper or something. I don't know much about writing news and stuff, but this is good.

The morning crew at Tops Market could hardly talk of anything else that morning: the dog, how clever it was, how angry Mr. Arden got, what they might do when they finally catch him. Everyone speculated on one angle of the story or another.

Stewart listened, but did not participate.

Mr. Arden appeared in the front of the store around half past nine.

"Listen, everyone. This dog situation, this . . . this embarrassment has to be stopped. The health department will shut the store down if they think we're letting the dog in. And then you'll all go home—and not get paid. No one wants that, do they?"

A murmur of nos answered his question, none of them truly enthusiastic.

"So—if we see him, we catch him. Okay? Stewart here, he's the one in charge of dog patrol. If you see the dog, call for Stewart. The dog is only going to come in the morning—that's his modus operandi—which is Latin for how he does things. It's always the morning. It's his pattern. So be on your toes. Especially you, Stewart. Everyone got that?"

A series of unenthusiastic yeses followed.

A voice from the back of the small group called out, "What if it has rabies?"

Mr. Arden glared in that direction. One of the back room stockers must have spoken out.

They're like crazy, those guys on the loading dock.

"It doesn't."

No one asked Mr. Arden how he could be sure of that fact.

"Now back to work. We don't want this store to be made a laughingstock by a criminal—even if it is just a dog."

With that, Mr. Arden retreated and everyone listened to the slow, complaining creaks of the staircase as he ascended to his office.

Halfway up they stopped, and a loud wooden groan escaped from the middle step.

"Stewart Coolidge, can you come to my office for a minute?"

Mr. Arden's voice drifted down like the echo of a specter,

Stewart thought. He tried to think where he had heard that metaphor, or simile, or whatever it was, as he climbed the stairs. Maybe in some Crypt Keeper episode.

"Stewart," Mr. Arden began as he leaned back in his chair, which also groaned as he did. "You stopped to take a picture of the dog? I thought you were supposed to be capturing the dog."

Stewart had worried that this question might be asked, and he'd spent an entire evening crafting a response that he thought made sense.

"Yes. I did get a picture. I was chasing the dog and it stopped and turned and growled at me, so I didn't want to provoke it in any way. No one wants any expensive medical claims for a dog bite and rabies shots and all that. And I knew that a picture would be valuable to show people what sort of dog they should be looking out for. And the dog is really fast. The paper asked for the picture and I knew that it would help in the search. That's why, Mr. Arden. I mean, I didn't write the story or anything. But I thought the picture would help in the search."

Stewart felt that it sounded more than a little rehearsed, like all the times he had to give speeches in high school, when the words rattled out like machine-gun fire in an effort to get them spoken before they disappeared from thought.

But Mr. Arden smiled as he explained it.

"That's good thinking, Coolidge. Good thinking indeed. Executive sort of thinking."

Chapter Six

T HAT EVENING, Stewart and Lisa spoke about her article for nearly twenty minutes while standing on their shared landing space on the second floor. Lisa bubbled with enthusiasm.

"They really liked the story. I think the editor wants me to do more like that. This is just so great, Stewart. It opened the door. And I owe it all to you."

Her phone began to ring, and she gave him a quick hug and slipped back inside her apartment.

I did not expect that. Not at all. A hug. Me? Her?

It was then that Stewart heard something—a growl or a bark from the backyard of the house, in the shadows of the even more ramshackle garage that was situated farther back.

Cautiously, he hurried down the steps and walked out onto the porch, thinking that perhaps a raccoon was into the trash again. The last time that had happened several bags of garbage had been strewn all over the yard. Stewart thought a shout would scare off whatever animal it was. He did not want to rake eggshells and moldy banana peels again.

He stood at the edge of the porch, the wood creaking as he did. It almost did not matter where a person stood in the house—something would creak in response.

He narrowed his eyes, trying to see into the shadows.

Instead of seeing a furry, furtive creature scuttling away into the shadows, Stewart saw a dog.

It's that dog. From the store.

The black-and-white dog slowly walked toward Stewart, his head turning to the left and right, as if he were assessing the possibility of threats or capture.

"Hi, doggy. How are you? It's me, Stewart. From the Tops Market. Where you steal rawhide chews. The bones, I mean."

The dog stopped walking and sat down, sniffing the air, staring at Stewart.

"It's okay. It's okay. You don't have to be afraid."

Later, Stewart would ask himself why he wasn't afraid. It was an unknown animal, coming out of the shadows. It could very well have been rabid or vicious, like he had lied about to Mr. Arden, or both. But Stewart would later tell himself that he simply was sure that the dog posed no threat. He just knew that dog was gentle and was lost and hungry.

"Are you hungry?"

The dog stood and took three steps closer, as if he understood the word "hungry."

"Listen. You wait here. I'll be right back. I have food upstairs. Wait. Please?"

Stewart took the steps two at a time as silently as he could. He seldom locked his door so he never had to fumble finding his keys. Besides, when he did try to lock it, one sharp jiggle of the handle was more than enough to pop the door open.

So much for security.

On the kitchen counter sat a full plate of macaroni and cheese. He had finished making it just as Lisa had arrived home. He had not touched it.

Dogs like cheese, don't they?

He grabbed the plate and hurried downstairs. He stopped

at Lisa's door and was about to knock, but he heard her voice, loud but lilting, talking about "the story."

She's still on the phone. I don't want to disturb her.

So he quickly padded down to the porch.

The dog was exactly where Stewart had left him. He looked up when Stewart reappeared.

Taking very deliberate steps down to the yard, Stewart moved slowly, making no sudden gestures or loud noises. The dog stood up and took one step backward. Stewart placed the plate on the ground, then backed up to the porch.

"It's good. I know it's only the store brand, but I like it a lot. I don't think I could tell the difference between this and the Kraft version—and this one is much less expensive. Try it. You'll see."

The dog sniffed a long time, then walked to the plate, lowered his head, and took a small, sample bite. He looked up at Stewart and smiled, a lopsided, canine smile, then went back to the mac and cheese. It was obvious to Stewart that the dog was hungry, or even famished, but he ate with dignity, with exactness, chewing with grace, not gobbling, not rushing, but tasting every bite, and apparently enjoying every bite.

In a few moments, the plate was empty, licked clean of any cheese residue.

"Good? I like it a lot, too."

Stewart made his way down off the porch, taking small steps until he was within arm's length of the dog.

I just knew he was a nice dog. I just knew. Sometimes . . . you can tell. You're just sure.

He crouched down and extended his arm.

The dog sniffed at his hand.

Then Stewart tried to reach around and pet the top of the dog's head.

The dog cowered and backed off and then turned, looking back once more, and ran into the shadows. Stewart heard the brush in the back crackle and break as the dog moved through it.

A sense of sadness nearly overwhelmed Stewart at that moment, sadness over what the creature must have endured and the cause of his fear. In a small nut-brown voice, Stewart called out after the dog, called out into the dark, "It's okay. You can come back at any time."

Stewart did not share what had just transpired with Lisa. He was afraid that she might get scared that the dog was lurking in the shadows of the house, even though Stewart was absolutely certain that there was no danger.

But it's better if she doesn't know. I think. For now, at any rate.

———

The dog scampered back to his makeshift den and sniffed about with care.

No other animal had been there since this morning, when he'd barked at the squirrel that was rooting through the leaves where the dog had slept.

The dog, now satisfied that the spot was just as he had left it, circled several times, flattening down the leaves, repeating centuries upon centuries of instinctual behavior. He lay down and put his head on his paws. For the first time in a very long time, his stomach felt almost full. He raised his head and listened. He must have worried that the human might follow him into the darkness, the gentle human with the warm food, and yet, he was also a little sad that the human did not follow him.

The dog sniffed the night air again. He knew it would be chilly this night, but not cold. That was good. He wondered if he might see that human again tomorrow. The dog's stomach growled again. The human's food was wonderful, but not sufficient to banish all his hunger.

Perhaps tomorrow he would take one more of those bones.

There was food in trash cans, he knew, but he was not a raccoon or possum who apparently relished going through the refuse of others. The dog did not want to lower himself to the level of a trash-eater.

He closed his eyes, thinking of that human again, thinking of the gentle tone of his voice, and the longing that showed in his eyes, that longing to belong, to be part of something other than himself.

It was a look that the dog understood without knowing the words.

The dog remembered when he was a puppy, with his mother and his brothers and sisters, when he was always safe and fed and warm and when all seemed right with the world, everything calm and at peace. He knew, without knowing why, exactly, that that was the way all things should be, even for a dog without a name, when he was part of something good and kind and caring.

⟿

There was a note on Stewart's door.

The handwriting was feminine and precise. It was from Lisa.

"If I write a follow-up to the dog thief story, I am going to call him Hubert. Stop for coffee after you get off and I'll tell you why."

A real invitation. That's good. Progress. Sort of. Maybe.

⟶

Bargain Bill Hoskins was the only occupant of the otherwise empty office of Bargain Bill's Dynamite Cars. The neon sign outside glowed *Bargain Bill's Dynamite Cars—You'll Have a Blast With Our Wheels!* all done in script, in bright greens and purples. Every fourteen seconds a neon explosion in red and ochre lit up, as if punctuating the slogan with a neon blast.

His car lot, situated on the east side of town, and just inside the city limits, was one of three used-car facilities in Wellsboro—a fact that Bargain Bill had agonized over on many occasions.

"There's not enough business for all three of us. One of the others should close and we would all be better off."

He had said that often over the last fifteen years, and neither of the other two used-car dealers had heeded his wish.

Bargain Bill, as most everyone called him now, even his long-suffering wife on occasion, read, with great interest, the saga of the bandit dog. He had driven past that very market this morning and had seen Mr. Arden, who drove an old 2002 Chevy Cavalier and who should be in the market for a newer car any day now, tacking up paper on the telephone poles by the store. Bill had slowed down and seen a picture of a dog under the banners WANTED! and REWARD!

Only now did he make the connection, after reading the story.

"He's getting a lot of free PR for his store out of this. It's a cute story, I have to admit."

The words "free PR" stopped Bill's line of thinking as an explosion stops all conversation within earshot.

Free publicity . . .

Slowly, an idea began to form in Bill's mind.

After a few minutes, he smiled widely.

"Free publicity. That's the ticket."

And then he grabbed his Rolodex and shuffled through his cards, looking for the personal phone number of the editor of the *Wellsboro Gazette*.

—

"I only have thirty minutes for lunch," Stewart explained. "I said I had to go to the dry cleaners."

"Do you?" Lisa asked as she slid a small latte across the table to him.

"No. Actually I don't think I own anything that needs to be dry-cleaned. Well, maybe my sport coat. And that's it, I guess."

Lisa's smile appeared genuine and unforced. Stewart felt that even if no relationship developed, he would still be able to say that she was a friend. At least he hoped he could. Lisa was the sort of almost nearly perfect girl who was well beyond even his most ambitious ambitions.

Pretty. Smart. Confident. All the things I'm not.

"So why Hubert?" Stewart asked.

Lisa grinned.

"It's an inside joke, sort of. When I was little, I went to Catholic school through sixth grade. The public school in town was terrible, so my parents, who weren't Catholic, made me go there instead. And we had to learn all about the saints. Saint Hubert is the patron saint of rabies."

Stewart was unsure whether to laugh or look concerned.

"I don't think the dog has rabies, though," he said.

"Oh, I know, Stewart. But it's a cool name, don't you think? No one names anything Hubert anymore. Distinctive."

"Yeah, I guess," Stewart replied, then said the name again, as if testing the sound. "Hubert."

"It's a good name," Lisa said.

"I don't know. I'm not sure he looks like a Hubert."

Lisa reached over and gently touched the top of his hand with her fingers.

"Maybe it will grow on you. Or him. If you see him again."

Stewart could not think of much else than her reaching across the table in the Wired Rooster Coffee Shop to touch his hand, so he nodded, quite energetically.

"Sure. Hubert. Maybe. Sure."

—

Contrary to his established modus operandi, his standard method of thievery, the dog, who was now called Hubert by at least two people, made his boldest move yet, appearing at the Tops Market only minutes past noon. The store was crowded, so a dog slipping past the doors hidden by a passel of incoming and outgoing customers became a simple matter of being confident, and quick. He grabbed the rawhide chew and was out on the street before Mr. Arden came hustling down aisle three, waving a broom, shouting to Stewart to bar the door.

Stewart was mid-bag at that point, and really didn't hear the shouted commands over the music incessantly played over the store's loudspeakers.

"Upbeat music makes people buy more," Mr. Arden had claimed once when a checkout clerk complained about the insipid music choices. "And perhaps you're not hep to the new sounds. Music works. It's a scientific fact. 'Subconscious retailing' is what it's called."

When Stewart saw his manager wielding a broom, he could not imagine him actually using it on the dog . . . on Hubert.

By the time Stewart had bagged the last two cans of Tops tomato soup into Mrs. Levin's brought-from-home, recyclable canvas bag, the dog had already made it outside and Mr. Arden was sputtering, in a veritable tizzy, almost, at the front of the store.

"Stewart—where were you? You're supposed to be on guard, aren't you? Didn't I tell you to watch for that mangy beast?"

Stewart looked stung.

"I was helping a customer, sir." He waited just a heartbeat before adding, "I'm supposed to be helpful, right?"

Mr. Arden sniffed loudly as if a disagreeable odor had just wafted into the store.

"Fine. Fine. For the rest of your shift, I want you to post more of these flyers—with the dog's picture. Someone is harboring this thief. Someone has to be held responsible."

So Stewart spent the last two hours of his shift stapling a series of WANTED posters up and down Main Street and Central Avenue.

Maybe I should catch him and turn him in for the reward.

Stewart smiled as he thought about it.

Probably a five-dollar gift card from Tops.

After work, he stopped in and relayed the latest episode to Lisa as she prepared him a small latte with caramel syrup.

"The editor says he wants a follow-up story for the next issue. Do you think your manager would talk to me . . . like in an interview?"

Stewart shrugged.

"I guess. If you mention the store a bunch of times. Sure. I think he thinks that people will come just to see if they can catch the dog. He is offering a reward, you know."

"I heard. Or saw. How much?" Lisa asked as the milk frothed in the small metal pitcher.

"I don't know. Maybe like a gift card to the store. He's not known for being generous, so I wouldn't think you could get all your Thanksgiving dinner stuff at once."

Lisa laughed again.

She has such a nice laugh. Inviting.

"Listen, I'll talk to you after work. You'll be home, won't you?"

"Sure. I'll be there."

Progress.

He walked out and caught his reflection in a store window.

Who am I kidding?

⌒

Bargain Bill Hoskins walked into the Insta-Print store with a copy of the *Gazette* in one hand and a pencil-drawn poster in the other.

"Can you make two hundred and fifty copies of this? And use this picture?"

The young man behind the desk, SAM written on his name tag with a dull Sharpie, looked at both, holding them up to the light and turning them one way and then another, as if he were examining a piece of fine art for being a possible forgery.

"You want me to make copies of this? The pencil lines are too light. It won't copy at all."

Bargain Bill appeared to slump and inch or two from exasperation.

"No. Good grief. I want you to use your computer or whatever it is you use and type this up—and make it look professional. But make it look like this. And with this dog picture from the paper."

The young man scrunched up his face.

"This picture is terrible. It will be all muddy."

"I don't care about that. People will know what the dog looks like. From seeing it in the paper. The words are what I want them to notice."

"Well . . . I guess. How soon do you need them?"

"Now. This afternoon at the latest."

Sam scrunched up his face even more, looked over his shoulder at the clock, then back to Bargain Bill.

"Okay. Two hundred and fifty copies? That gives you the best price. What kind of paper?"

Bargain Bill slumped even farther down, as if being deflated in stages.

"I don't care. I'm going to hand them out, maybe tack a few up here and there. Good paper. Okay?"

Sam took the two pieces of paper and, as Bargain Bill left the store, he began to type on the computer keyboard:

WANTED!! REWARD!!

LOST DOG!!

Anyone who finds my precious dog will receive a
REWARD from Bargain Bill Hoskins, owner and operator
of Bargain Bill's Dynamite Cars.

$500 REWARD!!

(in much smaller type, please)

Must be applied to your next car purchase from Bargain
Bill's.

When you find him, I will reimburse Tops Market for
any lost merchandise.

Signed,

Bargain Bill Hoskins

Chapter Seven

As THE DOG, Hubert, gnawed on his latest theft, he kept looking up and listening. From his protected spot in the brush he could see the back door of the human place where that human came out with the plate of food that tasted creamy and good. It was almost warm and that made it even better.

He chewed methodically, nipping off little pieces of the rawhide, swallowing them. He knew that this food was not the best food for a dog, not permanent food, but it did help. He would have to make some choices soon.

He had once thought his only choice was to go on, keep moving, heading along the river, and keep looking, hoping that he would find his way to another human who would help him. Or maybe, just maybe, he should stay here and let this human help. The dog was not adept at making decisions about what to do in the future, what to do after this one moment of the present moved into the past. Dogs, as a rule, he thought, were not overly concerned about what will happen next—only with what is happening now, and perhaps a little concerned with what has happened in the past.

The dog was not sure he remembered exactly why he was alone and why he'd had to fend for himself for so long. All he knew was that it seemed like a very long time since he'd slept inside a place where humans lived. He used to sleep inside. Then he closed his eyes and recalled pain, and humiliation, but when those thoughts and feelings came alive in him, he did his best to ignore them. He instead focused on his still-empty stomach. Or the cold. Or the scents that drifted in toward him. Or danger. Or a thousand other things that a lone dog encountered on his own.

His present, his "now," was all about being lost.

Some humans are not nice. The dog knew that. When the dog was reminded of that truth, when he went face-to-face with that reality, when he encountered mean humans, he did not like the experience; he disliked the jangly way it made him feel. When that occurred, he then thought of something else, something less puzzling, less confusing, less hurtful.

Not all humans are like that—mean. Not all humans are not nice. Some are nice. And kind. Like the one that gave me warm food. He was a nice human. He did not want to hurt me.

The dog believed he could now sense the intentions of humans by the way they smelled and the way they talked and how they moved and if they lowered down when they talked to a dog instead of making the dog look up. Some dogs did not like to look up. It hurt their necks.

He stopped chewing and raised his head, just an inch or two. The sun was halfway down in the sky. The air was warmer today. The dog felt comfortable. Almost.

He heard footsteps. It was that human. He could tell by the sound and by the scent. The human walked slowly up the steps and stopped at something, moving just a little as he did, then holding papers in his hands.

It was time for a decision. The dog closed his eyes, just for a moment, and tried to remember feeling warm. He tried to remember what it felt like to lie on a soft floor, feeling safe and without worry and without hunger and without pain and without threat. He shook his head and stood up, and made his decision.

He could not think about it more than he already had. It was time. He had grown weary of never being with a pack, of not being with a human. It felt unnatural. It was not normal.

He jumped over the log and crackled through the brush and weeds, heading toward that human who gave him the warm food. The pain of being lost and alone overwhelmed any hesitation he might have had. He wanted to belong again, and was willing to risk everything to get that feeling back once more.

─

Stewart looked up from the stack of circulars and solicitations that consistently made up the majority of his mail. He had heard something in the brush behind the garage.

It's that dog. He came back.

Stewart waited until the dog stopped walking, about a dozen feet from the porch. Then Stewart stepped to the backyard, moving very slowly, not wanting to make sudden moves that might be perceived as a threat.

When he'd made up half the distance, he knelt down, his knees on the damp earth of spring. He smiled, extended his hand slowly, and said softly, "Good boy. Good Hubert."

When the dog heard the word "Hubert," his ears perked up, as if it were a familiar word.

I'm sure it's not . . . but maybe it is. A long shot, but it could be.

"Come here, Hubert. I won't hurt you. I've got food upstairs."

The dog, now called Hubert, only hesitated a second, maybe two, then he stood and walked directly to Stewart and pushed his wet nose against the outstretched palm. The dog made a soft growling noise in his throat, as if trying to say that he trusted Stewart and that he, Hubert, as an unknown and perhaps a wild dog, would pose no threat, either.

After a moment, Stewart stood slowly. The dog watched him.

"You want to come upstairs? I have food upstairs."

The dog again tilted his head in response, as if he were trying to understand Stewart's odd accent and vernacular.

"This way. We have to climb steps. You're okay with steps, aren't you?"

Stewart, since he had seldom been in the company of dogs, wasn't certain that all dogs knew how to navigate stairs. He assumed that they did but felt it prudent to ask—or at least inform the dog that there would be steps involved.

Stewart walked up the three steps to the porch and the dog followed him, matching him step-for-step.

He must have climbed steps before.

Then Stewart opened the downstairs door and walked in. Hubert followed him in without hesitation. Stewart began to walk up the stairs and the dog followed a step or two behind, as if not wanting to rush his host.

Stewart opened the door to his apartment. The dog walked in right behind him, sniffing the air with enthusiasm, but not sniffing objects or furniture or anything else—just taking in the scents of the room all at once.

"This is it. This is where I live," Stewart said softly and extended his arm, indicating that what the dog was seeing was the extent of Stewart's home. The dog seemed to nod and smile.

And then Hubert sat down, polite and silent, and stared up at Stewart, as if to silently ask about the food that had just been mentioned downstairs.

—

What do I have that a dog would eat?

Stewart opened the refrigerator and peered inside. He had never gone in for fancy cooking—or much cooking at all—so the majority of the foodstuffs inside the appliance were made up of condiments: ketchup, mustard, mayo, and hot sauce.

And pickles.

He had three jars of sweet pickles—all of them opened, all of them half-consumed.

I'm pretty sure dogs don't eat pickles.

Then he brightened.

I have hot dogs. From just last week.

Tops had run a sale on them and Stewart had bought two packages of the store brand "All-Beef Franks."

He took two hot dogs out of the package, looked back at Hubert, who had remained seated, then took out one more.

He sliced them up into smaller pieces and placed the slices on a paper plate.

He could tell Hubert was excited about the smells, but he stayed seated and wasn't clamoring for the food like some starved animal. Stewart considered where to put the plate. A small alcove in the kitchen seemed perfect, and he set the plate down on the floor.

He had once read that animals like to feel protected when they eat.

"Okay, Hubert. Dinnertime."

Hubert did not move.

"It's okay, Hubert. This is for you."

Stewart stepped backward a bit.

"Go ahead. You can eat."

Hubert slowly rose, looking first at Stewart, then to the hot dog slices on the floor.

Maybe they don't smell as much when they're cold.

Hubert walked slowly to the plate and lowered his head. Stewart could see the dog's jaws moving. Hubert remained bent to the plate until he had eaten everything. It had not taken long, but it was longer than Stewart had thought it would take.

Maybe he's just being polite. For a dog.

Stewart grabbed an old bowl out of a cupboard, a metal mixing bowl of some sort that was dented and one that he seldom, if ever, used. He filled it with water and placed it next to the empty plate. Hubert backed up a step to let him do so. Then he bent to the water bowl and lapped up much of it, making noisy swallowing sounds as he did.

When he was finished, he stepped back and looked up at Stewart, water dripping from his chin.

Stewart thought the dog smiled at him.

"Did you like that? Are you full now?"

Maybe not full, but if he's really, really hungry, it's probably not a good thing to give him too much at one time. Might make him sick.

The dog seemed to nod in agreement, licking his lips in a satisfied manner.

"I'm going to make coffee now, okay?"

The dog sat and watched as Stewart put water into the kettle and measured out instant coffee and creamer into his favorite mug. When it was finished, the dog wrinkled his nose at the scent.

"I know. Dogs probably don't like coffee."

Stewart walked into his small living room, in the turret, and set down the coffee cup. Hubert followed him in, politely sniffing. Stewart picked his favorite chair and sat down. A thick braided rug filled up most of the floor. The dog stepped gingerly on it, sniffing at the ground, then circled three times. He stopped facing Stewart, then carefully lowered himself. Hubert put his paws in front and laid his chin on them, watching Stewart as he sipped at his mug.

The dog's eyes slowly closed. It was obvious that he was fighting sleep, but Stewart imagined that no domestic dog would sleep soundly outside, in the cold. He watched as the dog's eyes shut—and remained closed. In a moment, Hubert started to snore softly, sounding like a rabbit gnawing on a carrot.

So this is what it feels like to have a dog.

Stewart just stared at Hubert.

Not bad. Not bad at all.

⌒

Bargain Bill picked up his stack of flyers.

"They look good. The picture is fine. It's not muddy at all."

Sam nodded.

"I know. I called the *Gazette*. They sent me a PDF and I used that."

Bargain Bill had no idea what a PDF was, but he knew that the flyer would draw attention.

Maybe I can get a big write-up in the paper as well. Catch a free breeze of publicity.

Before he left, he turned back to Sam and said, "Okay if I put one of these up on your bulletin board? Never know who's going to come in, right?"

And before Sam gave his approval, Bill was already removing the fourth thumbtack from four other posters, tacking his flyer up in the center, then stepping back and admiring his handiwork.

"Not bad. Not bad at all."

Chapter Eight

*H*UBERT THE DOG seemed to be fast asleep. Even Stewart's standing and walking back into the kitchen to fix yet another cup of coffee did not rouse him.

They probably don't sleep good outside. I wouldn't. I'd be nervous all night. There are animals out there and all that.

He pulled out his phone and checked the time.

She'll be home in ten minutes.

He watched the dog sleep.

I don't want her to know about this. Not yet. She'll want to write about it.

Instead, he waited at the window, watching for her car to show up. When it did he ran downstairs to meet her.

"Okay if we have coffee at your place? Mine's a mess and I didn't get a chance to clean it up."

Lisa's face tightened.

"My place is a mess, too. You want to go out and get coffee or something?"

"This doesn't count as dinner, does it? You still owe me dinner. Remember?"

"I remember. And, no, this doesn't count. You want to walk? I'm almost out of gas, too, and I don't get paid until tomorrow."

"Sure. And I'll treat for coffee—or whatever. I got paid yesterday."

—

They walked back toward downtown.

"You want to go to Café 1905?" Stewart asked. "I would have said the Rooster, but since you work there, I don't think you want to go right back."

"The Café is fine. I like it there. I don't think many places like that still exist—being in a department store and all that."

"Good. I eat there sometimes. I'm not much of a cook."

Lisa turned to him and grinned.

"Neither am I. My mother told me to take home economics in high school and she seemed so disappointed to learn that they don't even offer home ec anymore at my high school."

"Home economics? What's that? I've never heard of it," Stewart replied.

"Way back, like in the olden days, I guess," Lisa explained, "girls used to take home economics. Guys did, too, I think. Sometimes. A few of them, anyhow. I guess they learned how to cook and sew and stuff like that. How to follow a recipe."

"In school? Really? They taught cool stuff like that?"

"I guess," Lisa said. "I sort of wished they still did."

"Me, too. That would be awesome. You know, to, like know how to cook things."

They sat down with coffees and Stewart ordered a cheesesteak sandwich.

"We'll split it, okay? I'm sort of hungry for lunch food," he said. "But not real, real hungry."

"Me, too. That sounds good."

"You can cut it, okay?"

Lisa handled the knife, deftly cutting the sandwich in two, and slid Stewart's slightly larger piece toward him.

"So you're pretty sure Mr. Arden would talk to me?"

"I guess. Some people say he's an all right sort of guy. But he yells a lot. And he always looks mad. Maybe you have to be that way to manage a supermarket."

As they ate their split Philly cheesesteak sandwich and talked and drank their coffees, neither of them noticed Bargain Bill Hoskins making his way down Main Street, holding a packet of flyers under his arm and a staple gun in the opposite hand, stopping at nearly every wooden pole, tacking his poster just above, or just below, or over the previous WANTED poster, smiling with every thwack of the staple gun.

~

That evening, just a few minutes past nine o'clock, Stewart's phone rang, scaring both him and Hubert, who had remained sleeping upon Stewart's return. The dog looked up, eyes wide and alert, but he did not rise.

No one calls me at night. Maybe it's Lisa....

He looked at the caller ID.

It was a familiar number. From Florida.

"Hi, Grams," he answered. His grandmother always called after nine. "That's when the rates are cheaper, Stewart. I have to be careful with my pennies, you know."

Stewart would have argued, claiming that there is no longer a discount for off-hours calls, but he wasn't positive that there wasn't anymore. So he did not argue with her supposition.

"Stewart, how are you?" she asked. She did not sound

pleased. But then again, Stewart thought, she seldom sounded pleased.

Some people are just that way, I guess.

"I'm fine, Grams. Things up here are fine."

Stewart's grandmother had sold her home, the only home Stewart had known, while Stewart was a junior at Penn State. The breakup of all that was familiar to Stewart had been disastrous, like four cars crashing into each other at highway speeds—Stewart, his mother, his father, and his father's mother, Stewart's grandmother.

No one escaped without injury. And some injuries remained unhealed, untended for years and years, the scabs turning into tender scars, the pain hidden by silence, civility, and forced smiles.

"Have you heard from your father?"

Why don't you just call him, Grams? He's got a telephone. He's your son, you know.

"Not recently. He's still in Coudersport. I guess he's still working for the county. I haven't heard otherwise."

Stewart's grandmother did not speak, and Stewart grew uncomfortable in the silence.

"So, Grams, how are you?"

I think she needs me to ask.

"I'm fine, Stewart. If you called me more often, you would know these things."

"I know. I keep forgetting."

Silence.

"So, how's sunny Florida? I think we finally have spring up here. Winter was hard, that's for sure."

"It's hot and humid here. Like it always is, Stewart. They give the weather for Florida on the Weather Channel."

"I know. I guess I don't watch much television."

"So . . ." she said, waiting, and Stewart held his tongue, not sure what she wanted him to say. "What about this dog business? That store that the newspaper mentioned—that is the one you work at, right? The Tops Market on Main Street."

How does she know about the dog?

"Yes. It is. And how do you know about the dog?"

"Stewart," she said, and then sighed loudly. "I may be old, but I don't live in the Dark Ages. There is a computer in the community room downstairs that is attached to that Internet thing. Sometimes, if no one else is hogging it, I read the news from Wellsboro. The *Gazette* is online—isn't that what they call it? I can't afford that sort of computer and all those fancy setups and wireless thingamabobs, you know."

"Oh. Okay. So you know that a dog has been stealing rawhide bones from the store. Mr. Arden is really upset. Put up posters all over town asking for help in catching it. Offering a reward, I guess."

Stewart's grandmother sniffed, as if an unpleasant smell had come across the phone wires.

"So, then, you're still working there. At a grocery store."

"I am, Grams. I'm looking all the time for something better."

Maybe she'll change the subject.

"Thebold's grandmother said he just got a new position with something called Goldman Sachs. What is that, Stewart? She said he has to move to New York City. I wouldn't do that for all the tea in China, but she said they are paying for his moving expenses. And a big salary, she said. What does that company do?"

"Stocks and securities, I think. Investing. Banking."

Stewart's grandmother sighed again.

"Maybe you could call him. You went to grade school together. Maybe he could get you a job there."

This time Stewart sighed, but very quietly. They were walking on familiar ground.

"Maybe, Grams. But I haven't seen him in, like, twenty years. And I didn't study finance."

"Please do not use 'like' in your sentences. Respect my years of teaching high school English."

"I know. I know. It just slipped."

"So what about this dog? Did they catch him yet? Do they think it has rabies?"

"Grams, I am pretty sure it doesn't."

At this point in the conversation, Hubert groaned quietly and stood up, shook himself, then sat back down and stared at Stewart as he spoke.

"Well, it would be best if you kept your distance, that's all. And who is this Lisa Goodly person? The name sounds familiar. Was she a student of mine?"

"No, she wasn't. She grew up in Johnstown. I think you met her during your last visit. She works at the coffee shop."

"That little twig of a girl? She wrote that? I'm surprised. It was actually well written."

Stewart decided to be proactive.

"And she goes to church, too."

A moment of silence followed.

"And how do you know that?"

"Grams, she lives downstairs—on the second floor. She saw that Bible calendar you sent me. She said she goes to church."

"Which one? Not every church is the right church, Stewart."

"I don't know. I didn't ask."

Stewart heard a sharp inhale.

"And what was she doing in your apartment, Stewart? Honestly? What would people say? What would Jesus say?"

"Grams, please. She came up to interview me about the dog, that's all. In the afternoon. She saw the calendar as she left."

Stewart could imagine his grandmother closing her eyes and rubbing the bridge of her nose—a gesture she always made when peeved, which was often.

"Stewart, I do not like this at all. Not at all. Perhaps you should rethink your decision about moving down here. The complex here is looking for a full-time pool attendant. You could do that, couldn't you, Stewart? And it would keep you out of trouble."

Hubert turned his head to the side as if hearing a high-pitched whine coming from somewhere.

"Move to a retirement village?"

"It's a senior housing complex."

"Grams, we already discussed this."

He hoped he sounded firm and final.

"Maybe you should try going to church as well, Stewart. For a change. I'm praying for someone to come into your life and change your priorities, Stewart. You need to repent. And be restored. That's what the Bible says, Stewart. You don't want God to be mad at you, do you? You're not doing things to make God mad at you, are you, Stewart?"

Later, Stewart would be unable to recall anything else his grandmother said that evening. He was pretty certain that it was nothing important. And making it harder to recall was the fact that Hubert came over to him and pushed his wet nose against him, trying to get his head under his arm, trying to offer comfort, Stewart thought, during a most uncomfortable time.

Chapter Nine

APPARENTLY HUBERT slept on the living room floor all night. There was no whining or barking. When Stewart woke, already ten minutes late, Hubert was standing, calmly, by the door to downstairs.

"Just a minute, Hubert. I have to take a quick shower and change."

Stewart prided himself on being low maintenance and could be ready for work, showered, shaved, dressed, in less than ten minutes. This morning, he accomplished it all in seven minutes. He would have to walk fast, but that was okay.

He stopped for a moment, trying to decide what to do with Hubert. He knew that dogs had to go outside—like every couple of hours?

And being already late, Stewart did not have time to wait for Hubert to accomplish anything and everything that he needed to accomplish in the morning. Nor did Stewart have any food to offer him.

I could cut up some hot dogs, but then what would I eat?

Hubert looked up at him with a knowing look, or at least that was how Stewart interpreted it.

"If I let you out this morning, will you stick around until I get back? I'll bring dog food back with me."

I bet the store has a private label brand of dog food. Or

maybe something is on sale this week. I don't often walk down that aisle.

He would have sworn that Hubert nodded as he explained his predicament.

"Okay. You promise to come back? Or hang around here— wherever it was that you hung around before. I'll be back in six hours. Maybe a little longer. Maybe I'll stop in and see Lisa at the coffee shop. But you'll be here, right?"

Hubert grinned up at him. Then the dog stood up and waited, his nose at the door.

"Okay. Let's go. But let's be quiet, okay? I don't want any-one to know you're here. Okay?"

Stewart would have sworn that the dog did indeed traverse the steps with care. Stewart didn't know how dogs normally walked, but going down the stairs, Hubert seemed to place each paw very deliberately and squarely on the carpet runner, and not on the exposed wood.

When they got to the first-floor door, Stewart looked out, peering in both directions. His landlord, who lived on the first floor, was not an early riser. Perhaps the rents were enough to allow him not to work. Stewart never saw him going out at any regular times. He did drive a pickup truck, more battered than new, always more dirty than clean, so perhaps he did odd jobs around town.

But this morning the pickup truck remained in its usual place beside the rickety garage, which held a plethora of bins and bags and odd pieces of lumber and plywood and cans, but never a vehicle. He saw no one in the yard.

Stewart bent down and looked Hubert in the eyes. The dog seemed to smile in response.

"I'll be back this afternoon. Stay out of sight, okay? I don't know what else to do—so I am going to trust you. Okay? Got it?"

Hubert moved his head and shoved his cold nose against Stewart's cheek, as if planting a canine kiss, or a peck on the cheek, actually, in an attempt to communicate his acceptance of the day's regulations.

"See you this afternoon," Stewart whispered loudly, and Hubert did not hesitate, but trotted off into the underbrush that was the backyard and, within a few heartbeats, was gone.

He'd better be back. He'd better.

⟵

Lisa rose a few minutes after Stewart did. She sipped at her coffee and thought she heard voices.

He never watches TV in the morning.

She went to her front door and pressed her ear against it.

I do hear someone talking. Stewart? Maybe.

Then she scolded herself for being a snoop.

I don't want to be Mrs. Kravitz—that's for sure.

She straightened up.

That's her name, right? Mrs. Kravitz. On that old TV show. On that TV channel that just shows reruns—which is the only thing to watch if you're not into the news, sports, or hunting shows.

Lisa screwed up her face, attempting to recall that specific show—a show she had not grown up with but had seen in re-re-re-reruns.

Bewitched. *Right? With Elizabeth Montgomery. That's the one. And they had two different Darrins. Like we wouldn't notice the difference.*

She sat down and looked at the front page of the *Wellsboro Gazette* for perhaps the hundredth time.

Bewitched. *I love that show.*

She smoothed out the crease in the paper.

And this is just so great. And I owe it all to Stewart.

She finished her coffee.

I wonder if there is anything I could cook for him that is easy and cheap. Maybe I should call Mom for some advice.

She put her coffee cup in the sink.

Or maybe not. I don't want a lecture—and that's what I would get. On cooking, if not life in general. Not that I blame her, really.

Bargain Bill—who for some time now had been thinking of himself, when he thought of himself, as "Bargain Bill," and not just "Bill"—came early into work. The used-car business, he often said, is unpredictable.

"Except no one comes in early. That I can predict. Nobody buys used cars before noon."

But today he hoped that someone might have called him about the dog and left a message on his answering machine. He knew he should replace his ancient answering machine with something more hip, more electronic, more digital. Was that what they were? Digital? Bargain Bill didn't know for sure.

"But this old one still works. I'll keep it until it breaks. It runs fine—like a good used car."

He opened the door with great expectations, but saw no blinking red light that would have indicated a message. He stabbed at the replay button anyway, and even then no message was forthcoming.

"Maybe it's better this way. The longer the dog stays loose, the more publicity I get. And the editor over at the *Gazette* did say that if the dog isn't in jail by Monday, he'll send a reporter over to talk with me."

Bargain Bill eased himself into his executive-style leather chair that groaned every time he sat down, or moved.

"I should probably come up with a good story of why this is my dog and how he got away and why I'm so heartbroken."

He looked out the window to his lot filled with cars under a canopy of red, white, and blue pennants, the spring breeze making the pennants flutter and crinkle like synthetic leaves on a plastic tree.

"And I'll have to tell the little woman to back me up on this. She can't go off on her own—like she normally does. No, this story has to sound convincing."

With that, he took a pen that had *Bargain Bill's Dynamite Used Cars* imprinted on the barrel and began to doodle, trying to think up a story that would make sense.

⟶

At nine fifteen the canine bandit struck again.

Stewart knew it was exactly nine fifteen because he had just completed his first break of the day and managed to down his first cup of coffee for the day from the communal coffeepot in the break room. It was hazelnut flavored, which Stewart hated, but it was free coffee, after all.

That pleasant spring morning, the dog now named Hubert

sauntered into the store, as he had done before, not slowing or stopping or hesitating at any one spot. As Hubert passed by Stewart, he grinned up at him, but did not slow. He quickly turned the corner to aisle five and hurried down to the display of rawhide bones, grabbed one, and was on his way out before anyone, with the exception of Stewart, had noticed his appearance.

This time it was Lucinda, a cashier on register three whom Stewart had never yet seen without chewing gum in her mouth, who sounded the alarm.

"Hey! Stewie! Call Mr. Arden! That dog swiped another bone. Or is swiping another bone. Present perfect tense."

Lucinda was attending college online.

At that moment, Hubert looked back over his shoulder and locked eyes with Stewart. Hubert managed to grin, despite clenching a rawhide bone in his mouth. He had to wait, for just a second or two, until someone stepped on the "in" door opener—and then he charged out.

Mr. Arden thumped down the steps, shouting, "Stewart! Go after him. Now!"

Stewart shrugged, put Mrs. Weaver's tin of kipper snacks back on the belt, and headed outside at a trot.

"You better get him this time!" shouted Mr. Arden as the doors slowly whooshed shut behind Stewart. He saw the tail end of Hubert heading around the corner on Main Street, heading back to where he lived.

What if someone tails him and connects him with me?

By the time Stewart made it to Main Street, the dog had vanished.

Stewart's steps slowed, then stopped.

"That is one fast dog."

A pedestrian down the street waved to Stewart.

"He went that way," the man called out and pointed to the east, to Maple Avenue.

Stewart mentally shrugged to himself and set off at a trot.

I have to make it look like I'm chasing him, don't I? I don't want to raise any suspicions or anything.

By the time he made it to the corner of Main and Maple, there was no trace of any canine.

The man who'd signaled to Stewart, Mr. Ralph Dickers, commiserated with him.

"That pup can sure run, Stewie. I say that if a dog don't want to get caught, you ain't catching him. I think I said that before, but if I didn't, I plumb sure should have. That was one fast pup, if you ask me. How many times has he gotten away with it? A bunch, I bet. That dog is one slick operator, for sure. Reminds me of a dog I had when I was a kid. I think I was five. Or maybe I was eleven. That's when we lived in Coudersport. I think I was eleven. Maybe the dog was eleven. It was a big dog. Brown. Or black."

Stewart knew it would be better if he didn't engage Mr. Dickers in conversation, or else the two of them would be there for the better part of an hour. Mr. Dickers was well known in town for carrying on long-winded monologues with a surplus of uncertain details, often with just himself as an audience.

"Gotta get back. Thanks, Mr. Dickers. 'Preciate it."

Stewart left him still talking about the dog, or his dog, or both, and hurried back to the store. He didn't feel that he had the time to stop by the Rooster and let Lisa know about the most recent burglary. He would catch up with her this evening.

Mr. Arden had composed himself by the time Stewart returned. Standing beside him was a uniformed officer from the town's police department.

"You didn't catch him, did you?"

Stewart shook his head no.

"See," Mr. Arden said, "that's why we need an armed police officer on site. The dog has stolen seven rawhide bones so far."

From Stewart's vantage point he could see the officer roll his eyes, just a little. The sun glinted off the revolver he had in his holster, resting casually against his hip. The gun had a lot of area on which to rest.

"Mr. Arden, I know it must be an inconvenience, but we simply don't have the manpower to spend on a stakeout waiting for a dog."

Mr. Arden sputtered, "But I pay taxes in this town. So does the store. Don't we deserve protection, too? Maybe the dog isn't as easy to catch as speeders on Main Street, but . . . the dog poses a danger. What if he bites a customer? What if the beast has rabies? Then who's responsible?"

"He won't bite anyone," Stewart said, surprising himself. Both men turned to stare at him. Mr. Arden glared more than stared.

"And how would you know, Stewart?"

He felt his face start to redden.

"Well . . . I mean, if he hasn't done anything other than steal so far . . . I mean, I don't see why he would start biting. And if he were sick, or had rabies or whatever, he would have already starting acting weird. He doesn't. He just walks in, takes a bone, and walks—or runs—out. He's probably a stray and is hungry, that's all."

The police officer opened his palms, turned them faceup, and made a gesture as if to say "Well, there you are."

Mr. Arden kept his glare and tried to intensify it.

"Still. No reason for the police to ignore the request of a citizen."

"Tell you what. I'll have the patrol car swing past a few times in the morning. Maybe we'll get lucky."

That seemed to mollify Mr. Arden, although it was apparent it did little to make Stewart feel better.

Mr. Arden put his hand to his cheek.

"Now, just so we're on the same page. If one of your men catches him—the dog, that is—as police, they wouldn't be eligible for the reward, would they? I mean, as a public employee and all, I would think that taking gratuities, like a reward, would be against some sort of code of police ethics. Am I right?"

The police officer, a Lieutenant Vardish, exhaled, as if trying to clean an unpleasant odor from his lungs.

"No. They couldn't take a reward..."

Mr. Arden beamed.

"...but they might ask you to donate the reward to the Tioga County Human Services. They always need groceries for the county's food pantry."

And with that, the smile left Mr. Arden's face, to be replaced by a glare directed at Stewart.

Chapter Ten

WORKING THROUGH the rest of his shift that day, Stewart felt Mr. Arden's glare on the back of his neck the entire time. Usually, the store manager spent most of his day hidden in his upstairs office, but today Mr. Arden patrolled the front of the store, making sure that the cashiers and bag boys accomplished their jobs with "Speed, Accuracy, and a Smile."

Hand-lettered on a sheet of white poster board, Mr. Arden had tacked the sign up in the break room a few days earlier. Every time he returned from a managers' meeting, he brought with him a new motto. Usually, the company had them printed—but, perhaps due to budget considerations, they'd left this one to each individual manager. Mr. Arden did not have a good sense of space; the word "Smile" had to be smooshed in tight to make it fit. Any number of less than enthusiastic employees—especially those who worked on the loading dock—had threatened to deface it. But each time someone with a smirk and a Sharpie came close to the sign, they were shooshed away by a long-term employee who did not want anyone to make waves—not even a ripple.

So the badly drawn poster had remained unpocked by graffiti, and Mr. Arden remained convinced that the words were helping inspire his entire crew.

As inconspicuously as possible, Stewart checked his phone

a dozen times during the last hour of work. Quitting time seemed to grow more distant, rather than closer, every time he flicked on his phone.

But finally the hour came, and he hurried to the time clock and punched out, hoping to avoid Mr. Arden, hoping to avoid any possible repercussions of his assessment of the bandit dog's health and motives.

I don't know if I should try to keep the dog. I mean, I have no business owning a dog. I barely make enough to pay the rent and buy food. And I bet Hubert can eat a lot of dog food. Maybe I'm not allowed to have a dog. I don't remember seeing that on the lease. And did I even sign a lease? I might have. And dogs might be off-limits. If I turned him in, I could get that reward from the car dealer guy. I could use a new car and $500 would be a nice down payment. I wonder if I could get both rewards? I don't see why not.

As he walked, he also thought of the dog looking up at him with a trusting look in his eyes, the look only two lost souls would truly understand.

If I turn him in, he'll probably get sent to the pound. And I guess most dogs don't make it out of there.

He turned on Rectory Lane, expecting to see Hubert bound out of the brush at every step. But he saw no dog. He knew that he shouldn't call out. And he knew that Hubert probably would not recognize Hubert as his name.

He made his way up on the rear porch, taking each step slowly, looking over his shoulder as he did.

That's where he came from yesterday. From the backyard.

Stewart heard a scuffling, shuffling noise, much closer than the backyard. He looked down and saw a black-and-white snout appear from under the porch. And then the rest of Hubert wiggled into view.

Looking over the edge, Stewart saw a small sliver of opening in the lattice that covered the space between the porch floor and the ground.

Hubert grinned and appeared to be suppressing a dancing hello.

"Hey, Hubert. You listened to me. That's so cool. Like an obedient dog. I mean, not 'like.' *An* obedient dog."

My grandmother's voice is way too loud in my head—sometimes.

"Come on up, Hubert. And let's be quiet, okay?"

The two of them hurried upstairs. Stewart poured a generous portion of Paws Premium Meaty Crunchy Kibbles for the Active Dog.

"It was on sale, too, Hubert. Our lucky day."

No one had questioned Stewart when he'd bought the bag of dry dog food. If they had, he had prepared a story that he was buying the food for his neighbor who had a bad leg and couldn't get out—Mrs. Kreger, and her miniature schnauzer, Rudy—no, Randolph.

But no one stopped him, questioned him, or even paid attention to him as he hurried through the checkout line after work.

Before Stewart put the food down, he refilled the water bowl. The back of the dog food bag said always to have fresh water nearby. The food did look a little dry and dusty, but Hubert did not seem to mind in the least. Again, he ate in a most dignified manner—for a dog, that is. He ate slowly and chewed thoroughly and stayed bent to the food bowl until the entire cup of kibble was consumed. He had a long, loud drink, then backed up and looked at Stewart, as if to say "Is that all there is?"

"Hubert, I can't give you more. That is supposed to be a full serving for an adult dog. A full cup. And I gave you a rounded cup. The package said just one cup. And if you eat too much after being skinny, you could get sick. I read that somewhere . . . or saw it on a TV show."

Hubert seemed to be paying attention to the explanation, almost nodding in response.

"Was it good? The kibbles. Being a store brand and all."

To answer, Hubert walked over to Stewart and pushed his head against his kneecap, in an almost intimate gesture.

"Good dog."

Hubert watched carefully as Stewart made coffee. Stewart thought he might wait until later to eat, since someone had brought an accidentally torn "Valu-sized" bag of Tops brand potato chips into the break room and Stewart had it timed perfectly and managed to eat nearly a third of the chips during his second break. It had been enough to dull the hunger. And he liked chips.

Stewart went to his favorite chair and sat down. Hubert walked with him and sat by his knees. Once Stewart seemed settled and situated, the dog stood on his back paws, his front paws on Stewart's knees, jumped, and, in a quick untangling of legs, managed to sit in Stewart's lap, facing him.

Stewart was pretty sure that he never had a dog in his lap, not once, so far in his life. It was a surprise, but not an unpleasant one, actually.

Hubert stared into Stewart's eyes. The dog's eyes were deep

and apparently thoughtful, the centers the color of black coffee, a deep cup of strong, black coffee.

"Hubert. What do you want?"

Hubert remained still, staring, memorizing, confident, at peace.

Then he stood on all four legs, a little wobbly because of the unevenness of Stewart's thighs, adjusted his stance a little, and then lay down, his eyes never once leaving Stewart's.

"You're really going to lie here?"

Hubert responded with a rusty growl, coming from deep in his throat—not an angry growl, not at all, but a growl that tried to convey contentment, and perhaps happiness. Stewart was not yet versed in reading a dog's emotions, but this emotion seemed easy to translate. Then Hubert laid his head down, his eyes still open. He wiggled once more, then closed his eyes and, in another moment, he was snoring softly, making his nibbling rabbit noise again.

Stewart reached over and stroked the crown of his head. He thought he could see a slight smile on the dog's face but wasn't sure if dogs could smile while they were asleep or not.

But it sure looks like he's smiling.

As Stewart stroked Hubert's fur, his finger ridged and fell where a dog should not be ridged—on his back and on his head. Stewart peered closer. Between a part in the dog's fur, two lines, puckered and jagged and uneven and twisted and discolored, on his head and shoulders, each running for many inches.

They must be scars. Big scars.

Hubert blinked his eyes open, just a little, and looked back at Stewart.

Stewart felt that he should whisper. He knew that a whisper would be understood.

"Are these scars, Hubert?"

Hubert appeared to nod. At least Stewart would have sworn the dog appeared to nod.

"Did some person do this to you, Hubert?"

Hubert shut his eyes for a long moment, as if he were trying to prevent a bad memory from invading and destroying the pleasant moment of the dog's "right now."

But he did let that memory come up on him, just a bit, and he nodded again, and kept his eyes closed and bowed his head as if he were trying to make himself small to avoid the blows that caused the deep and long and jagged and angry scars that snaked along his back and head.

"Someone was mean to you, Hubert?"

Hubert sat still, as if awaiting another blow.

"It's okay, Hubert. It's okay. You're safe, now."

Stewart leaned in close.

"I will never do that, Hubert. I will never hit you. I will never let anyone hit you again."

And the dog hesitated a moment. Then his stiffness disappeared, and he snuggled in closer to Stewart, tight into his lap.

"You and me have a lot in common, Hubert."

Hubert kept his eyes shut.

"We have pain in our past. I don't think I have any scars like you, Hubert, not real ones ... I mean not ones that you can see or feel, but there are scars. Words hurt people more than they hurt dogs, I guess. And sometimes not saying a thing hurts just as much. Like people who leave without saying good-bye."

They did that, Hubert. They both just left. I remember watch-

ing them both storm out of the house, yelling and shouting and throwing things.

"I didn't see my mother for five years after that," Stewart said in a whisper.

He rested his hand on Hubert's shoulder.

"Maybe we all have pain in our pasts, Hubert. But maybe some of it is worse than others."

And with that, Stewart closed his eyes.

Like two peas in a pod. Two peas in a pain pod.

Just before Stewart nodded off for a short nap, he chided himself.

It's probably not healthy to make fun of it—the past, I mean.

Then he stroked the fur on Hubert's back.

And maybe that's why we have to stick together, me and Hubert. We are sort of like brothers.

Then Stewart chided himself once again and shook his head.

Doesn't that sound just so pathetic? Good grief. Maybe my grams is right.

⟿

Perhaps an hour later, Stewart blinked his eyes open, almost startled, but not quite.

Was that a knock?

Hubert had not moved. The snoring continued, softly, like an intermittent power saw three blocks away.

The knock repeated. It was less of a knock and more of a gentle rolling of knuckles against the door—a fabric-soft knock, as it were, designed to alert almost no one.

"Who is it?" Stewart said.

The voice on the other side was as soft as the knocking.

"Stewart, it's me. Lisa. Can I come in?"

What do I do? What do I do?

In that instant, Stewart's thoughts raced as he tried to plot out a half dozen different responses and different scenarios and different plot lines that might sound plausible.

In the end, he decided that keeping secrets was simply too difficult. Or at least keeping this secret. And he could not come up with a logical made-up reason why this dog was sleeping on his lap.

Nothing makes sense. And, after all, it is just a dog. It's not like I've kidnapped anyone. Or held up a bank. The dog stole some bones. That's not a federal crime.

"Stewart?"

"Oh, yeah. Come on in. The door's unlocked."

It's almost always unlocked.

Lisa entered, smiling, beaming almost, then stopped suddenly as she saw what, or who, was on Stewart's lap. Her mouth formed a perfect circle—a cute circle, Stewart observed. He put his finger to his lips and mouthed the words, "He's sleeping. This is Hubert." He pointed down at the snoozing dog.

Lisa, now on tiptoe, made her way into the living room.

Her smile had returned.

She perched, as silently as she could, in the chair next to Stewart and leaned toward him and whispered: "When did Hubert show up? Has he been here all along?"

"No," Stewart whispered back. "Just yesterday afternoon."

"Such a sweet-looking dog. He has the face of an angel. He does."

"I guess."

"I know dogs, Stewart. And this dog is special. You can tell right away. He's smiling in his sleep. See? Only special dogs do that. My granny told me that. She loved dogs."

Even though they tried to talk in whispers, Hubert lifted his head and blinked his eyes. He offered a soft growl, a friendly, welcoming growl, toward Lisa, but did not move other than raising his head.

"Hubert, this is Lisa, my friend. She lives downstairs."

"Hubert, I am Stewart's good friend. And I think I have complicated everyone's life. At least everyone in this room."

Hubert raised his head and sniffed. It was clear that he had encountered the scent before. He unsnarled his legs and stood, a bit wobbly, then jumped off Stewart's lap with a furry clump and took one step toward Lisa and sniffed again.

"Can I pet him?" she asked.

"I think so," Stewart answered. "I mean, so far, he's been nothing but gentle and seems real nice. And he's been in my lap for the last hour, sleeping. Kind of big for a lap dog. My legs have been asleep for the last thirty minutes."

She reached down, softly saying, "Hello, Hubert, so glad to meet you."

Hubert snorked and sniffed and grinned and pushed his nose into the palm of her hand and then stood on his back legs so he could get a better view of Lisa's face. Lisa leaned in closer.

"You're a famous dog, Hubert. Or infamous, I guess. At least in Wellsboro, that is. I suppose fame is a relative thing."

Hubert licked at her and caught the tip of her nose. She wrinkled her face and replied, "Yuck," but in a genial, good-natured way.

"Sorry, Lisa. I can get him away from you."

"Stewart, we had dogs when I grew up. My granny always had at least one. They sometimes lick people. It's okay. Really."

"You sure? I never had a dog, so I don't know."

She began to scratch behind Hubert's ears and he closed his eyes, obviously relishing the careful, delicate, feminine attention.

"Stewart, I'm sure. And now that I'm up here, and we both have been with Hubert, I bet we are both guilty of harboring a fugitive. Or aiding and abetting. Or being an accomplice. Something. I am sure that they can throw the book at us now. You ready to go to the hoosegow for this pooch?"

Stewart looked to Hubert, who opened his eyes wide, staring back at him.

"I guess."

Lisa nodded.

"Good. That makes two of us, then. Or three, counting Hubert."

"Do you think they allow dogs in prison?" Stewart asked, and his question sounded very serious. Lisa laughed in reply.

I really like it when she laughs. Like the sound of a waterfall in the spring.

Hubert leaned against Lisa's leg as she petted him. He also closed his eyes, obviously enjoying the attention.

"You are such a sweetie, Hubert. I could tell you were a sweetie from the picture Stewart took. Just an angel of a dog."

Every word brought Hubert closer and snuggier to Lisa. It appeared that he considered climbing into her lap as well, but it was a much smaller lap than Stewart's, so he remained on the floor.

"Oh, yes, why I'm here," Lisa said, her words bright and full of cheer. She brushed a strand of blonde hair from her face.

Stewart wondered if she had fixed it differently today, or styled it differently. He was not sure which word was more correct. It always looked pretty to him, her hair, but today it looked prettier—and a little different.

I don't think I'm supposed to ask a woman about her hair. Or is that her clothes? Or tell them that they look nice. Right? Isn't that harassment or something? But she does look nice today.

"I forgot to tell you when I first came in."

Well, sure. She has not made a habit of dropping by. No one has, I guess.

"Anyhow, the editor at the *Gazette* is running my second story on Hubert. I interviewed Mr. Arden."

"Was he nice? I don't think I've ever seen him outside the store."

Lisa offered a small almost-smile in reply.

"He was nice enough. Very business-like. I went to his office."

"When? I didn't see you come."

"It was late in the afternoon on Friday. I knew you wouldn't be at work. And I didn't want to make a big deal about—I wasn't sure the *Gazette* was actually going to publish the next installment. So...you know...I didn't want to let everyone know, until I was sure."

"Well, sure, that makes sense."

Lisa wrinkled her nose.

"His office is tiny. I thought a store manager would have a better office. It's the size of a closet."

"Yeah, it is pretty small."

"And it smells...like lettuce. Does he keep lettuce up there?"

Stewart shrugged.

"I don't think so. But the whole store sometimes smells like a vegetable, if you ask me. Especially when some of the produce is getting close to being out of date."

Lisa wrinkled her nose again.

She looks pretty when she does that.

"Hubert stole another bone this morning," Stewart declared. Hubert sort of glared at him, with a dog's sort of glare, appearing a little offended, as if Stewart had just called him an importune name.

"Sorry, Hubert. I just wanted Lisa to know," Stewart said, and Hubert's expression softened.

"I know," Lisa replied. "It was all over the coffee shop in the afternoon. Seems like this dog crime wave has got the entire town talking."

"I know. A lot of customers make a point of asking if the dog bandit came in yet."

Lisa beamed.

"My story got a lot of attention."

"It should. It was funny."

"A lot of attention."

Lisa looked as if she was ready to burst.

"You'll never guess who noticed it. Never in a million years."

Stewart pursed his mouth, trying to appear deep in thought, even though he had no real idea who might be interested in the story and why Lisa was excited. It was a subject he had simply not considered.

"I don't know. I give. Tell me."

Lisa sat up straight.

"KDKA."

"Who?"

"KDKA. The big TV station in Pittsburgh! I think they have a radio station, too, but this TV producer called me. They say they want to come out and do a feature on the bandit dog. And they want to talk to me! Stewart! This is huge. KDKA. That's a real TV station. Not some cable show, I mean, like two guys in a van with an iPhone for a camera."

Stewart hoped his smile appeared genuine and authentic.

But right after he heard the word "Pittsburgh," he immediately developed a scenario in which Lisa was offered a job and she left Wellsboro forever, leaving him—and Hubert—forever, alone, bagging groceries at the Tops Market until he was in his forties and then almost dead, or something equally as bad.

"That's great, Lisa. Really great."

But I don't mean it. Not at all. I don't like being left alone. And I don't want it to happen again.

Chapter Eleven

*B*ARGAIN BILL was in a great mood—the best mood he had been in for months and months, even better than when he sold ten cars in one day.

"Ten cars! All by myself. Can you believe it?"

His wife had smiled that day when he'd entered the house, then nodded and gone back to doing her word search puzzle. She was never far from a book of word search puzzles. Their house was home to perhaps twenty different word search puzzle books, each one with a pencil stuck between the pages of the last completed puzzle. In the garage, there were seven plastic bins, the large size, filled with completed word search puzzle books. She refused to let her husband discard any of them.

"They're not hurting you. Just let them be. It's my hobby, not yours."

But none of that mattered just now.

His lost-dog ruse had worked. People were stopping in at the car lot, asking him about the dog—Rover, he now called it, "my sweet Rover"—and how he got the dog from that rescue shelter in Lewisburg, the one that just closed down, and how it ran off during a spring thunderstorm and how he was nearly heartbroken until he saw the posters in town and how he would do anything to get him back.

"The five-hundred-dollar discount is hardly enough—but it

is all that I can do. I am just a struggling businessman who lost his most favorite companion."

His wife simply nodded as he laid out his somewhat complicated scenario of the lost dog and the rescue shelter, and the trip to Lewisburg, and all the rest, but she had assured him, several times, that she would back up his story, no matter how outlandish she might have considered it to be.

"It's not a big enough lie for me to lose sleep over," she told him. "It's not like you embezzled or held back taxes. It's a dog. A dog no one wants."

This morning, the assistant pastor at the Good Hope Church stopped by to ask about the dog, but Bargain Bill came *this close* to getting him into a 2009 Mazda hatchback with low miles and new tires.

It's working. People are stopping in for no reason other than to ask about the mutt.

After the first blush of interest and calls and condolences, Bargain Bill had returned to the Insta-Print store and had Sam make a huge version of his original WANTED poster, and this time he had him print it on canvas, nearly six feet high and over four feet wide. He tied one end to the telephone pole outside his office and the other side he fastened to a faded red Ram pickup truck that had been on the lot for more than three months. The sign luffed in the breeze, flapping in and out, like it was alive and breathing.

That'll get people to slow down.

He stood back and waved at a car that honked as it went by.

And maybe it'll help get this truck sold.

Bargain Bill sauntered back to his office, full of high spirits and great expectations, knowing that this day would obviously be "a super-duper" day.

The good feeling almost made him wish that the dog really belonged to him.

→

Ralph Arden hiked up his work-grade khaki trousers with the built-in, absolutely permanent crease, and continued down Maple Street. The breeze was stout this morning, but warm. Strands of black hair were loosened from his carefully combed hair, hiding the bald spot that everyone could see, regardless of his mastery of comb and spray.

Regardless, Ralph felt almost pleasant this morning. Three cars slowed as they passed, the drivers shouting out to him questions about the dog and whether he had any leads and what the reward was up to today.

Well, there was that car filled with young hoodlum types who shouted out "Hey, Mr. Wiggins! Cujo goin' to get you, Mr. Wiggins!" as they passed, but they were, of course, hoodlums, or hooligans, who deserved to be ignored, which he did, with mature, adult condescension.

And who is Mr. Wiggins?

But even a packet of ruffians could not disrupt his mood this day.

Ralph Arden, of Meadville, originally, had been store manager of the Tops Market in Wellsboro for over six years now, and he'd never once felt as if he were considered a part of the proper Wellsboro society. He was not sure if there really was much to proper Wellsboro society—but whatever there was, he felt estranged from it.

They must have parties and dinners and go on picnics, but

I'm never invited. It's like a tight clique that keeps out outsiders, like me. I know I'm just the manager of the second biggest grocery store in Tioga County, and I suppose that doesn't mean anything to the locals here—but it should. I'm all but invisible to the movers and shakers in town.

But now, and for the last few weeks, he felt visible—very and completely visible. People stopped by his table as he had dinner at the Wellsboro Diner, and that had never once happened before—never, ever in six years.

Like the people in the cars this morning, they asked about the dog and wouldn't it be prudent to station a guard by the dog food aisle (too expensive) or perhaps move the rawhide bones to a higher shelf (goes counter to corporate's approved shelf plan-o-gram).

And no one—not even that snobby Wilson Demerrit who was picked to manage the new store in Erie—could get away with making changes in the plan-o-gram without corporate approval, and no one gets corporate approval.

His new friends stopped and chatted and commiserated and smiled and shook his hand and introduced their wives and/or children to him. It was like—being accepted.

And Ralph really liked the feeling.

Part of him, the part he would never reveal to corporate, ever, that hidden part of him, sort of almost hoped that the dog would not get caught, but he could never, never, ever tell a soul. The longer the dog was on the loose, the longer Mr. Ralph Arden would be accepted.

No, he had to be a good employee of the Tops chain and make sure that shoplifting and thievery were punished to the full extent of the law.

As he walked this morning, tilting his face into the sun, he wondered what sort of ultimate punishment a dog might receive, a dog who had already stolen more than twenty-five dollars' worth of merchandise.

That might make it a felony, right? Maybe it has to be more than that, but still ... criminal activity. And habitual. That makes it really serious.

Tucked away in a nondescript, steel-sided building edging toward the city limits, the offices of the *Wellsboro Gazette* were just a part of the publishing empire of Tioga Publishing—a rather small part of a small empire and that suited the current editor, David Grback, just fine.

"Yes, you spell it G-r-back, with no vowel in between the *G* and the *r*. Yes, I know it looks odd, but that's how they spelled it in the 'old country.'"

He had been tempted a thousand times to change it, either legally or just by changing it in his professional life, but he had never gotten around to doing so.

"It does make me memorable," he'd once explained to a former girlfriend, who had refused to leave New York City when David apparently lost his mind and resigned from the *New York Times* to take a job in a town that no one had ever heard of for a salary that the custodian of the Times Building would have dismissed as insulting.

After ten years of living in a fourth-floor New York City walk-up, with limited hot water and no views, with homeless people—aggressive, panhandling homeless people—living on each corner of his block, he had decided he'd had enough.

Wellsboro needed an editor and he needed out of New York.

And for the last seven years he had covered everything from city council meetings in which elected officials spent six hours deciding on paint colors for the new water hydrants in town, to high school sports, which he more or less liked, mostly because at that point the student-athletes were just that, both students and athletes and not jaded by culture or contracts or hordes of obsequious, sycophantic followers.

As an editor, David Grback had a pedantic obsession with his word-a-day calendar. He had three different copies in his office, each with a different level of difficulty.

As often as he could, he inserted one of the words into his weekly column—that is, unless the president of the company barked from his office that "no one outside of Daniel Webster would know that word. And maybe not even him."

David considered it a game that they both enjoyed. He was wrong, of course, but the company president knew his highly trained editor was working for the proverbial peanuts, so he never announced his great annoyance at the word games, at least not in public.

But over the last three weeks, David's quest for a quiet life in the valleys of central Pennsylvania had been mazed (January 17 on the real smart calendar), or befuddled or flummoxed.

That was when the story of the "dog bandit" first ran. David considered it a semi-cute human-interest story that might generate a chuckle or two, but was amazed—and bemused—at the interest it generated. The reporter, or rather the not-paid-at-the-time and now underpaid freelance contributor of the piece, a Miss Lisa Goodly, a mere slip of a girl but very bright and very energetic, had sparked something in town—something approaching a community-wide dialogue.

"Is the dog a criminal?"

"Is the dog a runaway?'

"You can't hold the dog accountable—he's just hungry."

"Can we blame the dog for the ills of society?"

Actually, the discourse never rose to that level, but people are talking about it. And I sense two camps: one that wouldn't mind catching the mutt for the rewards, and the other who would harbor the fugitive canine to keep it safe from the "man" and the evil authorities.

On his cluttered desk, he spread out an ad that Bargain Bill had dropped off the night before—a full half-page ad in the main section of the paper, and at full price. The ad featured a picture of the dog, taken from the *Gazette* files, with the same sort of wording as his poster but going into more detail about how heartbroken he and his wife were over the disappearance of their precious Rover.

The cynic in David, honed after nearly two decades of dealing with public officials who tended to treat the truth as if it were a dangerous narcotic and it would be prudent never to let the public have a taste, saw through Bargain Bill's subterfuge in a second.

It's not his dog. He just wants free publicity, he thought.

But David could not prove his intuition, so Bargain Bill's story, pathetic as it was, became part of the bigger story.

And his new reporting star, Ms. Goodly, covered it all, with

a keen eye and the wisdom, or cynicism, of a much more seasoned reporter.

*She'll make a good reporter one day…unless she marries
one of the hillbillies in town and has a passel of kids and spends
the rest of her life in a trailer drinking diet Mountain Dew and
eating store-brand Cheetos.*

While David loved the low stress of being an editor on the
Gazette, he had no love lost for some of the more countrified
aspects of small-town, bucolic life.

And today, well, today was proving to be one of those
perplexing days that could nonplus the most seasoned, jaded
newspaperperson.

Only moments after he arrived at the office, his phone warbled and the phone number displayed was odd, with more
digits than necessary. To his stupefaction, the voice on the
other end, in a garbled, time-distorted manner, announced itself as an "editor of the *Daily Mail* in England, the country and
not the New England in your eastern states."

Already David did not like this person, but he heard him out.

The man wanted information and pictures of the bandit
dog. Somehow he had picked up the story. David knew from
the paper's Web site that such features were its stock-in-trade,
but he himself never expected to be on their radar.

And even though he was pretty sure he did not like English
people, especially English people in the press, he agreed to
send copy and pictures that morning.

"We might spice it up just a bit, chap. You don't mind, do
you?"

"No. Just spell Grback and Wellsboro correctly. No *-ough*
on *-boro*, okay?"

"Right-o."

And won't our Ms. Goodly be pleased to see her story go international?

Only moments after he hung up with his snooty counterpart across the pond, his phone rang again. The caller ID lit up and announced the call was from KDKA Television in Pittsburgh—one of the three "big" TV stations in the tri-state area.

David closed his eyes.

It's going to be about the dog. I know.

And it was.

⌒

Jerry Mallick pushed the pile of mail from the table and it scattered on the kitchen floor like leaves in autumn—that is, if leaves were made up of bills, direct-mail advertising, political circulars, and faux magazines filled with coupons and half-price specials for duct cleaning.

He spread out the *Wellsboro Gazette* of the week prior, "borrowed" from that fancy coffee shop in town.

"No one was reading it," he told himself. "And it was already old by the time I took it."

Jerry Mallick was the landlord of the house where Lisa and Stewart lived, as he did himself, in the first-floor apartment. His third tenant, an older woman—Mrs. Glumper or Gumper or Gomper—had passed away last fall, and so far he had no takers on the ad that continued to run in the "Apartments to Rent" section of the *Gazette*.

You think they would give me a free newspaper each week,

since I been paying for this stupid ad and I ain't got a single re-sponse yet.

He slowly made his way through the story about the dog, reading twice, just to make sure, the paragraphs about the rewards being offered by Tops Market and that used-car guy on the east side of town.

Jerry had inherited the large Victorian from his mother fifteen years earlier. She had had enough of winter weather and had moved to a retirement community in Florida, where she'd died two years later from being hit by a bus filled with seniors on their way to Disney World.

Jerry did not relish the idea of being a landlord, but getting money for doing nothing was pleasant enough. He still did odd jobs, on occasion—hauling things in his truck, snowplowing in the winter—all things that could be accomplished sporadically and did not require new attire, or clean attire, for that matter.

"If that guy gives me five hundred dollars off . . . I could just about afford that Ram pickup that he has in his lot. If my valves get any louder, I 'spect the whole engine in the Chevy could go any minute."

Jerry bent close to the paper and the picture of the dog, trying to memorize the color and the features.

"I got nothing else to do. I can go hunting for a dog, I guess."

He stood up and shuffled through the letters and circulars on the floor, like walking through a forest in the fall. Then he stopped and checked his wallet.

"Five bucks."

He smiled. It was just enough for a gallon of gas and maybe a Slim Jim at that MinitMart over on Tioga.

"Now to hunt up that dog and make me some money."

Two floors above Mr. Mallick, Hubert sat and let the morning sun shine on his face. The dog's eyes were shut. The warmth of the sun felt good. It had been a long time since the dog had felt warm and safe with a nearly full stomach.

He wondered why the human gave him only one measure of food. He'd kept talking as he poured it out, so he must have some sort of reason for it. And while the dog's stomach was not totally full, it was fuller than it had been in a very, very long time.

It had not been this full since the dog had to leave the place where those other humans lived—the humans that were not nice, who were sometimes hurtful and mean.

An unpleasant expression came over the dog's face as this memory came to mind. His eyes closed tighter, just for a moment, as if he were bracing for something, or against something, and wincing in response.

Then he opened his eyes and stood and shook himself, as if he were wet from a rain.

He wasn't, of course, but the act of shaking provided a clearing moment for his thoughts, shaking the bad memories away as best he could. His left shoulder still bore a long jagged scar and it ached sometimes, but he did not bring attention to it, or whimper, or favor that side.

Dogs simply endured, and did the best that they could with the reality that was presented to them. Who would listen if they hurt? And there were only a few humans, that Hubert encountered, who would try to understand the language of a dog.

Hubert. He smiled slightly at the sound of that word in his thoughts—it sounded funny to the dog, that was all.

Hubert.

Hubert.

Maybe it was funny because it was like the sound of that bird that he once heard in the woods.

Hubert.

He had quickly realized that was the sound that this human made when he was speaking to him. It would do.

Hubert.

Hubert.

And, after all, a dog has little say in what sounds a human assigns to certain objects—or to certain dogs.

The dog, Hubert, looked up and stared at the ceiling.

It was the first time in many, many, many days that he could not see the sky and the sun and the clouds and the stars when he looked up.

This was different from his previous reality.

Not bad, but different.

He had forgotten, almost, how sweet the sleep felt when he no longer had to listen for the creak and the crack of the twigs and the rumble of some other animal clumping through dried leaves, perhaps a larger animal that had gained his scent. No, the sleep inside this place was sound, and real, and deep.

The dog sniffed. He had already memorized the scent of this human.

But when he looked in his eyes, the human's eyes, Hubert saw something else. It was the same expression that the dog had carried with him for so long. The look of being lost. The look of being confused. The look of being just a little scared.

The look was hidden, put away, but Hubert knew it was there. Kindred spirits know these things. Shared pain is not easily disguised.

Hubert then smiled. *I like him.*

And that other human, the smaller human who smelled like flowers. The dog liked her, too.

She knew exactly how to scratch and where to scratch, not too hard, not too soft, and in just the right place.

She lived here, but not here. She was behind that wooden thing on the steps. That must be her den.

The dog thought of his mother again, who was soft and kind and was the nicest dog any dog could imagine. This human reminded him of her.

The dog sat back down, and when he lay down his head remained in the sun.

It felt good to be warm and safe.

The dog knew, he simply knew, all during his lost days, that a dog should not be lost—and that someone or something watched over dogs and would keep him from more harm and lead him to a place where he could be warm and fed and a member of a pack once again.

That was the way dogs saw the world.

Dogs should be with those who loved them, who watched out for them, who could be trusted. That was the way that a dog saw as right and true and perfect—as perfect as nature allows.

He had spent too long by himself. Being alone was not how a dog's world should be. He needed to be part of a pack. He needed to protect others in his pack. They all needed to look out for each other. That was the way of the dog world. He knew it to be true. He knew it to be right.

And now, perhaps now, after all this time, the power that graced all of nature with life had brought him here to be part of this pack. The dog tilted his head, trying to understand if this feeling was correct and true and not just a desire born of cold and hunger.

No, he decided, it was true. He was supposed to be here. This pack needed him.

And he needed them.

The dog that needed to be found had found his pack at last.

And with that thought in his mind, he let sleep come over him again, with just a soft smile on his lips.

Chapter Twelve

AFTER WORK, Stewart planned to stop in at the Wired Rooster. He wanted to see Lisa but did not want to see Lisa. If she were dead-set on moving to Pittsburgh and forgetting all about him and Hubert, well, there wasn't anything he could do about it, so why should he invest the time getting to know her better when all she was going to do was break his heart in the end? *It's happened before,* he thought, *and this time is probably no different.*

And what about poor Hubert? He really seems to like you, too. You're just going to up and leave him? He'll be crushed.

Stewart took a deep breath.

Dogs feel crushed, right? Probably, anyhow. I bet they have feelings just like people.

Stewart stopped a block away from the coffee shop and thought about slapping himself on the face and telling himself to "snap out of it."

He knew he had a tendency to see the gloomy side of any situation, and also to take possibilities to the worst possible ending there was—well before any early indicators pointed in the direction of that grim outcome.

They just want to talk to her. And then they'll be gone and everything will be forgotten and the fancy TV reporters will move on to the next story in line. She'll stay in Wellsboro.

Stewart looked down at his hands and sighed.

That's what I thought about my mother, too. That she would stay here. And she didn't.

But Lisa is different than my mother was. She's nice. And she'll stay here. For Hubert, at least. The TV people won't make her leave.

Of course Stewart had no way of knowing, just then, that he was totally and disastrously wrong—concerning just about everything he was obsessing about at the moment.

⤚

"Hey, Lisa," he said as he entered, putting his best, most positive tone of voice out there so she would not suspect anything wrong.

"Stewart," she called out. "You stopped after work. This is so sweet of you."

He ordered a small latte, calling it a small and not a *piccolo latte* as it was listed on the menu.

"Listen, if you can sit with this for ten minutes, then I can join you on my break. Can you wait for me? Say you can, okay? Please?"

She is just so cute.

"Sure. I'm off work. I'll read the paper while I wait. I'll reread your story."

She laughed, and Stewart liked it when she laughed.

In eight minutes, Lisa joined Stewart at the small table in the corner, well away from the entrance. She carried a plastic cup filled with ice and water.

"After a day of making coffee, the last thing I want is another coffee," she explained as she sipped the water.

"Must be why I don't have any food or groceries in my

house," Stewart said, thinking it was a serious reply, but to which Lisa broke out in a loud peal of laughter, much like the sounds of bells chiming.

"You are so funny, Stewart. You lived upstairs from me for what, over a year, and I never knew how funny you were."

Neither did I.

"So when do the people from the TV come?"

"Tomorrow at one. They said that they may want the story for the late news that night—can you imagine? Me being on TV? Like a real reporter? They said they would have to drive back right after the interviews and pictures and all that. And if it was too late, they would use it in the morning."

Stewart nodded.

"It's at least a four-hour drive."

"I know. I checked on MapQuest."

See? She is thinking of leaving. Why else would she be looking at directions to Pittsburgh?

Stewart sipped his latte, now almost room temperature. It still tasted better, much better, than the instant coffee he made at home.

It should—it was several dollars more expensive.

"Stewart, this could be a huge break for me. And it might be nothing at all. But at least the editor of the paper knows me now. And if nothing else, I can keep writing things for the *Gazette*. Build up a portfolio."

"Sure."

I wonder what sort of portfolio I could build up for being a political science major.

"Hey, Stewart, can I ask you a question? You don't have to answer it, if you don't want to."

"Sure. You can ask me."

"Well, you know, you had that calendar on your counter, and I sort of assumed that you went to church and all that. The calendar with the Bible verses on it."

"Sure."

"Well, we're like friends now, aren't we?"

"Sure. Friends."

Lisa looked uncomfortable, or embarrassed, or perhaps even hesitant, but she pressed on.

"Well, since we're friends, maybe we could go to church together? I mean, we wouldn't have to go to my church. We could go where you go. I mean, just two people going to church. That's all. I've been going by myself for a long time. I know people there and I have people to sit with and all that, but it would be nice to go with someone. Do you know what I mean?"

"Sure. With someone."

What church do I go to? Which one? Not the Catholic church. I'm pretty sure she's not Catholic. Maybe that Lutheran one on Main Street. That looks like a nice place. It has stained-glass windows. That means it's a good church, right?

"So . . . do you want to . . . this Sunday?"

Stewart had never, ever been asked out on a date by a girl. He knew going to church was not exactly a date, but still, a girl had asked him, and that was a first.

"Sure. That would be okay. But we can go to the church you go to. Since you asked, right? You get to pick. Like going out to dinner."

She laughed again, then looked at her watch.

"My break is over, Stewart. Can I come up tonight and ask you about today's robbery?"

"Sure. I've got some video of it. Maybe you can show it to the TV people. Sort of the back end of Hubert."

He rose as she did and she leaned forward and gave him a quick hug, right there in the open, right there in the middle of the Wired Rooster and everything.

"I'll see you tonight."

"Sure."

As he walked outside, he took a deep breath.

Maybe she won't move to Pittsburgh. That would be really nice. If she didn't.

Chapter Thirteen

L ISA'S SHIFT ran through six o'clock, which she did not mind because it got her closer to forty hours and a more substantial paycheck—although even at forty hours the evaluation of *substantial* was debatable.

It was a different crowd of people in the afternoon than in the morning. Folks in the morning, the majority of them, were stopping in on their way to work. A few patrons, older folks, mainly, who had retired and had no real appointments, came in, sat, and talked for a while. They were her regulars and she knew many by name.

But in the afternoon it was a different crowd. They were older, but not old, and most of them were not skipping out of a job for a few minutes—they simply had no job to skip out of. They would buy a small coffee and sit and talk and stare out the window for hours on end.

I guess it would be better than watching afternoon TV.

Lately, many of their conversations centered on the "bandit dog."

They talk louder than the old people. Maybe because they spend too much time at bars shouting over the music.

One semiregular, Kevin or Kellan or Carl...

He has that backwoods accent that no one understands.

...was speaking about catching the dog.

"I wuz talkin' to crazy Jerry Mallick las' night..."

Hey, that's my landlord.

" . . . and he said he was headin' out dog hunting t'day. If he could scramble up 'nuff money fur gas."

Lisa usually did not enter into the conversations of customers, but the place was nearly empty and she could not stop herself.

"Dog hunting? What do you mean, dog hunting?"

Kevin or Kellan or Carl looked up, surprised that anyone was listening to him.

"Whale . . . huntin' dogs, ye know. That dog robber one. With the reward. Jerry said he got his shotgun all ready and that wuz that."

Lisa, in a perfect world, would have jumped over the counter and tried to throttle Kevin or Kellan or Carl, but the counter was high and she was not a tall girl and manhandling and beating on customers might be an offense that would warrant termination.

Maybe.

Lisa had to say something. "Listen, if you see 'crazy' Jerry, you have to tell him that there is no reward if the dog is dead. None. There actually may be a fine if it is harmed in any way."

Lisa sounded firmer, and a little angrier, than she had ever sounded before in the Wired Rooster, perhaps ever in her life.

"No reward?"

"None. The dog has to be alive. For Pete's sake, we're not dealing with a rabid grizzly bear. It's just a hungry dog."

Kevin or Kellan or Carl scratched his head.

"No reward for being dead? Whale, I'll b'sure to tell Jerry, if I sees him, ye know."

With that, Kevin or Kellan or Carl got up, made a show of tossing his empty coffee cup into the recycling bin.

"Safe the world, you betcha."

Lisa all but slumped over the counter, as if defeated.

The only other patron in the store was Nathan George, who often came in the afternoon after attending to matters at the county courthouse in town. He may have been a competent attorney, but whatever sport coat he wore, the garment was generally one size too small.

"Mr. George..." Lisa began.

"Nathan, if you would," he replied, offering her a sidelong smile that creeped her out just a little.

"Nathan, what would happen if someone in town actually owned that dog? Would they be liable—or whatever it's called legally?"

Nathan sidled closer to the counter.

"If I give you free legal advice, do I get another latte? Quid pro quo, as it were."

Lisa was the only staff person in the store at the time.

"Sure. A new *piccolo latte*. For advice."

She went about making him his coffee.

"With two shots of espresso, if you would."

"Sure."

"Back to your legal query. If the owner were local, and knew what the dog was up to, he might be fined. Could be fined. That is if you could prove that they knew what the dog was doing and did not do anything to curtail the illegal activity. Not an open-and-shut case, by any stretch of the imagination."

He added three artificial sweeteners to his coffee and stirred it with great deliberateness, licking off the stirrer before tossing it away.

"And they might face a fine for harboring a nuisance pet.

Or a destructive animal. Not using a leash. Not keeping the animal's vaccinations up to date. A plethora of possible ordinance offenses."

"Is that a lot of fines? Or money involved?"

"Miss Goodly, as long as you don't quote me by name in your next newspaper article—simply call me an 'unnamed legal source'—none of these violations reaches felony status. Unless the dog chews off the leg of the store manager—and that wouldn't bother me. That pompous Mr. Arden. It's a grocery store, for Pete's sake, not Tiffany's."

"So not a lot of money at risk?"

"If the DA wanted to throw the book at the dog's owner, maybe a thousand dollars in fines total. But that's a stretch. It is an election year, so I don't put anything past that incompetent law clerk of a DA that the wise citizens of this county have voted into office—for a third time."

"Thanks," Lisa said. "And the next latte will be on me as well."

"As long as you deny I said anything untoward about anyone, Miss Goodly, I will be your go-to, unnamed source for all things legal. Our little secret, okay? I still need to practice law in this backwater village."

"You have a deal . . . Nathan. Thanks."

And Mr. George gave her that lopsided, pickerel smile again and Lisa felt a cold shudder run up her back in response.

As he left, Lisa's pleasant, customer-pleasing smile disappeared.

I'm sure Stewart doesn't have that kind of money. A thousand dollars.

She wiped the counter.

But then, neither do I.

Chapter Fourteen

L ISA WAS UP early that morning. She had traded Wednesday
off with Janie and now had to work Saturday. But she did
not want to meet a real celebrity while smelling of coffee and
scones and steamed two percent milk. She did not own a large
enough wardrobe to agonize over her outfit selection, but she
did spend extra time ironing her blouse and making sure that
her shoes, while not highly polished, were not dusty and
coffee-stained, either.

She heard Stewart sneak out early, very early, speaking in
hushed tones. It was still dark outside and she knew he was
sneaking Hubert outside for a few minutes, before dawn broke
and everyone could see what he was doing.

On their return, she heard the soft clicking of Hubert's nails
on the steps, a slow, methodical climbing, so as not to raise suspicion on anyone's part. Stewart descended the steps again, not
much later, and she was very tempted to stop him before he left.

She was becoming fond of him. Sort of. Almost.

*I guess I have a history of falling for guys I date too early and
too fast. This doesn't seem like that, though.*

She adjusted the heat setting on the iron.

*And I was pretty sure that there weren't any guys my age in
this town who were normal.*

She looked out her bedroom window and watched him
walk toward town.

But Stewart is normal. Nice and kind and normal. Gentle. Maybe a little lost—but who isn't?

She hurried back to her ironing. She would not get dressed for several more hours but wanted everything ready when the time came.

And I'm not falling for him. Not this time. I'm not wearing my heart on my sleeve, like my mother says I do. Or did.

She had printed out a copy of her résumé, just in case, which she slipped into a leather-like folder that held a pen and a yellow legal pad.

It makes me look professional.

She looked at her reflection in the bathroom mirror.

That is if a fourteen-year-old masquerading as an adult can look professional.

―

The market was busier than normal. On Wednesday, everyone in the Wellsboro zip code received the Tops Market circular, and there was a full-page ad in the *Gazette*. That always brought out the bargain-hunters early in the day.

No sense in waiting to make the trip if they run out of Cool Whip halfway through the sale.

But Stewart thought today might be busier than the normal Wednesday. And he thought that there were more people carrying cell phones, out in the open, than he had ever noticed before.

That's odd.

He busied himself with stocking each register with a full complement of paper and plastic bags, emptying the trash cans at each station—or at least checking to see if they *really* needed emptying, all under the watchful eye of Mr. Arden. For the last few days he had positioned himself in the far corner of the front of the store for much of the day, perhaps so he could keep an eye on the front doors, and see if the police actually did what they said they would do and cruised past the store "more often than never," as Lieutenant Vardish had put it during yesterday's store meeting.

A few minutes after nine o'clock, when Stewart had run back to the soup aisle, aisle three, for a price check, he heard a small crest of sound, like a wave on a lake splashing against the shore driven by a slight breeze.

But he did hear, clearly, and above the modest din, Mr. Arden's high-pitched squeal, almost a squeal, porcine-like, nearly, "It's that dog! It's that dog! Stewart! Stewart!"

Stewart dropped the can of Top Valu cream of mushroom soup and sprinted over to aisle five, fumbling for his cell phone in his pocket as he ran. He had no intention of catching Hubert, other than on film.

And it's not film. It's digital—or electronic—but not film.

He arrived just as Hubert arrived at the bin of rawhide bones. Hubert looked up, puzzled, and turned his head to the side, as if hearing a high-pitched squeal of some sort.

Maybe Hubert is reacting to Mr. Arden's screeching.

It appeared to Stewart that Hubert recognized who he was.

For sure he knew who I was.

The dog stopped, for just a moment and smiled, wagging his tail.

Stewart said, "Hey, Hubert," but said it very softly.

Hubert nodded, sort of, smiled more, then took one of the rawhide chews.

Stewart grabbed his phone and managed to get most of the robbery videoed without much shaking or loss of focus.

Then Hubert stared at Stewart, with the bone protruding out of both sides of his mouth, turned, and jogged back toward the entrance, speeding up and sliding around the corner like a cartoon dog digging for traction on the tile floor and drawing a bead on the automatic doors, accomplishing this sliding, complex getaway maneuver with verve and precision, as if he had spent hours practicing the moves.

Stewart couldn't see what Hubert was doing, but he could hear.

"Stop that dog! Stop that dog!"

That was Mr. Arden, of course. Then he clambered into view, arms and legs akimbo, almost jogging toward the entrance, also like a cartoon character, going as fast as a sedentary, overweight grocery store manager could manage in a time of crisis.

"Bar the doors! Get away from the mats!"

That was Mr. Arden again.

"Didn't I tell you to get away from the doors! Doesn't anyone in this town listen?"

By this time Stewart had slid into register number five.

"I dropped the can. Sorry. It was eighty-seven cents," he shouted at the cashier—Josie or Josephine or Jay-Jay. (The name tag on her smock depended on her mood and hair color du jour.) Then he almost sprinted out the double exit doors.

Automatic doors are really slow when you're trying to run through them.

He made it outside and saw Hubert turn down Main Street, obviously heading back to Stewart's place. He ran as fast as he could and as he made the turn shouted out, "Hubert! Wait! Hubert!"

And Hubert slowed, then turned around, grinning wildly, the rawhide still in his mouth.

Stewart jogged up to him, stopping five feet away. He didn't want to scare him. And Stewart still wasn't sure just how a dog reacts to certain situations—like being chased with food in its mouth.

Stewart crouched down to Hubert's perspective.

"Hubert. How did you get out? You're not supposed to steal things. You know that, right? That's sort of in the Bible."

What in the world made me say that? The Bible? What does a dog know about God and His rules?

Hubert almost hung his head, a little, as if he were just a bit ashamed, but he did not drop the bone.

"Do you want to give it back?"

Hubert, not far removed from being hungry every day and all day for weeks and weeks and weeks, shook his head, indicating no.

"Hubert," Stewart said, trying to mimic the scolding voice he often heard his mother use, rising in inflection and drawing out the word.

Hubert shook his head again, then smiled, turned, and ran off down Main Street, taking a left on Maple, just like he had done before.

From behind Stewart came the screeching voice of an irate grocery store manager: "You almost had him! Why didn't you tackle him! Stewart! What's wrong with you people?"

Stewart stood and presented his thought-of-on-the-fly-hoping-it-sounded-authentic-and-heartfelt response.

"Maybe it had some sort of disease and if I caught the disease then the store might be liable and I didn't want to get you in trouble, Mr. Arden. I thought about grabbing it just like you said, but then the dog growled and showed his teeth."

Stewart wondered if he told the lie with enough honesty.

And a moment later, he knew.

Mr. Arden believed him.

After Mr. Arden left, sputtering and mumbling angrily to himself, Stewart took out his phone and forwarded his video to Lisa with the short message, "Use this on your interview. It's from this A.M. Somehow Hubert got out. Stewart."

Then he made his way back to the store, wondering if he had helped Lisa and if she would remember him and Hubert when she moved to Pittsburgh and became a famous TV reporter.

The store was still abuzz when Stewart returned, and everyone, or nearly everyone, wanted a second-by-second, frame-by-frame recap of today's daring daylight robbery—with which he was glad to comply.

It's better than just bagging groceries.

—

At twelve forty-five, Lisa positioned herself outside the Wired Rooster. That was where Heather Orlando said she and the KDKA News van would meet her. At one o'clock.

Is Orlando a real name? Or did she make it up? Heather Orlando. That doesn't sound real, does it?

Three minutes to one and Lisa saw the van coming, with a big radar dish or whatever it was on the roof and a long metal pole thing with wires coiled around, folded down for driving.

"That must be them," she said and offered a small, smiling wave as they slowed and pulled to the curb. "As if there are lots of those vans in Wellsboro."

"Lisa? Lisa Goodly?"

"That's me. Lisa."

Heather Orlando stepped out of the van looking like she would feel comfortable walking on some red carpet—maybe not at the Oscars, but she was really pretty and really professional, wearing her trademark pink suit. It might have been a Chanel suit, but Lisa did not automatically recognize high couture, which meant any fashion that wasn't sold in the Fashion Bug in Lewisburg.

"Heather Orlando, KDKA Action News Team 2. So nice to meet you."

"Likewise."

Likewise.

Lisa wanted to smack herself on the forehead.

Likewise? That is so stupid sounding. Likewise?

"Listen, Lisa, it has been a long, long drive up here."

Then she leaned closer to her, almost too close, and whispered something.

Lisa nodded.

"Sure. It's in the back. On the left."

And with that, Heather scampered away and hurried inside the Wired Rooster.

The driver slid open the van's door, revealing all sorts of electronic gizmos and blinking lights inside. He grabbed a large camera from the floor of the van and began to fiddle with the dials as another man exited carrying a big, furry boom microphone.

They nodded in Lisa's direction.

Then the cameraman stage-whispered.

"This is like the twentieth pit stop we've made since leaving Pittsburgh. I figure we got twenty miles to the bathroom break."

The cameraman laughed, or, more accurately, guffawed.

"You know who's worse?"

"Yeah. Jennifer Gill. She gets ten miles per."

Heather returned, her very high and very thin nearly stiletto heels clacking loudly.

"So, Wellsboro has a dog bandit?"

Lisa nodded. "It appears that way. It's given the town something to talk about, since not much else happens here."

"Ohh, that's good. Can you repeat that when we start rolling?"

Lisa managed not to shrug her answer.

"Sure."

The two of them chatted for ten minutes about the particulars of the incidents.

She's actually pretty sharp. She asks good questions.

"And I have some video of the robbery this morning."

"You do?"

Heather became very excited.

"Real video? That is great. Viewers love real videos. Can you show it to me?"

Lisa pulled out her phone.

"Clarence, come here and watch. Tell me if we can use this. Please tell me that we can use it."

The cameraman, obviously Clarence, came over and peered

over his glasses, which were halfway down his nose, at the small screen, watching the fifteen-second clip.

Clarence grunted. "It'll show okay. Decent resolution. E-mail it to me. I'll give you my card."

"Fantastic," Heather said with triumph. "This will run all day. And might even get picked up nationally. Wow. A video of the crime in progress. Fantastic."

Lisa beamed.

"Lisa, let's sit down inside. We can do the interview there, can't we? You said you work there, right?"

"I do. Until a real job comes up."

Heather leaned in close and whispered.

"I worked at an IHOP until I got my first real TV job. I know what it's like."

I like her. I do. She's nice.

Lisa introduced Heather to everyone, including the owner of the Wired Rooster, Gilbert Fenner, who wore a clean apron for the occasion and cleaned off the front table for them, shooing away a pair of retired county workers from their usual perch.

"I'll get you free coffees. Just move, okay? KDKA is filming here."

Lisa and Heather talked a bit more, then Heather called over to the crew.

"We're ready to start. Everything ready?"

Both men from the news van gave her a thumbs-up.

And Heather started with an introduction to the story, then moved on to Lisa, peppering her for details, asking about the town's reactions, about the multiple rewards being offered, if the police or animal control were involved yet, and a few dozen other questions that Lisa tried to keep up with, hoping that she was giving complete, cogent replies and not looking nervous or frightened.

After twenty minutes Heather stopped, pulled back a little, and did a quick twenty-second recap of the story.

"And special thanks to Gilbert Fenner of the Wired Rooster, and to Lisa Goodly, freelance writer for the *Wellsboro Gazette*. This is Heather Orlando in Wellsboro."

The cameraman leaned back and tilted the camera upward on his shoulder.

"That was great, Lisa. You should be a reporter. Good details. Funny."

Lisa swallowed.

Might as well try now.

"Actually, I did major in journalism and communication. Hard to break into the market, I guess."

Heather smiled. "You've got talent. I can see that. Keep trying."

"I am," Lisa replied.

"Tell you what. Here's my card," Heather said, fishing the card out of her suit pocket. "Call me later. Or better yet, send an e-mail. I can send your résumé around for you. If you want."

Lisa nearly dropped her leather-like portfolio.

"I will, Ms. Orlando. That is so nice of you."

"Least I can do. We professional women need to stick together. Right, Clarence?"

Clarence grunted. "Whatever you say, Ms. Orlando."

"Now, can you tell me how to get to the car lot of this . . . Bargain Bill?"

"I could come with you," Lisa said, a hopeful tone in her voice.

"Sure. That would save time. I hate getting lost. It's not far, is it?"

"Nope. Less than a mile. But three turns. Kind of tricky."

"Then ride with us. We want to stop at the newspaper office for a minute, and the grocery store, and then hightail it back home. You would be a help if you showed us the way."

"I would love to. I really would."

———

After work, Stewart walked home, as was normal, but today he kept looking left and right, and under bushes and checking out if a dog was hiding behind any large trees on his route.

There were no dogs, save that barky little white thing in the window of that house on Wilson Avenue.

And he barks at everything. I wonder how the owner stands it? Could be deaf, I guess.

He peered at the burgeoning greenery in the backyard and called out, softly, "Hubert? Are you out here?"

There was no Hubert.

He opened the first-floor door and walked slowly up the steps.

Maybe he's gone. Maybe he ran home. I guess he just needed a place to rest up for a few days.

When he opened his door, Hubert was sitting on the floor in the middle of the kitchen, his tail thumping on the tile floor.

"Hubert," Stewart said, and he knelt down and Hubert rushed him and grappled with him, licking and whining happily.

"How in the world did you get out? And back in?"

Hubert leaned to the left and stared at Stewart's front door. "You opened it?"

Hubert smiled broadly and tried to lick his face again.

The door handle was a latch/lever sort of doorknob, so perhaps Hubert had just risen up and caught it just right with his paw. The downstairs door never really locked—or closed completely—so that would be an easy obstacle to overcome.

The bone Hubert had stolen that morning was half under the rug in the living room. The plastic was still intact, appearing as if Hubert had simply placed it out of sight for safekeeping.

"You did a bad thing this morning, Hubert. Good dogs don't steal."

Hubert appeared to agree, nodding and growling—not really angry growls, but growls of acknowledgment.

"Are you hungry?"

Hubert launched himself into the air, and half twisted as he did, making soft yelping, happy noises as he bounced.

"Okay, I'll get your dinner. And instead of a cup, I'll give you a cup and a half. Maybe you're still hungry and maybe that's why you stole this morning."

Hubert kept up his happy yelps until Stewart filled his bowl with Paws Premium dog food.

Chapter Fifteen

MID-EVENING, both Stewart and Hubert were ensconced in two chairs in the living room watching an episode of *The Brady Bunch*, and they lifted their heads in unison and listened. They heard the soft and rapid footsteps of someone running up the steps. Obviously it was not the landlord, since the landlord had seldom, if ever, ventured up to the third floor. And if it was the landlord, there would be grunting and thumping. Since Stewart was on time with his rent and had no problems with the facilities in the apartment, there was no reason for Jerry to make the long upward climb.

The footfalls matched Lisa's light steps.

Instead of tapping at the door, she must have just leaned close to the door.

"Stewart. It's me. Can I come in?"

Both Stewart and Hubert rose from their chairs and hurried to the door.

Lisa stood in the open doorway, lit from the bulb behind her, face flushed and rosy, her blonde hair tied back with some sort of pink scarf/kerchief thing that made her face look even prettier, Stewart thought, showing her throat and ears and jawbone. The look made her appear younger and more delicate, like a painting or something artistic like that.

Like a model.

Hubert sniffed once and began to circle around himself,

yipping with restrained glee at having both his humans together again.

"Hubert!" she cried and bent down and embraced him, all the while his backside wiggling and joggling with canine elation.

Then she stood and gave Stewart just as passionate a hug, while Hubert danced around them, smiling and snorting as if he had been separated from them for days and days instead of a few hours.

"This has been such a wonderful, perfect day, Stewart. I didn't even mind having to go to work this afternoon when Lydia called in sick."

"Lydia?"

"The tall girl with purple highlights."

"Oh, sure. So what happened with the TV 2 Action News Team?"

"Well, you saw me at the market, right? With Heather Orlando? It was so much fun."

"I did. She seems nice. Real pretty. But sort of plastic, isn't she?"

Lisa crossed her arms and assumed a scolding schoolmarm expression. "Stewart, you have to look like that for TV. I probably should have used more makeup than I did."

Hubert finally settled down and sat, staring up at Lisa.

"You want a Coke? It's not actually Coke. It's the store brand—Tops Cola. And it's always cheaper. It's pretty good, though."

"Sure. A Tops Cola would be swell, Stewart. I just can't tell you how exciting today was."

Lisa curled herself into one chair, Stewart took the other,

and Hubert sat between them, turning to whichever one was speaking. That evening he looked at Lisa a lot more than he looked at Stewart.

"Hubert, you were a bad boy today, weren't you?" Lisa asked, and Hubert hung his head, his nose almost to the floor, when she scolded him.

"He didn't look guilty at all when I told him that," Stewart said as he handed Lisa the almost-Coke.

"You just have to do it right. Maybe women are better at it. Maybe their voice modulates differently. You get it from listening to moms. Who could make you feel guiltier—your dad or mom?"

"I guess it was my grandmother. She sort of raised me."

Lisa's face stayed neutral, as if she were doing her best not to show emotion.

"I'm sorry, Stewart. When did your mom . . . you know . . . pass away?"

"She didn't," Stewart replied. He knew this was not the right moment to bring up his fractured family, memories of abusive parents and all the rest, but the subject had already been opened.

Just the bare minimum, Stewart. If she hears everything, she might be scared off. I don't want Lisa scared off.

"She left when I was pretty young. My dad left at the same time. I think they both thought the other one was bluffing. And since we were living with my grandmother, I suppose they figured I would be taken care of regardless."

"They just left?" Lisa asked, her voice very small.

"Sort of. They weren't exactly Ward and June Cleaver at their best. More like *Married with Children*—you know, that old TV show with the guy that sold shoes?"

"Sure. It's on that station that just shows reruns."

"So they had this huge, daylong fight, and they both took off. My dad sort of stuck around the area."

"And your mom?"

"I didn't see her for five years after that."

Lisa looked down at Hubert for a moment.

I've said too much. She's scared.

"Stewart, I'm sorry. I didn't mean to bring up any hard memories."

Stewart took a deep breath.

"Hey, it's okay. It was a long time ago. And today was a good day, right? That makes things better."

There was a hitch in Lisa's voice, a pause in her eyes, as if she wanted to say something, anything, but simply did not know what that would be, those words that might make things better. She tried to smile.

"Well, Stewart, you're right. It has been a good day."

"Then everything is good. Really. And don't worry. The past is the past, right?"

"Right," she replied, her tone sounding not exactly heartfelt.

"And Hubert is the one who was bad today, weren't you, Hubert?" Stewart said, hoping that the change in the conversation would bring things back to normal, back before he said anything about his past, back to Lisa smiling and being happy.

Stewart thought, or hoped, that his deflection worked.

"He was a bad boy," Lisa agreed.

Hubert looked up at them both, as if his act of looking guilty was penance enough for whatever it was they said he did—whatever it was.

Lisa scratched him behind the ears and Hubert closed his eyes in deep satisfaction, groaning a little in pleasure.

"So tell me all about you and the news lady."

As she tended to Hubert, Lisa began to relate the facts of the interview at the Wired Rooster and the following interviews, starting with Bargain Bill.

"I just don't trust that man," Lisa declared. "I don't believe a word of what he is saying about Hubert. He's a perfect used-car salesman. I think he was even trying to cry when he was talking about 'his lost little doggie.' I could see him wincing, trying to get all teary."

At this Hubert's ear perked up.

"You don't know him, Hubert. Despite what he's saying. He just wants publicity."

Then she explained about the interview with Mr. Grback, the editor of the *Gazette*, and how he said that the story was "just so charming that he had to run it on the front page."

"He called it 'charming.' Can you believe it? He pretends he's such a curmudgeon, but he's really a softie. I mean, he called the story 'charming.' That's saying a lot. I think."

Then she elaborated about the filming at the Tops Market and the interview with Mr. Arden, "who seemed even more pompous and arrogant than when I talked to him. I mean, I think he is really offended at Hubert—like the bones he stole are going to be a major financial hit on the store. He doesn't seem to have a sense of humor at all. Heather was trying to give him an opportunity to say something nice, but he kept talking about criminals and how they need to be locked up for the good of normal society—locked up with the key thrown away."

"Yeah," Stewart said. "I watched you guys. I was having to deal with a 'clean-up in aisle seven.' Somebody dropped a jar of pickles. Sweet pickles, no less. I like them, but they are really sticky when they're all over the floor."

"So then Heather had the crew take a few more shots of outside the store, and I e-mailed them the video of Hubert that you took this morning, and she said that the story was so good that they were going to hurry back to the studio and edit it together so it could run tonight on the eleven o'clock news. You'll stay up with me to watch, won't you, Stewart? I need to share this with somebody. She said that the story and the visuals might even get it picked up by other stations. It might go national."

"Sure. I wouldn't miss this for anything."

Lisa sort of hugged herself.

"I can't believe it. And Heather gave me her card and said to send her my résumé. And that she would show it around if I wanted. Can you believe it?"

I knew it. I knew it. I knew it. She's going to leave me and Hubert and Wellsboro forever. And I'll be stuck mopping up pickle juice for the rest of my life. This is just my luck. Like something I deserve. Especially after what I told her about my crazy family. Like maybe I'm just used to seeing people walk away. Maybe it is what I deserve. That's what my grandmother said—when she was mad. People get what they deserve, she said. That's God's way, she said. God gives people what they deserve. And maybe I deserve being left.

Hubert had been watching Stewart's face for the last few moments. He rose, pushed his head against Stewart's thigh, then lifted himself up and placed his front paws on Stewart's lap. Hubert stared deeply in his eyes, smiling, then whining, then nudging at his chest with his head, as if to get his human to stop thinking bleak, lost, and alone thoughts and instead smile, because the three of them were together and warm and their stomachs were full.

Or at least his was full.

~

Later that evening, Stewart and Lisa pulled the two chairs in the living room closer together so they both had the same view of the TV.

Lisa checked her watch.

"We've got ten minutes until the news."

Stewart nodded.

"Time for another cup of coffee," he said and walked into the kitchen.

Lisa followed him.

"I think I'll join you. Although I don't need the caffeine to get amped up tonight."

As Stewart added water to the kettle, Lisa leaned against the counter.

"Stewart, have you ever gotten a bill for the cable TV?"

Stewart tilted his head.

"No. I haven't. I guess I thought it must come with the apartment."

"I don't think that's the way it works. I think our landlord is stealing the cable signal."

"Really?"

The water started to burble as it heated.

"Think about it. Why do we only get the network shows, hunting and fishing shows, sports, and that station that only shows reruns?"

Stewart smiled.

"Maybe it's the special Wellsboro backwoods package?"

At this, Lisa laughed so loudly that even Hubert stared at her, puzzled at her outburst.

"You are so funny, Stewart."

Back to normal. She's laughing again. That's good. Maybe she'll forget about what I said before—about my lunatic family and all. Maybe.

⤙

The news segment was called "The Canine Bandit of Wellsboro," and it ran just after the hard news section ended and before the sports segment.

"Heather said that if it runs early that means a big thumbs-up from the producers. If it runs before sports, we've got a winner on our hands, is what she said."

The segment started with a teaser, just before a commercial, and the teaser featured a close-up of Heather Orlando inside the Wired Rooster.

"She looks better on TV," Stewart said when the commercial started.

"I think she looked nice in person, too," Lisa replied. "It's just you're not used to it. No one in Wellsboro wears any makeup, or the right kind, that's for sure. I mean the women. I guess no one sees the need to dress up here. For anything."

Then the segment started—at the Wired Rooster. When Lisa

came into view, she reached over and grabbed Stewart's hand and squeezed.

No girl has ever grabbed my hand before. Or squeezed it.

And she held on during the entire segment.

"You look real good on camera," Stewart said quietly, not to interrupt the segment.

Lisa turned quickly, smiled at him, and turned back to the TV.

The interview with Lisa lasted nearly three minutes, which was, by TV standards, a long interview.

"You're funny, too," Stewart said, and Lisa squeezed his hand in response.

Then the scene shifted to Bill Hoskins' car lot—for just a brief shot of him by his new sign that had already been wind torn and patched with gray duct tape. A brief shot of Mr. Grback, the editor of the *Gazette*, followed, in which he scowled until Lisa's name came up and then he said it was all "charming."

Then came an outside shot of the market, which was interrupted by Ms. Orlando touting an exclusive of the "canine thievery as it happened!"

Stewart's video of Hubert taking the bone, smiling, and taking off down the aisle was shown three times while Ms. Orlando talked about it.

Hubert looked up when Lisa pointed at the TV with her free hand.

"That's you, Hubert. You're on TV."

Hubert stared but did not make the connection between the flat, flickering, two-dimensional image on the screen and himself.

Mr. Arden had a twelve-second snippet, in which he said, "All dogs that steal should be locked up and the key thrown away."

And the segment ended with Heather in front of the market, wrapping the story up, ending with a chuckle and a wide, toothy smile.

"I saw you in the background, Stewart. The camera panned around. I think I saw your back."

"Might have been me," Stewart replied. "Maybe."

The station's news anchors came back on.

"Delightful story, Heather," one said.

The other added, "You'll have to keep us posted on the investigation—and if they track the dog down."

Then they went to a commercial.

Lisa exhaled, loudly, squeezed Stewart's hand one more time, then stood up, obviously excited and simply needing to move because of that excitement.

"That was great, wasn't it?"

Stewart stood as well, and Lisa more or less launched herself at him, giving him a happy hug of congratulations.

And then she looked up at him, and he looked down at her. Later on, when he replayed the scene in his mind, he couldn't remember exactly how they wound up kissing each other. It was not for long, though not a short peck, either. Then they broke apart, both of them more embarrassed than not, Lisa looking up at him, sheepish, and Stewart looking down, disoriented, happy, but disoriented, and Hubert bouncing around their legs as if this was the perfect end to whatever that was on the glowing box they both had watched.

Within minutes of the totally unexpected kiss Lisa excused herself, saying that her mother was going to call and she just had to talk with her about today's events.

Stewart said he understood, of course, and stood at the top of the stairs until she got inside her apartment. She looked back, for a glance, smiled, and then slipped inside and out of view.

Stewart touched his lips, gently, as if making sure what happened had actually happened.

No girl has ever initiated a kiss before. Not that I'm experienced with this sort of thing. She did, didn't she? And it was unusual. Wasn't it? Or have I just been living under a rock for the past ten years? Do girls do that now?

Hubert noisily lapped up another drink and then circled the rug a few times and lay down.

"We'll have to go outside tonight, won't we?"

At this Hubert bounded up and ran to the door, looking back at his human.

"I don't have a leash and you don't have a collar—so you have to promise to stay near me, okay?"

Hubert appeared to nod and began his let-me-out-for-a-walk dance.

Stewart grabbed his cell phone. Not that he expected a call, but one never knew.

"We have to be real quiet going down the steps. Okay, Hubert?"

Hubert appeared to nod again, and slowly, and carefully, made his way down the steps, making sure each paw hit the center of the ragged and worn carpet runner.

When they were outside, Stewart said, "Let's go this way, away from town. It's darker this way and there's less traffic. But then there's never much traffic around this town after dark."

The two of them walked, Hubert keeping pace, veering off

every so often to examine some scent or another, never becoming more distant than ten feet or so.

As they walked, Stewart's phone warbled. He recognized the number. Hubert turned his head as Stewart said "Hello," obviously not understanding the function of a cell phone.

"Hi, Dad. How are you?"

"Crappy. Like always. Nothing changes. Always the same."

And just how do I respond to that? Do I say "That's nice"?

"Saw that story about the dog on the news. That's the store where you work, isn't it?"

"It is."

"They talk to you? That Heather What's-her-name reporter? The one that always wears pink?"

Maybe that's why Lisa was wearing a pink scarf.

"No. Just the store manager. And the girl who wrote the story for the newspaper."

"Figures. No one I know ever catches a break."

"It's okay, Dad. I thought it was a cute story."

It doesn't matter what I call it. Whatever I say it was, he'll say the opposite.

"Cute story? It was stupid. And they should just put a cop outside to shoot the dog the next time he comes. Watching it was a waste of my time."

What do I say now?

"Well, I just wanted to see if that was your store. You still bagging groceries?"

"I am. But I keep looking for other jobs."

"Well, good luck. This economy is in a cesspool, if you ask me. Should have bought gold when I wanted to and not listened to your mother. I'd be on Easy Street right now. Her fault that I still have to get up every morning for this stupid job."

"I know. Hard to time the markets, I guess."

"You guess right on that, Stewie. Well, I gotta go. Just wanted to see if that was where you work. You take care, okay. You come up this way, we'll get coffee or something. Or hoist a cold one. Okay?"

"Okay."

Stewart stopped walking, ended the call, slipped the phone back into his pocket, and took a deep breath. Then another.

Maybe a few more will get my blood pressure back to normal.

Hubert came over to him after scratching around at the base of a large oak tree and looked up. The moonlight caught Hubert full on and there was a most plaintive expression on his face, like he was attempting to commiserate with Stewart, or offer some emotional comfort.

"It gets tricky, Hubert. Very tricky."

Hubert appeared to nod.

"Thanks for understanding, though."

And Hubert yelped, just a little, just softly, and as empathetic as a dog yelp can be.

⌒

"Wasn't it great, Mom?" Lisa gushed as she talked with her mother while walking around her apartment. She was too wound up to sit still.

And that kiss ... what was that all about?

"She seems really down to earth. I know she wears a lot of makeup, but they have to when they're on TV, I guess. And she gave me her card and said to e-mail my résumé to her and that she would send it around to people that she knows. This could really be a huge break for me. And it's all because of Stewart."

"Who?" her mother asked.

"You know, Stewart. He lives upstairs. You met him when you helped me move in. Tall, dark hair, intense eyes. He's just a nice guy, you know. Normal."

"Lisa, you're not rushing into anything again, are you? Remember what happened last time. You need to be careful. I love that you want to trust, but there are a lot of people, young men especially, who will take advantage of that."

Lisa glanced out the window overlooking the street as her mother talked and saw Stewart looking about furtively. Then Hubert came into view. Lisa smiled.

"Yes, Mother. I will be careful. I know what happened last time. You told me like a thousand times already. Okay? That I was too much in a hurry. Okay. I got it. But this is different. Stewart goes to church. He has a Verse-a-Day calendar on his counter."

"You were in his apartment?"

She took a deep breath.

"Not like that. I was only up there for a minute. I had to ask him a couple of questions. He works at that store so he saw everything."

"A minute this time. But that's how these things start. And if he lives just upstairs, things could get out of hand far more quickly than you want them to."

Lisa leaned against the kitchen counter. "I know. But we're just friends. It won't be like before. And I am over twenty-one, you know."

"I know. I just don't want to see you hurt. You're still my little girl, no matter how old you are."

She closed her eyes. "Yes, Mom. But what happened the last time will not happen again. I've told you that like a thousand times. I learned my lesson. I don't want to get hurt, and I don't want to hurt you again, Mom. And I promised I won't. I'll be careful. I won't let this get complicated. But he seems like a nice guy. We might even go to church together this Sunday."

"That's...nice. But—okay, I won't start up again. Just, please be careful."

She looked out the window again and Stewart and Hubert had slipped out of view. "I will, Mom. And thanks for getting so excited over this story. It means a lot to me. It could be the start of a career—who knows?"

"It's worth getting excited about. I love you, sweetheart. And I'm so proud of you!"

The street remained deserted.

"I love you, too. Thanks."

⤙

They had walked five blocks, away from downtown, and the last street lamp they passed was now a block distant. While Stewart was not unnaturally afraid of the dark, he wasn't all that fond of it, either. As if sensing his discomfort, Hubert walked next to him, almost at heel, back toward the more well-lit sections of the residential area of Wellsboro.

"Good dog, Hubert," Stewart said, and Hubert responded by rubbing his head along the side of Stewart's leg.

Then his phone warbled again.

Twice in one night?

"Hello, Grams," he said, doing his best to keep his tone neutral and his breathing calm, as if he were sitting in his apartment doing a crossword puzzle. She would not understand the truth of this evening—that a girl had kissed him, that he was out for a walk near midnight, and that he had a dog living in his apartment.

None of that would make sense to her.

"I saw the story on that horrid dog on TV, Stewart. Well, on the computer. In the community room. They have computers. I told you that I couldn't afford one of those gizmos, didn't I? I had to go walk there, in the dark, to see it. They show the news on the computer. News from anywhere, I think."

"How did you know it was on TV?"

"Edna called me. You know her. Edna from the Cut 'n' Curl. She said her husband saw the TV van or something in town. She called me because she knows you work at the grocery store. Her grandson is a teacher, did you know that? Over in Scranton. Why don't you look at getting a teaching position?"

"I don't think so, Grams."

"So you're content with bagging groceries, is that it?"

"No, Grams. I'm looking. You know that."

"Don't get snippy, Stewart. I'm just trying to help."

Stewart remained silent.

"That blonde girl the reporter interviewed—is that the one you mentioned? The little twig of a girl?"

"She's not a twig, and yes, that is the one I mentioned."

He heard his grandmother sniff dismissively. "I thought she wore too much makeup. And that blouse . . . it was very tight, if you ask me. She doesn't look like a girl you should be interested in, Stewart."

Keep calm. Keep calm. It does no good to argue.

"I'm not 'interested' in her," Stewart lied. "She's a friend. She lives downstairs."

"How convenient for the two of you."

Stewart had a few possible responses and did not use any of them.

"Well, Stewart, you should start going to church. I know you haven't been. Edna says she has not seen you at church in over a year."

He stayed silent. Hubert looked up at him with that same plaintive, understanding look.

"All I'm saying, Stewart, is that if you want to get ahead in this world, you better start going to church."

"Okay Grams. Listen, it's late and I have to be at work early tomorrow. I'll call you this weekend."

She didn't speak for a moment.

"Have you heard from your father?"

Stewart made a quick decision.

"No."

"Well, if you have to hang up on me, go right ahead. I'll be here all weekend. Like always. Where am I going to go, anyhow?"

"Okay. I'll talk to you soon."

Stewart hung his head and let all the air out of his lungs.

"Hubert. Never get married, okay? It doesn't seem worth it. Or even have a family. Or a relative, either."

⟼

The next morning, when Stewart woke up, it was still dark and the streets empty. He knew that Hubert would need to go outside, and when he opened the front door he saw a small envelope on the welcome mat. It bore just a single word: "Stewart," done in a most feminine handwriting.

He carried it outside and waited until they reached the second lamppost on the second block away from the house.

Stewart,

Thanks for everything. I so appreciated your help.
Forgive me for that kiss. I don't know what came over me. I am not usually that forward.
What about going to church with me this Sunday? Are you still up for it?

Thanks,
Lisa

Stewart looked back toward the house. He could still see it in the shadows. Other than the single light coming from his apartment, the rest of the house remained dark.

And this is the first time a girl asked me out on a date.
Curious life is . . . as Yoda would say.

Chapter Sixteen

*H*UBERT SAT on the floor in the small bedroom as Stewart began to obsess over what he might wear to church. If he had asked his grandmother, she would have said a three-piece suit with a sedate tie and wingtips would be the only truly theologically appropriate attire. His father would have just snorted and claimed that going to church was for suckers and that all churches wanted was your money.

He was on his own today.

And Hubert was no help.

He held up his only sport coat, a blue jacket he'd bought expressly for job interviews. He'd worn it twice so far—and not for the interview with Tops Market.

"I could wear this with a button-down shirt, Hubert. What do you think?"

Hubert leaned forward and sniffed at the coat as Stewart proffered it to him. Then he looked up at his human with a puzzled expression, as if to say he really had no idea what he was being asked to decide.

"I could wear it with jeans, Hubert. Makes it both casual and dressy."

Hubert happily nodded, smiling.

They had been out early and Stewart and Hubert had both had breakfast. Hubert had been given a few bites of toast, which he certainly seemed to enjoy.

"Okay, the sport coat, a blue shirt, and jeans. The good jeans and not the ripped ones. That sound good to you, Hubert?"

Hubert appeared to be satisfied—and happy that the questions had stopped.

And in that moment of dialogue it became clear to Stewart that he was getting acclimated to having a dog in his life. Not just acclimated, but he was enjoying having a dog in his life.

He reached into the closet and found his good blue shirt. It was more wrinkled than not. He returned to the closet and slid hangers back and forth. His other blue shirt, the not-as-good one, was much less wrinkled. That was the one he selected.

I'm not too good at ironing. And I don't have an ironing board.

It did not take long to put on the outfit. He pulled out his leather loafers. They had not been worn since his last job interview and were only a little dusty, which Stewart took care of with a single sheet of Tops brand paper towels.

He checked his phone.

Nine o'clock.

"Well, Hubert, I said I would get her at nine. And it's nine. It's off to church, I guess."

At this Hubert stood, and danced about, just for a moment, as if he were celebrating this event, as if he knew what the word "church" meant, as if he knew what going to church might lead to.

The dog appeared to be genuinely and sincerely and totally happy.

"Okay, buddy. See you in an hour or so."

↩

The two of them, Lisa and Stewart, were a good match—fashion-wise. Lisa had jeans on as well, but much nicer jeans that probably cost more than Stewart's entire outfit. But then, girls had to buy clothes like that.

"You look so nice, Stewart," Lisa said as she put her arm into his as they walked toward town.

"You do, too," he replied.

"I sort of forgot to tell you that you didn't have to wear a suit and tie to church or anything. A sport coat would be fine. More than fine, really. But you look very nice. Handsome."

This is the first time a girl has called me handsome—and appeared to actually mean it.

"The church is casual, sort of. Some of the older people still dress up. But you see shorts and T-shirts as well. No one minds."

They walked along.

"Well, maybe some of the older folks do mind. But no one says anything. At least not to anyone's face, I guess. Maybe over lunch afterwards."

"I know. When my grandmother was still living up here, that's what she did afterwards. I wanted to tell her to bring a clipboard with her with an evaluation sheet for everyone. But I never did. She wouldn't get the humor in it."

They walked to the end of the block, then turned right. Lisa reached down and took his hand in hers and they walked, without talking anymore, until they reached the church on Pearl Street.

"Saint Paul's?" Stewart said as they stopped. "I thought all the saint churches were Catholic."

Lisa giggled.

"You're funny, Stewart. I really like that about you."

I wasn't being funny. That's what I thought. But if she thinks it's funny...well, I like that more.

⟵

Despite the fact that Stewart was not a regular, every-Sunday churchgoing person, the service at St. Paul's was both familiar and not familiar. He actually recognized a couple of the hymns from his sporadic church attendance as a child, but today he was never quite certain when to stand and when to sit.

He simply followed Lisa's lead, and managed to keep up with only a second of delay or so.

Lisa had chosen to sit on the left side, about halfway back.

"This is my usual spot. Funny how we are all such creatures of habit," she said before the service began.

"I know. I see people at the market wait in huge lines just so they can get 'their' checkout person."

"Really?"

"Sure. And after a while, I can almost guess what certain people will buy on certain days. Some people buy milk only on Wednesday and bread only on Friday. I guess they think it gets delivered that day so it's fresher."

"Does it? I mean, get delivered then?"

"No. Maybe it used to be—like in the old days. But now everything comes in all the time—no set schedules that I can see. But that's what they believe. So who am I to tell them the truth and burst their food bubble?"

The service started and Stewart followed Lisa's lead.

I didn't mind the preliminaries at this church at all. And a couple of the songs sounded almost modern.

The pastor walked up to the pulpit. He wore a dark suit, a white shirt, and a red tie.

He dresses up.

And then he began.

Afterwards, if he had been asked, Stewart would not recall all the details of the message, but some of it. The verses and chapters and numbers and the Greek words and translations—*well, all that was all Greek to me,* he thought—but the rest of his story made sense.

The pastor spoke about the story of the lost sheep.

Stewart wanted to remember that it was in Luke.

I'm pretty sure he said Luke. Because I might want to read it again. And Lisa may ask me about it afterwards. I want her to think that I know something about this religion stuff.

"I know you have all heard the story of the lost sheep and how the shepherd will leave all those in the fold, or flock, in order to search for the one he has lost. And how he will rejoice on finding that one sheep. And his neighbors will rejoice with him. As all the angels in heaven will rejoice when one sinner returns, rather than rejoicing over those who are already righteous."

I think I have heard this story before. At my gram's church, maybe.

"Today, instead of focusing just on the shepherd and how he will seek the lost out, I want to spend a moment talking about that one lost sheep."

So far I'm following him. Not too many thees *and* thous *and no one is hollering or shaking or falling over.*

"Think about it. If every sheep stayed with the shepherd, he would have no reason to worry. He would have no reason to search for any of the sheep. He would know that they are all safe and sound and protected."

"But that one sheep, maybe it's bull-headed—although a bull-headed sheep might be a mixed metaphor; my apologies to all of our English teachers."

Everyone laughed. Maybe there are English teachers here. I don't see any of my old English teachers.

Lisa laughed as well and looked over to Stewart.

"He can be funny sometimes," she whispered.

The pastor continued.

"Now it's the lost sheep that makes the shepherd search. It's the lost sheep that makes the shepherd prove that he truly loves each and every sheep in the flock. If it wasn't for the lost, we might never know that he cares."

I guess I follow that . . . sort of.

"And you know what? We are all that lost sheep. The reason Jesus has come is to find us. Each and every one of us. We are all lost and alone and scared and in need of protection and safety."

That's just like Hubert. He was lost, and now he is found. He's talking about Hubert . . . sort of.

"That poor sheep, alone in the wilderness. There were wolves and lions ready to eat him. There were brambles and thorns to get tangled in. But all of that worry stopped when that sheep saw the shepherd coming. He was on a mission to find the lost. He sees it in your eyes—that you are alone and scared and lost and, maybe, just a little bit desperate."

That's Hubert.

"And that is each and every one of us. We're lost. Let yourself be found. Let Jesus find you. Let Him find you. Look for Him. He's coming for you. Let Him find you."

Stewart looked over at Lisa.

She looked back at Stewart, then reached for his hand again and squeezed it.

"No one is outside of His care. No one. Let Him find you. Stop running away. Let Him find you."

The pastor talked a lot more that morning—well, not a lot, but more, and Stewart sort of stopped listening at that point, so taken by the imagery of being lost, like Hubert was lost.

And that sort of makes me like a shepherd, doesn't it. Hubert came to me and I found him. That's kind of cool.

Afterwards, they walked back home. Lisa had to work later that day.

"That's the one thing I really don't like about working at the Rooster—having to work on Sundays sometimes."

"I know. I have to sometimes as well," Stewart replied.

"How's Hubert getting along?"

"He seems real good," Stewart said. "I think he likes having a safe place to sleep, and regular food."

"I wonder how long he was out there, by himself?"

"I don't know. But I sort of feel like the shepherd guy your pastor was talking about. Finding the lost, and all that."

Lisa looked up at him, a hopeful look on her face, as if Stewart was about to admit something intimate to her.

"Well, we are all lost, just like he said," she replied, waiting for Stewart's confirmation.

"For sure Hubert was. I know dogs don't matter...you know...to God. Well, I'm sure they matter and all that, but not in the same way people matter. Right?"

"Probably," she said. "But He does search for the lost."

"I bet," Stewart replied, which left an odd half smile on Lisa's face, as if she had been hoping for something more expansive and did not hear it.

"Thanks for coming to church with me, Stewart. It was nice."

Stewart quickly nodded.

"It was. Maybe we could do it again next week?"

Lisa brightened.

"Sure. I would like that."

"Swell. I would, too."

⟿

That night, when the evening was spread against the sky, Hubert waited by the door as Stewart got the new leash he had purchased just that afternoon. He had waited until now to get the collar out, thinking that Hubert might be spooked by the whole something-around-his-neck process.

But he was not fazed in the least.

Stewart sat down next to him and spoke in calm tones.

"This is a collar, Hubert. You have to wear one since you live in town. I think that's the law. And then I can clip the leash to it. Because, you know, now that we've found each other, I don't want you to get lost again. You can understand that, can't you, Hubert? I like having you with me. It's like...having someone to talk with. And you really seem to understand what I'm saying. Like you were lost and are now found. That's in a song or something, I think."

Hubert sat staring back at Stewart, his eyes locked on the human's eyes, as if trying to understand. Or perhaps he wanted Stewart to understand something.

Either way, Hubert remained motionless as Stewart carefully fastened the collar around his neck. Then Stewart leaned back and Hubert leaned back and shook his head, his ears flapping, the small metal loop on the collar making a tiny, metallic clicking sound.

Hubert seemed to smile, as if to say he was pleased with the choice of a simple black leather collar—no studs or rhinestones, thank you very much.

"Now, shall we go for a walk? With the leash?"

Hubert bounced to a standing position and danced by the door, his hips doing his version of a canine rhumba.

They slowed at the landing, Stewart leaning closer to the door. He did not hear any noise coming from Lisa's apartment.

It is late. Maybe she's in bed.

They continued down to the first floor.

Or maybe she's out.

The pair walked away from town again, thinking that minimizing any potential contact with anyone would be best for all concerned. Stewart took great care not to pull or tug on the leash, thinking that if he had a collar on, he would not want whatever sort of human-master to be jerking his neck out of place if he stepped too far out of line.

But Hubert took to the collar and leash, obviously having experienced them before. He sniffed at the leash once or twice when it went slack, but seemed to be totally fine with being tethered to another creature.

"I liked the church today," Stewart said, and Hubert turned his head and smiled. "I did. I was surprised. After that deal with my grandmother, I didn't think much of going to church, you know?"

Hubert seemed to nod.

"You do know what I'm saying, most of the time, don't you, Hubert?"

Hubert smiled.

"It's called anthropomorphism, Hubert. I had to look it up. I sort of half remembered it from Mrs. Davis and eleventh-grade English, but just barely. That's when people put human emotions and characteristics onto animals."

Hubert looked like he was nodding again, but it also might have just been the bobbing motion Hubert made when walking.

"But, with you, it really seems like you do understand. I mean, you having been lost and all—maybe your perceptions are more attuned or something. And maybe some dogs are just really smart. After all, you have to be smart to keep stealing from the store—and never coming close to getting caught. That means you're real smart. And, well, I think you understand me. You know, you get what I'm trying to say."

Hubert slowed, then stopped, and looked up at Stewart. The harsh glow from the street lamp at the end of the street seemed softer in Hubert's eyes, and appeared to show a deep empathy with what Stewart was trying to explain.

Hubert sat, as if expecting a long monologue.

Stewart did not seem surprised that Hubert was waiting for an explanation. The sidewalk was empty, the street was empty, the air was still, and there were no house lights shining, illuminating their way. The two closest homes were dark and quiet and shuttered for the evening.

It was a perfect spot to talk, to explain, to try to understand.

"Hubert, you were lost. I found you—or you found me. And now we are both found, I guess. That makes me feel good. And because of you, Lisa and me are now friends—maybe a bit more than just friends, but we'll wait and see on that."

Hubert sniffed at something in the night air, but his vision remained locked on Stewart.

"It's what that pastor person said—we're all lost, sort of."

Stewart looked at his hands for a long moment without speaking.

"You know, Hubert, I guess I don't think about being lost too much. I learned about not thinking about things when I was young. The bad things, I mean. Thinking about the bad things. Or, not thinking about them, I guess. If you don't dwell on something, then sometimes that thing just goes away. I learned ignoring things sometimes is the only thing that you can do. When you're little and people are always fighting and all that . . . well, there's not much you can do when you're seven. So you try to ignore things. You know? Ignoring things, hiding things, that makes the bad stuff go away. Sometimes."

Hubert stood up and bounced his head against Stewart's thigh—not just once to get him moving, but several times, then looked back up at him with a pleading look in his eyes.

But Stewart did not get the hint, or the nudge.

"Okay, I get it, Hubert. Let's keep walking. I know you don't like sitting and waiting."

Hubert remained standing and it took two small, gentle tugs on the leash to get him walking again, as if something had been left undecided there, on that lonely sidewalk, out in the dark.

Chapter Seventeen

O N MONDAY, after work, Lisa drove home in a rush, changed out of her caffeine-scented clothes, freshened her minimal makeup, recombed her hair, and set off again for an assignment.

"The editor actually asked me to do this story," Lisa told a co-worker that morning. He said if I could get it done by Tuesday, he would run it in this week's paper. And this guy, he said, is a big advertiser, so I shouldn't make him sound like a monkey, even if he is one."

Lydia laughed.

"He called him something else, but I don't like to use those words. Gives horses a bad name."

She drove to Bargain Bill's Dynamite Cars and pulled in next to a battered and faded Chevy Malibu with ripped upholstery in the back. On the windshield, written in white marker, were the bold words: "Good Runner & Student Car."

If your student is an auto mechanic, I suppose. And blind.

Bargain Bill was outside, his hand extended, even before Lisa managed to switch off her car's engine.

"You're in luck, little lady. I have just received the most perfect lady car today—a cream puff if there ever was one—and in red. I know you ladies love red cars. Am I right? Am I right? Red to match your lipstick."

Lisa might have laughed, or gotten angry, if Bargain Bill

had not been so earnest, so naïvely transparent and cheerful. He radiated enthusiasm, even if it was artificial enthusiasm. He would be the type of person at a party whom Lisa would try to avoid—not because he was offensive, which he was, though in a naïve way—but because his resolute enthusiasm would be exhausting, like a clueless uncle.

"No, I'm not looking for a car today," Lisa said with professional cheeriness. "I'm Lisa Goodly. With the *Wellsboro Gazette*. The editor, Mr. Grback, said he called. I'm here to do an article on you. You know, an interview."

Bargain Bill's face went from crestfallen to wildly happy in a nanosecond.

"Of course. Sure. The *Gazette*. You want to ask me about...Rover, right? About how heartbroken I am about the loss of my dog and how I am crushed that he has resorted to a life of crime. Besmirches the good name of our town—and me, I guess. Looks bad to have a criminal in the family, am I right?"

"Sure. I guess," Lisa said. "Can we talk in your office? So I can take notes?"

Bargain Bill ushered Lisa into the trailer that served as the car lot's office, waiting room, and sales force headquarters. All three were ensconced in the sagging double-wide trailer parked at the far corner of the lot, braced up by railroad timbers rather than depending on threadbare and suspect tires on the undercarriage.

"Coffee? I have Coca-Cola in the mini-fridge, if you'd like. And water. What's your pleasure, little lady?"

Lisa smiled demurely, trying to hide the fact that she would have taken offense at being called a "little lady," but the way he said it felt a little off-key charming and nostalgic at the same time.

"I'm fine, Mr. Hoskins. Really."

"Well, you just let me know the minute you're not, and I'll see what I can do to make you feel fine again. A deal, okay?"

"Okay."

Lisa flipped open her steno pad and began to ask the first question on her list of twenty-one prepared questions. In one of her journalism classes, the professor had been adamant that an interviewer needed to have twenty-one questions before the interview. "It forces you to think about the subject. It forces you to prioritize the information you want. Even if you don't get a chance to ask them all."

Bargain Bill Hoskins started with a brief personal history: raised in Scranton, attended public school, dropped out of college because of financial pressure, started working as a car salesman, and saved up to start his own lot nearly twenty years ago.

I guess I never thought about how these businesses start. I sort of assumed that they were always here.

She followed those questions with a few "How's business" questions and the state of used-car sales and the like, then she moved into the core of her story—or at least what she hoped would be the core of her story: his lost dog, "Rover."

"I adopted poor Rover just three months ago from a shelter in Lewisburg—the one that closed just days after I found the dear, sweet...dog."

Lisa wrote this all down as best she could. No one studied shorthand anymore, but she'd been a most proficient note-taker in college. She knew she was getting some good quotes to use.

Most people don't remember exactly what they said, so all I need is to come close and not change the meaning.

Bargain Bill actually stopped talking for a moment, and wiped a tear away from his right eye.

"Pretended to wipe a tear away" is what Lisa wrote in her notebook.

"And now, my dear wife is home, heartbroken, losing herself by doing word puzzles because poor, sweet Rover has run off. I just hope he is found soon."

Lisa noted that as well.

He also made sure that she knew it was not exactly a cash reward.

"I'm just a struggling small businessman. If I could give away five hundred dollars, I surely would. But a discount is just like money, isn't it?"

Lisa smiled professionally.

"I'm sure it is."

She had filled up six pages of notes—more than enough for a 500- to 750-word article.

As she gathered up her coat and purse, Bargain Bill made sure that she had one of his promotional pens shaped a little like a stick of dynamite, two refrigerator magnets that looked like a small stack of dynamite, and a car freshener in the shape of a single stick of dynamite.

"You have any questions, you call, little lady. I'm here six days a week."

She waved as she pulled out of the lot.

He didn't adopt Hubert. That much I know.

She wasn't angry at him for his subterfuge. Not one customer had come even to browse the whole time she was there.

I almost feel sorry for him, all that energy and all by himself most days. That has to be hard.

Chapter Eighteen

T HE TALK of the early Wednesday morning crew at Tops Market was centered on Lisa's article on Bargain Bill Hoskins.

"The poor man," one of them said. "To lose a dog like that. Sad."

"He sounds like a real character," another added. "We haven't ever bought a car from him—but he seems like a nice enough guy."

"You read what he said about this place? That Tops hasn't spent a dime updating our dog security system. That was pretty funny."

Ralph, a long-haired, nighttime shelf-stocker, nodded sagely. "I liked it when he suggested that all we had to do is move the bones up a shelf." Then he added, in a loud whisper, just in case Mr. Arden was lurking nearby, "And we all know that next to the Bible, the shelf plan-o-gram is sacred and never to be deviated from."

"He said that he didn't think old Rover has committed a felony yet," Jackson Bennet said. "Doesn't a felony need to be over two hundred and fifty dollars? Didn't the article say that? The paper said we probably throw that much away every week in brown lettuce. I bet Mr. Arden is really gassed at that remark."

⌐

Mr. Arden was not "gassed." He was incensed. He stood behind his desk in his small upstairs office, fuming. He would have liked to have paced the floor, back and forth, in anger, but he didn't have enough room for serious pacing. Two steps, maybe three, if they were small steps, were all it took to get from one side of the room to the other.

So, instead, he simply stood and gritted his teeth.

The teeth-grinding stopped, then Mr. Arden placed a wry, semi-twisted smile on his face. He flipped open his address/ phone book. Then he punched the numbers into his phone and sat back down. The phone cord was so badly tangled that if he tried to stand and make a call, the cord would pull the receiver part of the phone off the desk. He actually had to lean in closer to the phone to talk.

"Yes, I want it bigger than his. What's the biggest you can print without multiple panels?"

He listened.

"Good. And change the reward. I'm offering two hundred and fifty dollars. Not cash. Good heavens. On a gift card for the store."

He listened again, scowling.

"Do I have to say that on the sign? Could I just put an asterisk or something?"

He took a deep, unsatisfying breath.

"I know you're not a lawyer. Then just put in 'gift card' in really small letters. And a gift card is just like real money, you know."

He hung up the phone and leaned back in his chair, smug and almost happy.

No dog is going to make a fool out of me.

He wrote on a Smith & Sons Produce notepad, "Pick up sign. Insta-Print. This P.M."

That's the trouble with this town. Everyone wants to make a fool out of me.

"I can get a couple of the bag boys and the ladder in back and we'll hang the sign between the telephone poles out on the street," he said aloud, even though he was alone. "Everyone will see it. And then we'll see who gets the dog first. Grocery money will beat out a fake discount on a beat-up wreck of a car any day."

Jerry Mallick checked his gas gauge again. The four dollars of gas he'd pumped yesterday had hardly made a dent in his tank and barely budged the needle above the red empty line. But, from experience, he reckoned he had another thirty minutes of cruising time left before he had to coast to a stop or pull up the front seat cushion and root for loose change. He had done that seven months ago and come away with nearly five dollars' worth of lost dimes and quarters. The pennies he had left where they were, as a primer for future cash-searching expeditions under the seat.

"That stupid dog has to be around here somewhere. I figure he's no more than ten blocks from the store, holed up in somebody's backyard or under a porch or something."

As he drove, he let his left hand dangle out the window, still holding on to three-quarters of the beef jerky strip he'd bought at the gas station.

"Dogs like meat, right? And they got good sniffers. He'll smell the jerky and come running and I'll have myself a new truck in no time."

After several trips circumnavigating the downtown area of Wellsboro and seeing not a single dog, Jerry decided that he had pushed his luck just far enough for today. He headed home, the truck sputtering slightly as he turned into the gravel driveway.

"I think I got a gas tank in the garage for the lawn mower. Maybe. Or does that got oil in it for the snowblower?"

If it did, the gas was two years old, since the snowblower had stopped working two winters ago.

"Rents aren't due till next week."

The truck door squealed as it opened.

"I really need a new truck," he muttered as he slid to the ground.

"I can drain what's left in the lawn mower. Maybe there's some left in the snowblower, too. That'd be enough to catch that darned dog."

At that moment, Stewart turned off the sidewalk and headed to the mailboxes.

"Hey, Stewie, you seen that dog around? You know, the one with the reward."

Stewart shook his head. "I haven't. But I keep looking. I know a lot of people are looking. I hope I get to him before they do."

If Jerry had been a student of human expressions, he might have detected that Stewart was beginning to spin an elaborate falsehood. But Larry was not such a student.

"Tell you what, Stewie. If you see him, and maybe like, you can't catch him 'coz your car's not running, you tell me and we'll both go out in the truck after him. I'll split the reward with you. Okay?"

Half of that discount is still like . . . a couple hundred dollars, right?

"Sure, Jerry. I'll keep my eyes open."

Jerry started toward the garage, then turned back.

"Hey Stewie, if you see that Lisa, could you tell her to keep an eye out as well? I saw on TV the other night that women are better at spotting hidden things than guys are. I think that's what the guy on TV was saying. I ain't never seen a woman hunter that's any good, but I figure they can't say stuff on TV that ain't true. Right?"

"Probably," Stewart responded.

They both heard a dog bark, off in the distance.

"That ain't him," Larry declared. "That's Simpson's stupid mutt over on Walnut. Mangy dog tried to bite me once when I was plowing their driveway. Stupid dog. I remember barks."

Again, if Jerry had been observant, he might have noticed how nervous Stewart had become, glancing up to the steps and then to the small window in his kitchen that overlooked the backyard.

"Well, thanks, Stewie. I got some gasoline to drain. Hey, you have any gas in your car? I mean, it ain't running, is it? I could siphon it out. Probably no good anymore, right?"

"You know, Jerry, I think the tank is just about empty. You're welcome to try, but I don't think there's much in it."

"Hey, thanks, Stewie. I might try. If I can find a hose. I had one, but I don't know where now. Probably lost it. Or somebody kipped it out of the garage."

"Okay."

"And you keep an eye out for that mutt. We'll split the reward. Maybe we can both get new wheels. Okay?"

"Sure thing, Jerry," Stewart replied and hurried up the stairs, obviously anxious and in a sudden hurry—and without checking his mailbox at all, which was most unusual.

Unusual, if Jerry had been observant, that is.

Which he was not.

Chapter Nineteen

THE BREAK ROOM at the Tops Market was again all atwitter with the brazen return of the dog bandit. The canine had struck again only twenty minutes prior to the break.

"Another daylight robbery," Dennis King said, pushing his straggly hair behind his ears and then capturing it with a faded SeaWolves baseball cap, the minor league team from Erie. "Somebody should call the *Gazette*."

Stewart had already sent a text message to Lisa outlining the bare basics of today's heist.

"Somebody said the dog's already a felon. That's pretty bad, isn't it?"

That was Darlene Killeen, a very young and very naïve cashier, less than a year from walking the halls at Wellsboro Area High School as a Lady Hornet on the pep squad.

Dennis waved his hand in dismissal.

"Nope. A felony has to be five hundred dollars all at once. You can't steal a bunch of little things over a month and be charged with a felony."

Darlene nodded, sipping on a Diet Coke.

I wonder why all our stock people are well versed in felony matters? Stewart thought to himself as he typed another text message to Lisa—this one about the felony discussion.

"The dog looks healthy," Darlene said. "I got a good look at him as he scampered past. I only looked because I heard Mr. Arden screeching from over in Dairy, I think. Or maybe it was Produce."

"It was Dairy. He was complaining 'bout how the chocolate milk was stacked. We had so much in the back cooler that we had to use two rows instead of the one on the plan-o-gram. He made us pull it all out and reset the whole case. And stick the rest in the back reefer. A definite pain."

"Well, anyhow," Darlene continued. "The dog looks healthy enough. Like he's being fed somewhere. Not like a runaway dog or anything. He's got to belong to somebody—somebody who doesn't care if he's like a criminal or something."

"But not a felon," Dennis added as he finished off his large can of Monster. "Just a simple misdemeanor, that's all. A fine and a week in jail, tops."

"What about the owner?" she asked as she stood up to return to work, smoothing out her apron and making sure it was correctly tied and adjusted symmetrically.

"That's who I was talking about," Dennis said firmly. "The dog—well, maybe they'll put it down. Dogs in grocery stores, that just ain't right. Probably a public nuisance or something. Or a health hazard. And for a dog, being a public nuisance or a health hazard ain't good."

As the three of them walked down the stairs and back to work, Stewart wondered if Dennis actually knew what he was talking about or was simply playing at being a semi-hardened criminal to impress the easily impressed Darlene.

⌐

When Stewart arrived home that afternoon, Hubert was sitting in the middle of the kitchen, his tail wagging happily, a smile on his face. Stewart knew he was excited, as if Hubert could barely prevent his haunches from ecstatic wiggling.

Stewart knelt down and in three jump-steps, Hubert was nose-to-nose with Stewart, whining softly, a happy whine, offering gentle head butts against Stewart's chest.

"I'm glad to see you, too, Hubert."

After a few moments Hubert settled down and Stewart sat next to him on the kitchen floor.

"Hubert," Stewart said, his voice rising on the end of the word.

Hubert immediately lowered his head.

"Did you come to the store today?"

Hubert lowered his head farther.

"Did you steal a rawhide bone?"

Hubert then looked up, just an inch, with his eyes focused on the living room.

Under the corner of the rug were two rawhide bones, still wrapped in plastic, slipped under the corner of the rug, almost totally covered, but not really.

"Hubert, why did you steal another bone? You know that's wrong."

At this Hubert lay down, put his head between his paws, his chin on the ground, and closed his eyes.

Maybe he's just hungry. I've been feeding him just like the bag said. And even a little more.

Then Stewart looked to the bones again.

He's not eating them. He hasn't even chewed the plastic wrapping off.

After letting Hubert wallow for a moment in guilt, Stewart reached out and put his hand on the back of the dog's head and stroked him a few times.

"It's okay, Hubert. I know you don't know right from wrong. At least people's right and wrong."

Hubert jumped up and almost enveloped Stewart between his front paws, demanding, as it were, to be hugged back, to be forgiven, to be loved.

—

"You have to remember, Stewart," Lisa said as she sipped at her tea in Stewart's kitchen, "Hubert is a dog of deprivation. We don't have any idea how long he was out on his own."

Stewart liked Lisa in his kitchen. He liked having her near. He'd even bought a new box of tea, thinking that if she ever wanted tea in his kitchen, he would have fresher tea than the four-year-old box of Tetley tea bags he'd had since his senior year in college.

He didn't smile when he looked at her, though he wanted to. He didn't want to make it too obvious. Perhaps his lips formed a slight smile, just a snippet of a smile, and that was all.

"What if he lived around here? Maybe he's local and he's just a bad dog?" Stewart said.

At this Hubert growled, just a little, just to register, as it were, his complaint with Stewart's personal assessment and character assassination.

"I don't think so, Stewart. I talked with Mr. Grback about it, and he was virtually certain it wasn't a local dog."

"How would he know?"

Hubert got up from the rug in the living room and walked to Lisa and sat next to her, looking up at her with both admiration and expectation. She smiled at him and began to scratch behind his ears.

"He said he's been running that free classified section in the *Gazette* for lost pets since he's been editor. He said that no one loses a pet that they don't call him for a free ad. He said it doesn't matter if it were a gerbil or a mouse or a moose. People call because they know the ad is free. So if Hubert had an owner in town, that owner would have called."

Stewart shrugged. "Maybe."

"He said somebody probably dumped him off on a back road somewhere. Or even on the interstate. It happens all the time, he said, because people don't want to pay the twenty-five dollars to a shelter to take an unwanted animal. And he said that most people are jerks."

Stewart laughed.

"He's a keen observer of human nature."

Lisa's face beamed. "He just likes being gruff with reporters. Like he's still in New York City, I guess. But I like him. He's smart."

"Of course he is. He's printing your stories, right?"

Lisa tilted her head and smiled at Stewart—more than just a smile, a thank-you sort of expression on her face.

Stewart let it be silent for a long moment. It was obvious that the both of them enjoyed that moment.

"But the hard part of all this is I can't figure out how to keep Hubert inside," Stewart said, finally breaking the silence.

"Your lock still doesn't work?"

"It never did, really. All it takes is a little push—or pull—

and the door opens. And if I ask Jerry to fix it, which I doubt he will—or can—he'll see Hubert. He's already asked me to be on the lookout for him. Wants to split the reward. And Hubert growls a little bit when someone is at the door—even me. Larry would hear him."

"I know. It's kind of touching, that Hubert wants to protect you like that. What about a little hook-and-eye latch on the outside of the door?" Lisa asked.

"I thought of that. But if Jerry sees that, and he will for sure, he'll know something's up. He has some sort of idiot-savant radar for spotting things that don't belong. He noticed when I bought a new tire when the Nissan was still running. Who looks at tires? Anyhow, a hook-and-eye I could understand on the inside—but not on the outside."

Lisa nodded her understanding.

"I guess I could try to put a chair or something in front of the door—but then how would I get out?"

Lisa switched hands on Hubert.

"And the door downstairs doesn't lock at all, so that's no help either," he added. "I watched him open it with his nose in about two seconds. So no barrier there."

Lisa sipped at her tea.

"This is really good, Stewart. Thanks for getting it just for me."

Stewart hoped his blush did not show. Hubert offered a contented growl.

"Thanks. It's the store brand—but the good store brand. There's good and then a little better. This tea is from the little better section."

"Well, I like it," Lisa said with finality.

At that, Hubert looked up at Lisa and rumble-growled

again, but it was a pleasant, happy growl, as if he were in on the discussion.

Which Stewart was pretty sure he wasn't, but then, he could never really be sure with Hubert.

After the tea and coffee had been consumed, after evening had come upon Wellsboro, Lisa picked up her purse and stood.

"You want to go to the Frog Hut?" she asked, surprising Stewart, surprising him a lot. "For ice cream?"

Again, girls don't normally ask me out—ever.

"I didn't think it was open yet."

Lisa's face scrunched up in thought.

"I think it's open all year. Pretty sure, anyhow. But it's open now for certain. I saw people coming out at lunch. I feel like an ice cream cone. Want to go for a ride?"

"Sure."

Hubert danced about, happy that something was happening and that Stewart and Lisa appeared to be happier than normal.

"No, Hubert, you can't go."

Hubert appeared crestfallen.

"No, he can go," Lisa said. "It's dark enough to sneak him into the car. And I think Jerry is over at the Moose Lodge tonight. Two-for-one draft beer special, I think."

"Oh, yeah. That is tonight, isn't it? Well . . . okay. But do dogs like being in cars? I never had one."

"They love cars. My grannie's dogs did. And I bet Hubert does as well. Right, Hubert?"

At this, Hubert jumped up and down, in excitement, obviously not knowing what was about to happen but excited that he was being included.

⤙

Hubert walked quickly to Lisa's car, walking between Lisa and Stewart, not looking left or right, but head down, taking deliberate, firm steps, as if he knew that he had to remain hidden, at least in the vicinity of Jerry, the dog hunter. Hubert jumped up into the car without a second of hesitation, though he did have to be persuaded to climb over the center console to the backseat.

"When I was young," Lisa said as she backed out of the driveway, "my grannie used to take me and one of her dogs with her to get ice cream at the Dairy Mart in town. Back then, she said, they used to give away doggie cones for free. Or maybe she said they did that when she was young. But now they cost a dollar."

Stewart rolled the window down, letting the full force of the brisk air wash over Hubert.

"I'll treat tonight," Stewart said. "Since you're driving. I'll even pick up the tab for Hubert."

"You don't have to, Stewart. I can get my own ice cream."

"I know. I don't mind. And how much can ice cream cost?"

⤙

Nine dollars and forty-five cents.

That was what it could cost.

A couple of deluxe sundaes and a doggy cone apparently cost $9.45.

The three of them sat outside on one of the benches and ate, while the humans alternated holding the cone for Hubert to lick at delicately as if it were some forbidden pleasure food.

The dog kept looking around, as if to make sure no one was sneaking up to steal this chilled and creamy delicacy. After the top of the cone was consumed, Hubert took the rest in his mouth and crunched it noisily, smiling as he did, with streaks of vanilla soft serve dripping from his chin.

While they sat, another couple, an older man and woman, shuffled outside and stopped suddenly, as if hitting an invisible force field. Without speaking, they turned to each other, and then back to Stewart, Lisa, and Hubert.

"Is that the bandit dog?"

Lisa spoke up first, with confidence.

"No, we get that all the time now. Some bad dogs just give mutts like this a bad name."

Hubert growled a little at the term *mutt*, but Lisa ignored him.

"We see the resemblance, but our dog is much taller. And he has more white on his paws than the criminal dog."

Hubert looked up and stared at Lisa, as if asking *Just what dog are you describing?*

"Well, it sure looks a lot like the bandit dog. I bet you could turn him in and get the reward."

Lisa offered a gay laugh.

"We've thought about it. But we could never do that to poor Hubert here."

The woman's face pursed, as if she were eating a lemon.

"Hubert? Odd name for a dog. Hubert."

"We like unusual names, I guess," Stewart added.

As the older couple shuffled away, Stewart, without leaning close to Lisa, whispered loudly, "Let's get out of here before they call the cops."

Lisa was already standing and pulling the keys from the pocket of her jeans.

"One step ahead of you, Clyde."

Puzzled, Stewart walked beside her to the car.

"Oh, as in Bonnie and—"

"Exactly. Now let's get Baby-Faced Hubert hidden in the backseat before the feds catch up."

Stewart wondered, as he put on his seat belt, if Lisa would drive faster on the way home.

Chapter Twenty

Y ES, HE has the dog now, Mom, but you have to promise not to tell anyone. Ever."

Lisa paced in her living room, twirling a strand of her blonde hair as she talked, thinking that she might need a haircut soon.

Or maybe I could dye it brown. Make me seem more serious than a "dumb blonde," I bet.

"Who would I tell? I don't know anyone in Wellsboro besides you. I don't even know anyone who knows anyone in Wellsboro besides you."

"I know you don't know anyone who knows anyone in Wellsboro, but news like this goes fast."

She looked out onto the street. She had just left Stewart's apartment. They had shared a meal, finally—a pizza that Lisa picked up from Pudgie's Pizza. Hubert had tasted some of the crust, with a little sauce and cheese, and had decided it was delicious. He sat and stared at them for the rest of the evening as they ate.

Lisa gave Stewart a quick peck on the cheek as she left, and was pretty certain it had taken him by surprise.

He blushes easily.

"And you and Stewart are still hanging out together?"

"Yes. But before you say it, I know, Mom. Slow. I won't jump into anything. Honest."

She would not tell her mother about tonight's dinner with Stewart. Even if friends did go to dinner together.

And now she watched the darkened street out front, waiting to catch a glimpse of Stewart and Hubert as they went out for their furtive nightly constitutional.

"He's a really nice guy, Mom. He's not pushy like Mark was. Not at all. Very laid-back. Sort of shy, really."

"Sounds like he might be more than a friend."

"I don't know, Mom. I mean, he's not. We're just friends. Like I said—slow. I have learned my lesson. Please don't nag."

Stewart edged out of the shadows below her window and looked back up toward her apartment. She went to the window, smiled, and waved.

Stewart waved back, and then he and Hubert scurried off to the west and into the shadows again.

"Caring is not nagging. You talk about this Stewart all the time. And it's just too familiar. You acted the same way when you met Mark."

"I know I need to be careful, Mom," Lisa said, her tone growing edgier and just a bit petulant. "But not every guy is like Mark."

"You'd be surprised. A lot of people lie. They tell you what you want to hear because they want something from you. They may not even think of it as a lie."

"I know."

I have heard this nearly every time we talk. I was young and made a mistake. It scared the both of us. Okay, call it a sin. And it was. I know, Mom. I know.

"Mom, I've told you a hundred times. What I did was stupid and dangerous. He said he believed. He said he went to church. He made promises and I thought he meant them. We made a mistake. I made a mistake. It won't happen again. Okay? I can't do more than what I've done."

Lisa tried not to think of that painful experience in her past. Mark had been handsome and charming and duplicitous and deceiving. Lisa fell quickly and hard—believing everything he said. She thought it was love. She thought it was mutual. And she'd allowed Mark to go way too far, farther than she had ever gone, at least in that most intimate of ways. She regretted the terrifying scare that her actions—their actions—had caused her. The sleepless nights until she found out from a health clinic two towns over. The terrible regret and guilt. The shame of what had happened and having lied to her mother like that.

That was all in the past, she had declared. She had turned over a new leaf, both physically and morally.

She listened to her mother repeat herself one more time.

But Stewart is nothing like him—or any of the guys I dated before. Stewart has Bible verses in his apartment. He went to church with me. He's one of the good guys.

"I know he has to be on the same page as me, Mom. I know. And I know I have to be careful with my feelings. There won't be a repeat of the last time. Really. You have to trust me."

Lisa lay back on the couch and stared up at the ceiling, which had a feathering of cracks in one corner. She had thought about asking Jerry to fix it, but decided that making the request was not really worth having him blunder about her apartment for days and then having the finished project not much better than when he started.

"And I know you don't want what happened to you and Dad to happen to me. But it won't."

She took a deep breath and hoped she sounded convincing.

"Besides, since I might be moving to Pittsburgh someday, there's no way friendship becomes anything more than just being friends with a nice guy. Honestly, Mom, I have more sense than that."

I mean now; maybe not so much before.

She stood up and walked to her bedroom.

"Okay. I know." Her mother sounded resigned. For now, at least. "I just worry, that's all, with you living so far away. I miss you."

"I miss you, too. I'll send extra copies of this week's paper. The editor really likes what I'm doing—so much so that he is actually paying me now."

"That's wonderful! How much?"

She sighed. "Well, it's not much, but I am a real journalist now, and getting paid for it. That's what I've always wanted."

"As long as you're happy. I love you, sweetie."

"I love you, too. Good night." She pressed the off button on her phone and entered her dark bedroom.

He does have faith. He does. He has to.

⌐

"Stewart, I don't want to hear about you and this woman. You're too young. And inexperienced. I saw her on TV and I know that type. She knows what she's about. And don't think that just because I'm not there that I don't know what you're doing. Edna said she saw you and that woman at some ice cream place in town, looking all lovey-dovey."

Stewart toyed with the idea of just hanging up and later

170er Kraus

claiming that the battery had run down. But since his grandmother still only had a landline, with a single phone in her apartment, he did not think she would buy into his excuse.

So he gritted his teeth, silently, and did his best to remain civil.

"We just got ice cream. There was nothing lovey-dovey about it, Grams."

"So Edna is a liar now. That's what you've come to?"

There were a lot of things he wanted to say. He took a breath and held it. Did she want him to be alone forever? Wasn't dating normal in your twenties? Most people in her day were married in their twenties, weren't they? But he knew better than to start an argument he'd never win. He'd just upset her even more.

"The pool boy position is still open, Stewart. I asked about it. They said you sounded like a perfect candidate for the job. Just come down and talk to them. Is that too much to ask?"

"Grams, you're in Florida, not around the block. And I bet the pool boy position pays even less than what I'm making now. So no, I am not coming to Florida to sweep out pools in a retirement village."

He seldom defended himself with such firmness. He was a little nervous as to her reaction, but he could not bear to hear about the pool boy position one more time.

"It's a senior living facility, Stewart. Not retirement. And you are just like your father. Stubborn. I loved him, but he was as stubborn as a blind, deaf mule."

He closed his eyes.

That's the ultimate insult, according to her—being like my father.

"Just remember that women these days...well, they're not like when I was young. And that girl, I don't trust her, Stewart. Maybe she is just looking for a meal ticket. Did you ever stop to think about that possibility?"

Stewart did his best not to laugh out loud.

I'm a bag boy at a supermarket. That's a meal ticket?

"Grams, I will be careful. I promise. Oh, and Dad said to say hello."

That will put her off balance.

She did not respond for perhaps twenty seconds. Stewart waited, knowing that she had not dropped the phone, or hung up.

"That's nice. Real nice, Stewart. Talking about me behind my back."

Stewart remained firm.

"He just said to say hello. That's all. No talking behind your back."

More silence.

"Well, okay, then. And I have to go now. This long-distance chatter is costing me a fortune, I bet. And I'm on a fixed income, Stewart, or didn't you know that?"

"I know, Grams. We'll talk next week. Take care."

And the phone went silent.

Stewart slumped farther into the chair, this short conversation almost as tiring as two fast laps around the block.

⟶

The only illumination in the apartment came from the streetlight halfway down the block. But it was enough for Hubert. He, like all dogs, could not see perfectly in black, inky darkness—not like cats, but well enough. Dogs, wolves, were nighttime hunters, and could navigate without trepidation in the absence of a moon, or a streetlight.

Hubert walked to the window and put his front paws on the sill and looked out, slowly peering down the street, and then the other way.

All was quiet. He saw the shadow of a raccoon across the street as it edged along in the dark, looking for trash or leftovers, or whatever else might have been discarded on trash day.

Hubert sniffed, almost in derision.

Trash-eaters.

Hubert walked to the chair and jumped up and awkwardly circled three times and then lay down, his chin resting on the arm. From there, Hubert could see the glistening sliver of the spring moon.

He tilted his head, hearing a rustle from the small room where Stewart lay sleeping. Hubert did not like to sleep in there. The space was too hard to protect. Not enough room to maneuver in case some evil appeared, some toothed creature looking for food. And Stewart tossed and turned while he slept.

Hubert felt better in a chair, or on the rug, where the moonlight could find him.

He blinked his eyes.

That person who is Stewart needs to be in a pack—our pack. But he does not know it. I think he wants that, but then maybe he doesn't. He's like a dog that runs from other dogs. That is not the way things should be. I may not be a smart dog, but I know what I know. I know that good dogs should be part of the pack. That is the way the force of nature wants it to be. And it is more than just nature. More powerful. More everywhere and always. But I am just a dog and do not have words for everything in my heart.

That person Lisa smells like flowers. She wants to be part of us. She understands that.

Hubert stirred a little, readjusting his back legs.

But Stewart is not sure. Maybe someone hurt him, too. But all I can do, because I am a dog, is to protect him. Maybe that person Lisa will know what to do. But I will do what a good dog can do. And what a good dog should do. That much I know. That much I am sure of.

He held his eyes shut even though he heard the swooping of an owl outside.

I like owl creatures. They look funny. With big eyes.

He sighed deeply.

And they know. They are very aware.

Just before Hubert drifted off to sleep, one more thought came to be.

I know that I should stop taking those bones, but what if the Stewart person runs out of food? It is good to have bones stored in case of hunger. Having extra food is good, even if Stewart was not happy the last time I brought one home. Maybe he will see it is a good thing, too.

Hubert's breathing grew deep and rhythmic.

To be part of a pack. That is the right and good and best thing to be. Stewart will have to find that truth. And I will do what a dog can do to make that happen.

Chapter Twenty-One

LISA STOPPED just for a moment, just by the door to her apartment, and texted Stewart "Good morning," then ran down the steps and into her car. She checked her phone again, this time for the time.

I'm almost late. If I get the green light at Maple, I'll be fine.

The Wired Rooster was too small to have a complicated and expensive time clock, so employees were on their honor, more or less, to start and stop at the correct, preapproved times. And Lisa took pride in being on time, in never slipping out a few minutes early, even though her shift manager did cut a few minutes off his workday all the time, brazenly and without any apparent regret.

She busied herself with her setup tasks for the morning, putting up two sheaths of paper cups, filling the appropriate slots with lids and sleeves, making sure the sugar and sweetener bins were full, filling the metal containers with milk and half-and-half—all the sort of things that most customers took for granted.

As she worked, a few sleepy customers wandered in, looking ruffled and a bit disoriented. Robert, her shift partner most mornings, was able to handle their simple orders without any help.

"Black coffee."

"Coffee with cream."

"Coffee with cream and sugar."

As the morning progressed, customer orders became progressively more complicated, as in "a double decaf shot, no-fat, no whip, caramel, iced, two-story latte, with room for milk."

Early is easy, later is complicated. Like life, I guess.

As she worked, she began to replay her conversation with her mother over and over in her mind. Lisa attempted to find a context for her mother's nearly overwhelming anxiety. Lisa was well aware that her mother had suffered in a cruel marriage for over a decade, leaving her husband, Lisa's father, when Lisa was only six. And as a young girl, Lisa was not fully aware of the pain a bad marriage, a bad partnership, created, and the long-term ripples of caution and heartache it caused.

Maybe she is right . . . that I should wait. I should make sure. I should have waited before—but I was sure we were in love. Love and sex. Sex and love. They're confusing.

She arranged the yellow packets of artificial sugar in the small metal bin.

Maybe I'm just hearing the ticking clock . . . but I have a long time for that. Maybe not as long as I think, but I have time. Another twenty years, right? Or is it fifteen, now? They say to be safe, all of those choices should be made by the mid-thirties. So that leaves at least ten years.

She took a spray bottle and began to clean the inside tables. It was still too chilly for anyone to sit outside in the morning. The afternoon shift could clean off the tables outside when it was warm enough to do so.

Most of my friends from school are married. Some with kids already. Some with two and three kids already. And here I am in Wellsboro, single and without a career.

She took a broom and swept the sidewalk outside, to get any stray leaves or paper that appeared overnight.

Am I sure he believes? That's what my mother keeps insisting on. "Make sure that the two of you are on the same page spiritually." Mark and I weren't. Mark was a big mistake. I was so sure he was the one. He made everything sound so good—and he was a liar. We went too far. Too far and too fast.

She closed her eyes for a moment.

But that is water under the bridge, right? Time to move on. Time to hit the restart button.

She stopped sweeping and looked down Main Street. Traffic remained light. Wellsboro was a small town, after all, and traffic never became congested, not really.

My mother has been alone since I was six. She made one mistake and is still paying for it. I don't want that to happen to me. Maybe it's better to be safe. I don't want to be sorry. One scare was enough.

—

The e-mail was only two lines long, but Lisa was ecstatic.

"The last article was great. Keep it up—you'll be working in Pittsburgh in no time."

The e-mail came from Heather Orlando.

In Pittsburgh.

The Heather who was on television.

On Pittsburgh television—on a real news show.

She must be getting the paper in the mail—or is reading it online. This is great. She knows who I am—and what I can do. Wow.

Customers at the Wired Rooster confirmed Miss Orlando's

evaluation. Without a single dissenting opinion, Lisa had collected dozens of kudos after each article appeared.

"Makes the *Gazette* almost worth reading."

"You're really funny. Why are you working here?"

Indeed. Why?

"Are you going to work for the paper full time? You should."

Besides the congratulations, another group of customers acknowledged seeing the article, and they left it at that.

"Saw your thing in the paper."

"I liked the picture of that dog. He's a cutie."

"They hiring here?"

At least that's better than saying they hated it.

Lisa decided if she was going to be an actual reporter, she needed to do some real reporting.

The Hubert story is really cute. But I probably need to show more depth than just cute.

That afternoon she returned to her apartment, changed into more business appropriate attire, put fourteen dollars of gas in her car, and headed to Lewisburg, some seventy-five miles to the south.

She had called the number of the now shuttered dog rescue organization and heard an electronic voice announce that the phone number was no longer in service. The Web site was still operational, and from that she found the names of the two co-directors. She looked up their personal phone numbers, and addresses, but rather than call, she decided to investigate in person. She carried her notepad and pictures of Hubert, as well as one of Bargain Bill Hoskins.

She wanted to make sure his story was true—about Bargain

Bill claiming he had adopted Hubert just before the shelter had closed its doors.

Sounds too convenient, if you ask me.

The drive took longer than expected.

Everything on these back roads takes longer than expected.

The first name and address she had was for an Emily Sillers on St. Paul Street.

The man at the gas station said, "You can't miss it. If you see the airport, you've gone too far."

Lisa never saw the airport and parked in front of an untidy ranch house with a full lawn of uncut grass. The garage door was lined with rust stains and leaned a few inches askew. She got out and walked toward the front door.

A door creaked open from the house next door.

"You looking for the Sillers?"

"I am. I'm Lisa Goodly. With the *Wellsboro Gazette.*"

She said it firmly, as if that association gave her the right to come, unannounced, to a stranger's house and pepper her with questions.

"They ain't here no more. At least she ain't. The mister, I ain't sure of. But she moved a couple of months ago. Right after she closed that dog shelter of hers. I heard it was some sort of what-cha-call 'marital discord.' I ain't saying that for sure, but that's what I been hearing. And he was never round much, anyhow. So now I got to cut their grass or else the neighborhood looks like it's going to hell in a hand basket, pardon my French."

Lisa tried to remain professional and not appear crestfallen, even if she was.

"Oh, I am sorry to hear that. I wanted to ask her about the shelter."

The voice came out from behind a storm door, the glass so cloudy that Lisa could not be sure exactly who or what she was talking to. She stepped a little closer. The voice belonged to a man, an older man, no doubt retired, from the casual looks of his mid-afternoon dress: baggy work khakis and a scooped-neck white T-shirt. Or at least a mostly white T-shirt. His white hair formed an incomplete halo around his ears and the back of his head. He took a half step outside, holding on to the doorknob.

He's got a kind face. Just dresses horribly.

"You might try that other lady. There wuz two of 'em. Two ladies who ran it. The shelter. I thought they were both sort of odd, you know what I mean?"

The pot-and-kettle cliché.

"Not in that sort of weird way. But taking care of strays and protesting at the mink farm out on Henderson and saying that eating a cheeseburger is wrong. That kind of weird, you know?"

"That would be Judy Kubista? Am I saying that name right?" Lisa asked as she flipped her notepad open.

"Beats me. I knew there wuz two ladies. She used to live over on Washington. You know, around the corner from Domino's Pizza. But I heard she moved."

Lisa was striking out.

"Would you know where?"

The old man shook his head.

"Nope. I mean, she used to work over by Dor-Day's Sub Shop. I saw her in there a few times. Taking care of dogs and making subs don't appeal to me much. Maybe they know where you might find her."

"Do you know the address?"

"Over on Market. You can't miss it. It's like downtown, sort of."

Lisa scribbled down the name in her pad and closed it.

"Well, thank you so much for your help. Really appreciate it."

The old man grinned widely. He was in need of some serious dental work as well.

"No problem. I had no idea that you Wellsboro people came all this way to sell your newspaper subscriptions. Long drive, if you ask me."

Lisa was about to explain that she was not selling newspapers, but stopped herself and decided not to go there.

"Now, I ain't been getting newspapers here since Truman. Got no use for 'em. All a bunch of lies, you know. You seem nice enough, but I ain't got use for them newspaper people or them television people. You tell your editor that I ain't interested in subscribing. Okay?"

Lisa smiled at him, her best walking-backward-while-keeping-an-eye-on-someone smile. "I will be sure to tell him that. Thanks so much for your help, though. And have a good day."

The old man nodded several times.

"You, too, young lady. You, too."

⌣

Hubert was spread out on the rug in Stewart's living room, letting the afternoon sun warm his stomach.

He could not remember how long he had been cold and miserable. Dogs are not adept at recalling numbers or accurately judging the passage of time.

All Hubert knew was that he had been cold for a very, very long time, many, many days and nights—so cold that he, once or twice, had dipped into despair, all but certain that he was simply a dog, disposable and forgotten, and that he had no business thinking that someone, somewhere, was watching out for him and leading him and keeping him from undue suffering.

The cold can do that to your soul.

And now Hubert luxuriated in allowing the sun to beat down on his chest and stomach, making them warm—nearly hot, actually, and letting the heat sink deep into his being and his bones.

Then his eyes snapped open.

He scrambled to his feet and shook himself aware.

He knew what to do. Or at least, he knew what to try to do.

The thought simply appeared in his mind, and because of the sudden and total surprise, he knew. Sometimes dogs just knew. It was the way nature worked.

Hubert was pretty sure that while he was a smart dog, he was not skilled in formulating complicated plans.

I know enough to get by today. Tomorrow will take care of itself.

Hubert smiled a canine smile, to himself, happy that the idea was there. That he knew what to do next.

They need to be together. And I need to help. I need to do all that a good dog can do to make that happen. It is so simple.

He listened for the sound of footsteps outside the door. All was quiet.

They need to be together. I can try to do that. I can.

He took a deep breath.

I can try to get that Stewart and that Lisa person together. I can do that. I can try to do that.

He smiled again.

That is a very good plan. A very good plan indeed. Everyone needs to be part of a pack and this will make our pack stronger.

Then Hubert walked to the door and sat down. He thought that Stewart person would soon be home and he wanted to be ready when he arrived. He wanted to greet him, but he also wanted to think more, with Stewart in the room, of just what he might do to get them together.

It is what a good dog must do.

꘏

Everyone at the Dor-Day Sub Shop (no superfluous "-pe") knew Judy Kubista, and no one knew where she went.

The manager on duty, a small, wrinkled woman with WENDY written on her name tag, said, "She came in one day, got her paycheck, and said, 'I quit.' No one seen her since."

The rest of the afternoon crew, consisting of two teenage boys, nodded in agreement.

"Judy, she used to live over by the elementary school. But I go that way to pick up my grandkids sometimes and I saw her house was empty with a FOR SALE sign on it."

Lisa tried not to appear disappointed.

"You a relative?" Wendy asked, as if suddenly realizing that Lisa was a stranger—and from out of town, probably.

"No. I work for the *Wellsboro Gazette*."

It's only sort of an exaggeration.

Wendy's face remained as blank as those of her two teenager assistants, and that was pretty to mostly blank.

"It's the newspaper in Wellsboro. I was doing a story on animal shelters and I heard Judy helped run the one in town here."

"So you're not trying to collect on a bill or anything, are you?"

"No," Lisa replied. "I just wanted to ask Judy a few questions, that's all."

Wendy shrugged.

"Sorry I couldn't help. I would tell you I'll keep a lookout for her, but people like that...once they leave, they leave for good," Wendy explained, as if disappearing from Lewisburg was a relatively common occurrence.

Well, maybe it is.

⌐

As Lisa was facing her disappointments in Lewisburg, Stewart was home dealing with a most unexpected phone call from his father.

"So, what's the weather like in Wellsboro?" his father asked.

Stewart held the phone away from his face for just a second and stared at it, as if a stranger had hijacked the conversation.

"Dad, we're only fifty miles away. The weather here is the same as the weather there."

He heard his father snort in derision.

"Not always, kiddo. Sometimes it can be ten degrees colder here than where you live. That's nothing to sneeze at, you know. Ten degrees is a lot."

Stewart closed his eyes, almost as if in pain.

"The weather here is really nice, Dad. Almost seventy degrees today. Sunny."

His father listened and replied.

"'Bout the same here. This time, anyhow."

He never just calls me. Maybe he needs money. Or is sick. Or something.

"Well, your grandmother called me. Out of the blue."

"Really?"

Really?

"Yeah, been 'bout a year, maybe two, since we talked."

What do I say to that?

"She's all worked up. Which is normal for her, but still . . ."

I have to ask, don't I?

"About what? I mean, what's she upset about?"

He heard his father sigh loudly, as if giving up. That was one of the things he remembered very clearly about his father: his long sighs of resignation. Other memories were more painful.

"She says you're datin' some hussy. I ain't even sure what a hussy is. You went to college. I didn't. Is this girl a hussy or what?"

Stewart would have sighed as deeply as his father just had but did not want to emulate him—not now.

"Dad, she's a very nice person. We're only friends. And Grams doesn't know her at all. She met her once when she was up here visiting two years ago for like a minute. So she has no idea what she's really like. And we're just friends, for Pete's sake."

"Okay, okay. I believe you. But your grandmother insisted

that I call you and straighten you out. She also said you have a job waitin' for you in Florida that you just don't want. Like jobs grow on trees these days. Is that what you think?"

This is all too complicated to straighten out. Too much triangulation.

"No. I don't think that. And I'm not moving to Florida."

"Hey, suit yourself. You never listened to me and you're not listening now."

Stewart looked down and saw that he had been clenching his free hand, much too tightly, and the skin over the knuckles had gone sheet white.

Even Hubert had stood and walked carefully to Stewart, nosing at his clenched fist, whimpering softly.

"And this girl—her name is Lisa, by the way—she's very nice. We even went to church together."

Oh man, I should not have said that. What was I thinking?

Stewart heard a low guttural snort from his father.

"A Bible-thumper? Really? You're hooked up with a Bible-thumper? You forget what happened to your mother? Don't get me started on those holy rollers."

Why did I say that? Why did I tell him that?

"Stewie, you saw what happened to your mother and me, right? You ain't going there, tell me you ain't going there."

"Dad, she is just a friend. That is all. There is nothing going on."

Another snort.

"Your mother—you were there. How them crazies at that church broke up our marriage. It was all their fault. You know that, Stewart, don't you?"

No, they didn't. It was because you drank too much, were

*abusive, and ran around. That's why. That's why she took off. It
wasn't their fault. And it wasn't my fault. It was your fault.*

"Hey, Stewart, if that's what you want to do with your life,
then go ahead. Just don't expect anything from me, okay?"

Stewart took a deep, silent breath.

"Okay, Dad. I won't. And tell Grams if she calls back that
everything is fine. Okay?"

"Yeah, sure thing, sport. If you say so."

Stewart ended the call and slumped into a kitchen chair. In
a moment, Hubert was standing on his rear legs, his front paws
on Stewart's thigh, whimpering and pressing his nose into Stewart's cheek, as if trying to reassure him that everything was
going to be all right.

Chapter Twenty-Two

STEWART HEARD Lisa pull into the driveway that evening. He remained in his chair near the window, muted the TV with the remote, and waited. Hubert heard Lisa arrive as well, and danced silently over toward the door, hoping she would be coming up to visit.

Stewart heard the soft closure of her apartment door. Hubert did as well, then looked back to Stewart, his dog face marked with obvious disappointment.

"She must have had things to do, Hubert. We'll see her soon. Maybe tomorrow."

Hubert did not appear to be assuaged, not at all, and circled in front of the door several times, perhaps whimpering just a little, then lay down.

Maybe they're right. Maybe my grandmother has a sense about these things. After all, I am just a bag boy at a supermarket. What sort of career path is that? And Lisa is probably going places. She has talent. I could see her moving to Pittsburgh. And what am I doing? Bagging groceries.

He did not unmute the TV. He stood and went into the kitchen and prepared a cup of instant coffee.

You know, maybe that's good enough for me.

He did not bother to turn on the kitchen light and drank his coffee by the blue flickering light from the TV.

—

Lisa wandered about her apartment.

At least I have some room to pace. Poor Stewart would cross his entire place in like four steps.

She placed her empty notepad on the kitchen table and glared at it.

What a waste of an afternoon. Some reporter. I should have called. Saved a lot of driving time and gas. What was I thinking?

She opened her refrigerator and pulled out a can of store brand diet cola. The can hissed as she popped it open and she sat at the table. She did not bother turning on the lights.

It feels better to be in the dark.

She sipped silently and stared out the window.

I wonder if Stewart and Hubert went for their walk. I could watch for them.

She shook her head.

No. Not tonight. And maybe my mother is right. That I'm moving too fast. I don't want what happened with Mark to happen again. Stewart is nice and all, but if I move to Pittsburgh, then what happens? Hurt feelings all around. I don't think I can go through that again. Better just to stay as friends. Only friends.

She drained the rest of the cola and placed the empty can carefully into the bin she had set aside for recyclables. It was lined with a recyclable paper bag.

Better to be safe than sorry.

—

Upstairs, Hubert stood and paced, as best he could, in the small apartment.

Up until this moment, the cozy closeness of Stewart's small apartment had felt warm and inclusive and safe, like a protected den in a rock pile in the forest.

But tonight Hubert felt as if the walls were growing closer and closer, pinning him in.

He wanted to nudge open the door and run down the steps and nudge open that door and keep running until the trapped feeling left him.

I could do that. It would feel good.

But he looked over to Stewart. Stewart did not hide his loneliness well. His face was a road map for loneliness. He did not hide the pain behind his eyes. Hubert could not imagine what caused that pain, but Hubert knew pain and knew what it looked like. He knew pain like that—loneliness like that corroded the soul, rusted the heart.

Hubert walked into the living room and stared at Stewart.

In an instant, a fear spread over him, causing him to shudder, just a little.

What if Stewart doesn't want to be part of the pack? What if he is too broken inside to know that?

Hubert shook his head and his body followed, as if shedding an unwelcome bath of water.

That can't be. I will make it work. It is the way that—the way that things are supposed to be. Together. Safe. Fed. Warm.

Hubert narrowed his eyes.

I will do all that a good dog can do to help him see. Stewart, you have to open your eyes—to Lisa and the truth of the pack.

—

In the dark, the clock on Stewart's countertop microwave, purchased during a "Blow-out After-New Year's Sale" at the Tops Market, glowed 10:00.

I have to take Hubert out. No fair to him to make him wait any longer.

He snapped on the leash and then waited at the door, opening it just a little, and listened.

All was silent. He heard no noises from Lisa's apartment. And there was no loud ESPN chatter booming from Larry's apartment on the first floor.

Must be two-for-one beer somewhere in the area.

He tried to walk down the steps as quietly and as softly as he could, avoiding the third and sixth steps, which creaked loudly every time anyone stepped on them. He actually held his breath as he approached the landing on the second floor.

But Hubert had not been briefed on their stealth walk. He stopped at Lisa's door, sniffed heavily, just to make sure he was in the right place, then whimpered loudly and scratched at the door.

Stewart whispered-hissed, "Hubert! Stop!"

Hubert faced him, midscratch. His canine face seemed to communicate that he was intent on rousing Lisa from whatever she was doing.

"Hubert," Stewart hissed again.

And Hubert whimpered loudly again, adding a little twist of a growl as well.

Stewart heard footsteps inside and closed his eyes for a moment, hoping that she would peer out the spy hole in the door and not open it.

She may have looked. But she also opened the door.

"Hubert. Stewart. What are you doing here?"

Stewart took one step closer.

"We were sneaking out for a walk and Hubert suddenly stopped and started acting all weird—like he deliberately wanted to get your attention."

"That's sweet, Hubert."

"He's never done that before."

Hubert bounced, in more or less a sedate manner—a complex dance routine devised, no doubt, to encourage Lisa to accompany them on this evening's walk.

Hubert looked back at Stewart with a pleading, child-like look on his face, as if to ask, "Can she come with? Please? Please?"

It would be no use to ignore the dog, of that Stewart was certain.

"Would you like to come with us? Hubert seems to want more company tonight."

Stewart would have thought for sure that Lisa would say no. He saw the "no" in her face. But Hubert whimpered again, a puppy-like whimper, designed to bring out a motherly-comforting-take-care-of-the-lost-soul-and-pitiful-dog response.

And it did exactly that.

"Well, sure, I guess. Let me get a coat. And shoes."

In a trice she joined them on the landing. They all tiptoed out onto the porch, Hubert's tiptoes less delicate than his human companions', and hurried across the driveway and onto the sidewalk, heading away from the house and the town and down the darker, less-lit streets.

A half block farther and Lisa and Stewart began to breathe easier. They had evaded detection one more time.

—

"I'm goin' ta catch that mutt," Larry said to no one in particular as he sat at the Duncan Tavern downtown. He had run out of gas money for his truck, and this establishment was within walking distance. And they served inexpensive local brews.

The bartender was well versed in barroom chatter and bravado.

"What makes you say that, Larry?" he asked as he wiped glasses dry. "A lot of people are looking for him now. I hear Bargain Bill is going to up his reward to seven hundred and fifty. Well, up his discount, anyway."

"I'm going to catch him, all right. I got people looking for him. Like a posse. We'll split the reward."

"Other people have help, too, I bet," the bartender said. Business was slow that night, so discussing anything was preferable to listening to the drone of the TV showing a Phillies baseball game.

"Maybe. But I'm the one that really needs a new truck. I had to walk here. Ain't that pitiful? A grown man having to walk?"

"I guess, Larry. Good exercise, right?"

"I hate it. Walking is for dopes and losers."

The bartender finished drying the last of the glasses, arranging them like a line of soldiers behind the bar on a mirrored shelf.

"Good luck, Larry. I wish you well."

"It's that mutt that needs luck. To escape from me. That's who needs luck."

Hubert seemed to be very deliberate about how and when he veered off the sidewalk, pulling Stewart steps closer to Lisa every time. The first two times it happened, they both laughed about it. The third and fourth time, they exchanged knowing glances, or unknowing glances, silently questioning Hubert's motives and tactics.

"Hubert," Stewart said firmly. "You can stop your games now. We're all on a walk together like you wanted. No need to do anything else, okay?"

Hubert stopped and when he looked up, it was pretty obvious that he was a bit offended by Stewart's accusations. But after a moment, the dog grinned, turned, and continued walking, staying in the exact middle of the sidewalk.

"So your day was bad, too?" Lisa asked, after she had recounted her fruitless trip to Lewisburg.

"My father called. He never calls. Seems my grandmother called him. And she never, never calls him. Lots of triangulation. They have some nasty, deep-seated mother–son issues."

Lisa nodded, then replied, "Triangulation? About what? Unless it's none of my business. And that would be okay. I mean . . . you know. Friends."

"Sure."

And how do I answer this? Do I tell her what they've been talking about?

Stewart swallowed and began. "Lisa, my grandmother's friend—Edna—saw us together at the Frog Hut and called her and now she thinks we're in a serious relationship and actually called my father so he could 'talk some sense into me.' And she wants me to move to Florida to take a job as a pool boy in her senior center. That sort of triangulation."

I'm tired of hiding things.

"Oh."

Lisa stared at her feet for a long moment as they walked in silence.

"That is a bad case of triangulation. I mean, not us being together—not that that's bad—but—oh, I don't know how to put it."

Lisa did appear to be honestly flummoxed by Stewart's revelation.

"I know," Stewart said. "It is confusing."

Lisa stopped and placed her hand on Stewart's forearm—not the one with the leash, but the other one. Hubert noticed it, stopped and sat, and stared at them, rapt.

"Listen, Stewart, my mother...well, she sort of said the same thing. It's a long story."

"Everyone's story is long and filled with all sorts of twists and turns."

That was almost poetic. Where did that come from?

Lisa offered him a crooked, knowing smile—affectionate, intimate.

She brings it out in me. It's Lisa.

"They seem to be worried—I mean, our families—your grandmother and my mother—you know, are worried about us following in their footsteps. Or missteps, I guess. Neither of them—or none of them, I guess, would be more proper grammar—none of them had the best of marriages or relationships."

Stewart nodded.

"But just because they had a bad experience, that doesn't mean we have to shut ourselves off from the world, does it?"

"No. It doesn't."

"We're friends, aren't we, Stewart?"

Lisa's voice had gone a little trembly and a little pitchy, as if she were doing her best to keep it in an even tone.

"We are."

"And we don't have to worry about what other people think, do we?"

"We don't."

Lisa looked up at Stewart; her eyes glinted with a trace of a tear, but not a sad tear—a tear of awareness.

And then Stewart decided to take the lead, after Lisa had taken the lead in all the previous encounters of a close physical nature. He stepped closer and enveloped her in a tender embrace—not a hug, not fierce like that, but a gentle and kind embrace, enveloping. Just a protective embrace. An understanding embrace. No more than that. Lisa stiffened just a bit, then relaxed and embraced him back, there in the dark, far removed from any streetlight or prying neighbor or parent or the rest of the world.

And Hubert stood and danced about them whimpering with happy growls, tangling them both in his leash, tangling them so badly that they broke the embrace with laughter and smiles.

The next morning, after Stewart left for work, and after Lisa left, Hubert made his way to the door. He stood and placed his front paw on the shiny metal thing and pushed down. The metal thing yielded with a click and the door opened an inch. Hubert pushed his nose against the door and nudged it open. He sniffed. He carefully made his way down to the landing where the Lisa person lived. He sniffed again and smelled flowers. Then he listened for a long moment, listening for the person who lived below them all. That person carried a musty smell of sweat and some acrid scent Hubert recognized from a long time ago, a stale, fermented scent.

He did not like it, any of it.

But that scent made that person easy to locate, even from a great distance.

Hubert stood behind the door on the porch, still hidden. He sniffed again, deeply.

The other person was not here. He was sure of that. The scent was here, but not strong.

Hubert nudged the door open and hurried across the backyard, not looking left or right, not running, but trotting fast. He jumped over the log where he had stayed those first few nights. He sniffed. There had been no visitors. He did note the scent of squirrels and a possum, but those were common and near universal.

Hubert shook himself, snorted once, and set off at a fast walk.

He was headed to town. He was headed to the store.

That person Stewart said it was bad. And maybe he means it. Maybe I shouldn't do it. But that Stewart person has probably never been hungry. Not as hungry as I was. He doesn't under-

stand. I don't want to be hungry again. That Stewart person would do the same if he were hungry.

Hubert trotted on, his eyes moving left and right, seeing everything, making sure that no one noticed him, staying hidden in the shadows as best he could.

And afterwards, with the bone in his mouth, he heard the shouts, the high-pitched squeals of someone, the footfalls of a human person giving chase, the panting of a human person who could not run fast nor long, a pursuer who never came close to catching him.

And in a few moments, in the time it took a fast dog to run several blocks, Hubert was home, the first door open and the second door open.

He buried the bone next to the three other bones he had stored under that flat, soft thing. The bones would be safe there.

The other bones have been there for many days and that Stewart person has not seen them. He is not a very good hunter. Or maybe he's just not hungry yet.

Hubert let his breathing come back to normal. He took a long drink of water, then circled on that flat, soft thing several times, lay down, and let the sun cover him in warmth and happiness.

Chapter Twenty-Three

THE TOPS Market felt more crowded than the normal Wednesday. Everyone in the break room remarked on it.

"It's because of that stupid dog," Troy said with an exasperated groan. "He's making me work harder than I want to work."

Several of the cashiers agreed with him.

"Seems that everyone wants to come in to take a chance on seeing the dog bandit in action."

Stewart thought it best if he entered into the discussion, making it clear to everyone that he had no knowledge of the dog's whereabouts—or, worse yet, whether someone in town was actually harboring a fugitive and choosing not to call the proper authorities.

"And now that he's stolen another bone today, we'll be even more crowded tomorrow. I think the *Gazette* is doing another article on it," he offered.

A chorus of groans and mumbled objections were offered in reply.

"Somebody should tell that rag of a paper to lay off. We're tired of having to work harder. I mean, I didn't sign up for this."

Stewart nodded enthusiastically.

I haven't really worked all that much harder. A little busier, but it's not like before a holiday or anything.

"Well, they better catch that stupid animal soon. Did you

see that cop slip and fall chasing him? Makes you proud of the city's finest, don't it?"

"Come on now. That dog is fast. And the cop was wearing new shoes. They're slippery when they're new."

A few eyes rolled in response to that.

The buzzer went off announcing the end of break. Stewart stood and stretched and made it look like he was overworked as well, even though he wasn't. He couldn't be sure, but he thought some of his fellow employees had been giving him the once-over as he spoke—as if he were withholding some information on the canine bandit.

Or maybe I'm just being paranoid.

⌒

That evening, Stewart tapped at Lisa's door.

"I bought two subs at the deli today. They're on sale. Have you eaten yet? Hubert wants you to come up and join us for dinner."

Lisa smoothed back her hair as Stewart spoke, as if she had been napping on the couch when he knocked, which she had—but she didn't want him to know that.

"Uhh . . . sure. Can I bring anything?"

Stewart hesitated, not knowing what sort of answer might be expected.

Subs are dinner. What is she asking? Bring what?

"Maybe some soda—if you have it? I have chips."

Lisa smoothed out her blouse as she hurried to her refrigerator.

"Two cans left. Diet okay?"

"Sure."

They sat at Stewart's kitchen table with a sub wrapped in white deli paper in front of each of them.

"Maybe I could say grace?" Lisa asked with a tired smile. "Since you cooked and all."

"Oh. Sure. That's fine. Grace. Sure."

Lisa folded her hands together and bowed her head. Stewart did, too, but kept his eyes open. He wasn't all that certain what might be expected and he didn't want to be surprised, midgrace, as it were, by having to add something.

"Dear Lord, thanks for Your blessings. Thanks for friends. Thanks for this food. Bless it to our bodies, in Your name, Amen."

That's it?

Stewart added an "Amen" as well, remembering how people on TV do it when someone prays.

Stewart unrolled his sub and began to tell Lisa of the semi-pandemonium Hubert had caused at Tops this morning.

"We all thought Mr. Arden was about to have a heart attack. He came screaming out of the back room like he was on fire when someone shouted 'Dog bandit in aisle five!'"

Lisa put her hand over her mouth to laugh, obviously thinking that laughing with an open mouth filled with a partially chewed Italian sub was poor table manners.

"He and the policeman who was in the store for some totally other reason—and not there watching for Hubert—nearly crashed into each other. And then the cop slipped and fell over rounding the corner from the parking lot to Main Street. It was like a TV show."

"I should be taking notes on this," Lisa said between bites and laughter, "but it's too funny. I'll write it up later. And then you can jog my memory if I forget anything."

"Sure."

For the first time in months, perhaps years, Stewart felt at peace—not totally, not completely, but more at peace than he had felt since...well, since grade school.

And maybe even before that.

Lisa must have noticed that he had grown quiet. She smiled to fill the silence.

Hubert sat on the floor, midway between them, staring at each as they ate, obviously hoping that something would fall from the table to the floor, some small part of a sub, as it were, so Hubert might be able to taste the food that they were eating, which smelled delicious.

His head went back and forth, as if he were following a tennis match from the top row of a large stadium.

Then he stopped for a moment, and simply stared at Stewart, as if he were seeing him anew.

Stewart noticed his increased interest and stared back.

"Lisa, does Hubert look different to you?"

She shrugged and swallowed.

"I don't know. Hubert, look at me."

Hubert reluctantly turned to her.

"How do you think he looks different? Good or bad different?" she asked.

Stewart's face scrunched up as he tried to put his feelings, his intuition, into the right words.

She's better at this than I am. She would know just the right words to use.

"I don't know exactly. But like he has a plan? Like he's figuring things out."

"What sort of plan?" Lisa asked.

"I don't know. But he's looking at us differently. Different than when he first showed up."

Lisa tilted her head, like a dog hearing a high-pitched whistle, and pursed her lips.

"Maybe."

"It's the way he looks at me, or you, or us, when we're together. That's what different."

Lisa folded the paper that her sub came in, neatly, into a perfect square.

"Maybe his plan was to get us together. Dogs like to be part of a big group. I read that on the Internet. The more dogs, or people, the safer they feel."

"Maybe that's it," Stewart said. "He does seem happier when you're up here. Like he's been thinking of how to get you here, and now you're here, that makes him more content, happier. I see that in his eyes. I think so, anyhow."

Lisa reached over and gave Hubert a palm-sized piece of yellow cheese.

Hubert loved cheese in any form. He ate it quickly and looked up at her with undisguised affection.

"Maybe that was his plan. It's working, if it was."

Stewart crumpled up his sub paper into a small ball and tossed it toward the open wastebasket, coming within a few inches of making the shot. But he didn't, so he retrieved it and placed in the wastebasket.

"The garbage can isn't covered. Hubert doesn't pull things out of the trash?"

"No. Do dogs do that?" Stewart asked.

Hubert growled softly, and looked as if that would be the last thing he would ever consider doing.

"My grannie had her garbage can under virtual lock and key. She had a few garbage-loving dogs. But not Hubert?"

"Nope. Not once. He doesn't even sniff garbage cans when we pass them on our walk. I thought dogs did that sort of thing."

Lisa shrugged. "Hubert has good manners."

"And a plan," Stewart added.

"And it's working, isn't it?" Lisa added. "It's a good plan, isn't it?"

This time she blushed, just a little, confirming the truth of the situation.

"It is. Thanks, Hubert."

And Hubert growled happily in response.

When Lisa left Stewart's apartment that evening, she scratched Hubert's neck, making him growl/whimper in appreciation, and gave Stewart a short kiss on the cheek, again, and again. Stewart appeared nervous and jittery by her closeness.

Hubert glanced at her as she kissed Stewart, and it appeared to Lisa that the dog acknowledged her power over Stewart.

It's not power. He just gets all teenagery when I'm the least bit forward.

She returned to her apartment and switched on the light by the sofa, took her shoes off, and placed them in a rack of cubby holes for shoes she'd bought at the Target in Selinsgrove when she first moved in.

A place for everything, and everything in its place.

She liked Stewart's apartment, and while he was by far the neatest man she had encountered in some time, she liked the neatness and order in her apartment more. The coffee cups were lined up in two rows. The drinking glasses took three rows. Cereal boxes in her small pantry were lined up by height and/or thickness. The clothes in her one large closet were ordered as well: all darks on one side, all other colors to the other side, short tops in the middle, growing longer as you moved to the end of the closet rod.

How can you operate when things are messy?

She put on an old sweatshirt (bottom drawer) and a pair of track shorts—her standard bedtime attire. The outfit she had worn today went carefully into her laundry hamper, with the fabric bag forming the liner, so when she went to the Plenty O' Suds Laundromat all she had to do was grab the bag and head out.

You save a lot of time not having to pack a laundry bag.

She positioned her phone on her nightstand and plugged it into the recharging cord.

As she did, it danced and vibrated in her hand.

She did not recognize the number, but it was in the 412 area code—the original area code for Pittsburgh.

"Hello?"

"Well, if it isn't our star reporter. Hi, Lisa, this is Heather Orlando."

It took a moment for the reality of that to sink in, and another moment until Lisa had found the wherewithal to answer the phone in a cogent manner.

"Ohh . . . sure. Hello."

She didn't do a great job of assembling herself in a cool, collected manner.

"I have been following with great interest the ongoing saga of the bandit dog of Wellsboro. Seems like no one is any closer to catching him, are they?"

"No," Lisa replied, getting her bearings now. She related the latest incident of thievery.

Heather was laughing as she told the tale.

"I've been following your stories, Lisa. They're good. Very good."

Lisa wanted to demure and say that they were only puff pieces and they weren't that good and that the *Gazette* is an awfully small paper, but she held her tongue.

"Thank you," she said instead.

I read that declining a compliment is like insulting the person who gave you the compliment—like they're not smart enough to see the real truth.

"I get the feeling that you don't think Bill Hoskins is telling the truth about the dog."

"And you would be right." Lisa hesitated for a moment, unsure how much to share. "This is between us, right? Off the record, as it were."

Heather laughed again.

"Of course."

"He's lying through his teeth."

"I got that impression from your last article."

"It wasn't that obvious, was it? I didn't mean it to be obvious."

"No, no, not at all," Heather replied.

Lisa thought she sounded more blonde and more pretty on the phone than most normal people.

"But after a while, Lisa, you get a sense about people. And you get a sense about good reporting. I'm just reading between the lines, that's all."

"Thanks. I guess."

"No, that's a compliment. And I've shared your work with a few people in the newsroom here—and with a few people I know over at the *Post-Gazette*."

At a loss for words, Lisa felt her mouth hanging open in surprise.

"So when are you coming to Pittsburgh? There are people here you should meet. And who want to meet you."

"I . . . I don't know. I don't have anything planned."

"Tell you what, Lisa. Plan on coming down. Whenever. Just for the day, even."

"Well, sure. I could do that."

"Great. And you promise me that you'll call me right away if something exciting happens with the dog, right? We had such a great response to the last story. I want to be able to give the audience at least one more installment. They're all pulling for the dog, you know. The pictures just set off a flood of calls saying they would adopt him."

"Really?"

"Well, perhaps not a flood. But more response than most stories ever get. The station manager even said it was a good piece. And he hates everything that smacks of human interest."

"Well . . . I'm glad that people liked it."

"So you'll plan on coming down, okay? And make sure you call me before you come," Heather said in a very authoritative reporter's tone.

"I'll call. I will. Promise."

"Good," Heather said, putting her stamp of insistence on the request.

And that evening, even though the clock on her phone blinked 12:30, Lisa was no closer to sleep then than she had been at 9:30.

And she continued to note the clock until a few minutes after 4:00 A.M.

And this was with the alarm set for 6:00 and the start of the early shift at the Wired Rooster.

Chapter Twenty-Four

M R. ARDEN flapped out of the Wired Rooster, his arms aflutter, as if attempting to fly back to the Tops Market in indignation.

City council members Kevin Connelly and John Stricklin sat at their usual table, in the back, where it was a little more private, all but dazed mute by the early morning tirade from Mr. Arden.

It began as most typical citizen tirades began, by his claiming to be a taxpayer and, thus, the boss of whomever was being addressed.

"I pay your salary," was the one sentence most often repeated by irate city members—especially when no one was paying attention to them as they preferred to have attention paid.

"And the agreement is most often made moot," Kevin often said, "when they learn how little we get to attend each meeting. Barely covers the coffee I have to buy to stay awake."

Today, Mr. Arden held forth on the city's responsibility to track down the horrid "dog bandit of Wellsboro" and put him behind bars—or worse.

"I'm losing valuable merchandise. This has to be stopped."

Mr. Connelly and Mr. Stricklin assumed their "earnestly listening" poses, and both of them knew it was indeed simply a pose to put people at ease. It wasn't that they weren't listening, but people with complaints needed to see head nods and hear a few "I see"s as they rambled on and on.

Both councilmen did that this morning.

Both councilmen knew that they had little authority to rein in a stray dog—a very clever and resourceful stray dog that had already eluded Wellsboro's finest on several occasions.

"Mr. Arden," Kevin began, in response, waiting until Mr. Arden's volume had lowered and his velocity had peaked somewhat. "You are an upstanding citizen of Wellsboro and Tops Market is a key employer in the city. We are all aware of the outstanding contribution Tops has made to the local economy and to the town as well—what with the float in the Fourth of July parade and all. We want to make sure that you hear us hearing you. We understand your frustrations and we are doing everything in our power as city council members to alleviate the problem and find a solution with some alacrity."

Mr. Connelly was also a devotee of "word-for-the-day" calendars.

"Alacrity" had been last Tuesday. Even though he wasn't sure he was using it correctly, he plowed forward.

"And as a result of your concerns for the safety and well-being of your customers, also citizens of Wellsboro, Mr. Stricklin and I, this very morning, have discussed issuing a 'special council order of enforcement' concerning this specific stray animal. The special order will endeavor to keep the animal, this menace as you call it, off the streets."

Mr. Arden looked at first puzzled, then almost gratified at being heard. Mr. Stricklin, a fellow councilman, also appeared puzzled at first, then leaned back in silent admiration of what the brilliant Mr. Connelly had just performed.

Mr. Arden puffed himself up, like a pigeon, then said, loudly, "Well, good. See that you do."

And then he glanced at the large clock over the condiment table.

"Good heavens. I'm almost late for the frozen delivery."

And he took off, out the door, tilting sideways as he made the turn onto Main Street.

In the silence that swallowed up the two councilmen in his absence, Mr. Stricklin—or John Jay, as most people in town referred to him, seeing as how Jay was his middle name— brought his hands together in a very exaggerated clapping motion, without really making a clapping sound.

"And just what is a 'special council order of enforcement'?"

Kevin shrugged.

"I have no idea. But doesn't it sound officious and puissant?"

"If 'puissant' means really smart, then yes."

Kevin drained the last of his coffee.

"I need to get to the office. I'll call the city manager later and see if there is anything like a 'special council order of enforcement' on the books. If anyone would know, it would be him."

John Jay stood as well.

"And if there isn't?"

"Well, Mr. Arden would probably need to hire an attorney to find out. And we both know he's not going to do that, is he?"

John Jay held his smirk. After all, the Wired Rooster did lie in his district and he did not want to go overboard and offend anyone—if anyone had been eavesdropping, that is.

"No. He won't," he replied, then added in a whisper, "but it did calm him down. Maybe he won't be sending me so many angry e-mails this week."

"Maybe. Good thing he lives in your district and not mine," Kevin added with finality as the two councilmen walked out and on to their real, paying jobs.

↩

Despite having only a couple of hours of uninterrupted sleep, Lisa felt great this morning.

Superb. Outstanding.

She almost wished she had taped the previous evening's conversation—but she had been replaying the salient parts of it over and over in her mind.

Especially the part about coming to Pittsburgh.

"There are people here you should meet. Who want to meet you."

I know that doesn't mean I'll get a job offer or anything like that. But they know who I am. They read what I've written. This is just so wonderful.

She had daydreamed her way into three mistakes this morning: using whole milk instead of soy in a chai latte, using regular coffee when decaf was requested, and spilling an entire large frothy something or other onto the floor.

What sobered her up, what brought her back to reality, and her normal professional self, was the thought: *What about Stewart?*

↩

At the same time Lisa was on her hands and knees mopping up the caffeinated spill, Stewart was on his way to work—walking, of course.

*One of these days, I'll have enough saved up to fix my car—
or, better yet, buy a new one. That would be great. To have a car
that actually starts all the time.*

As he turned the corner onto Main Street, he noticed one of
several posters tacked to the telephone pole.

Bargain Bill had indeed upped his offer to $750—still in the
form of a credit, of course.

*But that, with the few hundred dollars I've saved, and a few
hundred dollars for my old Nissan—I could almost swing something newer.*

As he considered that, he knew what it entailed.

And then Lisa's face popped into his thoughts, stern and almost angry.

"You can't even think about that. Hubert has to stay with
you. He has to. He loves you."

And while Stewart agreed with her, or at least he agreed
with the image he had of her in his mind that morning, he also
added, with just a dusting of bitterness, *But you don't have to
walk to work every day. And try dating without a car. It's not
easy.*

↢

That evening, the Wellsboro City Council debated, with not a
single member cracking a smirk or a knowing smile, the "special council order of enforcement" concerning the nefarious
dog bandit of Wellsboro.

Even the city clerk, an acerbic and dour man originally from
Schenectady, went along with the charade.

"Everyone has endured the same e-mails, multiple times. If

this works," he said quietly, in a hallway aside to Councilman Stricklin, "then I will write it into the city charter...somehow."

The motion passed seven to zero.

And just as the gavel sounded, Hubert was leading Stewart and Lisa into a darker section of the residential area south of town.

"It feels like Hubert has been here before, doesn't it?" Lisa said. "Like he knows where he's taking us."

Stewart nodded. He had not said much for the last four blocks, ever since Lisa took his hand in hers, at the end of their block. Stewart wasn't really sure where they were going. He wanted to look over at Lisa as they walked, but wasn't sure that was proper, so he tried to focus on just walking and not thinking about how small her hand felt in his and how delicate her fingers seemed in comparison to his calloused and meaty appendage.

Hubert took another turn, away from town, where the only lights were from houses. The moon was out, not quite full, but buttery and gibbous that night, so the absence of street lamps was not as perilous as it would be when the moon was hidden.

Stewart thought Lisa actually moved closer to him the darker it got. And as she did, it appeared that Hubert had a bigger bounce to his step, as if his master plan was falling into place and that made him happier—at least as happy as a dog could be in the dark on a leash without eating.

The trio stopped at a small rise that opened up to the south. The moon hung just an inch or two off the horizon, as if skipping off the ridge of mountains that ran south from the city, all the while illuminating the hills and fields in a pale light, turning the landscape sepia.

Lisa slipped her arm into Stewart's arm and pulled him close to her.

Stewart was aware that in certain situations, the male of the species should take charge of things, sort of, and make the proper moves. But Stewart was at a loss to know exactly what those proper, preprescribed moves might be.

Stewart had dated some in college.

Well, to be honest, he would never describe the number of dates he'd had as "some."

"Infrequent" would be the term he would use to describe his dating past.

It was not for lack of interest. It was for lack of confidence.

What do I talk about? Grams always said I was "backward" with girls. Because of my mother, she said. She blamed a lot of stuff on my mother. Maybe she was right.

That question of ease of conversation seemed to have worked itself out with Lisa. Even though the subject of Hubert was their first and primary focus of conversation, they also talked about all sorts of other things. Conversation came easily with Lisa. Stewart wondered if that would have been the case with other women, but decided it would not have been.

Only certain gears mesh, he thought.

They stood there, the three of them, staring to the south, marveling at the brilliance and the distance and the size and the luminosity of the moon, hanging like some sort of ripe peach, just out of reach.

Peach isn't the right fruit—but I don't know any white fruit. And cauliflower just doesn't work.

He felt her move and he turned to her, just as she turned to him.

Now what do I do? This is so difficult.

Lisa tilted her head back, just an inch or two.

That must mean something. Right? But what?

Stewart felt Hubert butt against his shin, and that caused him to look down even more, bringing his face and her face closer together.

That was when Lisa closed her eyes.

Okay. Okay. Okay. I can do this.

He leaned in closer to her, closing his eyes as well, but first making sure of the proximity of lips and noses and all the rest.

And then he kissed her.

It was not the sort of mad, passionate kisses that occur in the movies, in which one partner appears hungry and intent on devouring the other person.

This kiss was more delicate, more chaste, more refined, more meaningful than any kiss Stewart had ever seen on TV or at the movies.

It was a perfect kiss.

An absolutely perfect kiss.

It did not last for multiple moments. There was no groaning or murmuring.

It was simply the most perfect kiss that Stewart could ever imagine sharing with another person.

And when the kiss stopped, and they both returned to their normal heights and positions, that's when Hubert barked loudly, three times, almost shouting with joy, and then bouncing, like a kangaroo, in the moonlit darkness before them, as happy as an animal could ever expect to be.

And that's when Lisa hugged Stewart, and that's when Hubert barked again, and that's when two porch lights snapped on, from opposite sides of the street, and that's when Lisa whispered loudly, "Run!" and that's when the three of them took off, two of them giggling and laughing and one of them woofing with great canine joy, through the dark neighborhood south of town.

⟿

Stewart had read somewhere that a gentleman remains a gentleman at all times. He wasn't sure what that entailed, but when he said good night to Lisa, instead of another kiss, which perhaps would have been anticlimactic, at least for this one particular evening, he hugged her. It was a soft hug, tender and gentle, and as Lisa closed the door she kept her eyes on Stewart until the last moment. And he read that as her reluctance to say good night and that she had had a good time on their walk.

This is all so confusing, he thought to himself. *Happy, but really confusing. For a novice. I guess I'm doing okay. Despite what Grams said. Despite my mother.*

Stewart did not see the small sliver of apprehension in Lisa's eyes as she closed the door, thinking that this night had been magical, and wonderful, and memorable, if only the word "Pittsburgh" hadn't kept popping into her thoughts.

And for Stewart, all that emotion times two, but he also worried as he closed his own door behind him.

What now? I mean, I'm a bag boy at a supermarket. That can't be what girls dream about, can it? Meeting some guy whose most important daily task is asking "Paper or plastic?"

While the two human players in this drama were happy but

confused, the canine player seemed beside himself with joy. He continued to head-butt against Stewart's leg, demanding to be petted and paid attention to, grinning wildly, grinning as if everything he had hoped had come to some sort of fruition.

But dogs can't see ahead. I read that somewhere. Their sense of the future is just not there. He's happy now. So am I, actually. But I'm worried about what's going to happen.

He scratched behind Hubert's ears.

And he doesn't know what's going to happen.

And, unknown to both more advanced players in this evening's activities, Hubert did understand what the future meant. And while he could not foresee what was about to happen, it was also obvious that he had perfect peace in the path that their lives, or loves, would take.

He grinned up at Stewart.

Just be patient. We will help Stewart see.

Chapter Twenty-Five

T HE FOLLOWING MORNING, just a few minutes before seven, Stewart stumbled out of bed, responding to a soft tapping at the door.

It was Lisa.

He did a quick body scan. He was wearing athletic running shorts and a Penn State T-shirt. That was enough coverage for company.

"Listen, I can't stay since I'm already almost late. But I needed to tell you something."

Uh-oh. I did do something wrong.

"Hubert has to see a vet. All this time, and I haven't even considered that. He needs to be checked. He could have some sort of disease or parasite or something. And he needs a rabies shot. What if he accidentally bites someone? He's got to be protected. We have to get him to a vet. Like right away."

Stewart thought about trying to smooth his hair into a less wild style but thought it would only draw attention to it. Lisa seemed too preoccupied to notice.

"Okay," he said.

"What time do you get off work?"

"Two."

"Okay. Meet me back here as soon as you can. I heard about a vet in Coudersport that's really good. And she's open until six. I checked."

"Coudersport? That's like an hour away."

Lisa nodded, as if in a hurry.

"Yep. But if we go to a vet in town—well, they've all seen the posters and the *Gazette*. They'll turn us in. We have to go out of town for this."

"Oh. Yeah. You're right."

"Good. Then I'll see you back here at two."

"Okay."

Lisa stood in the doorway for just a second, then turned back.

"And last night, Stewart, was really, really special."

"Oh."

"I mean fireworks sort of special."

What do I say now?

"Well . . . for me, too. Really special."

She smiled, a sort of knowing smile.

"Good."

And that was when Hubert barked, not loudly, but loud enough, and Lisa hunched over, shut the door quickly, and hurried down the steps. And Stewart turned to Hubert, put his finger to his lips and hissed, "Shhhh."

Lisa drove faster than Stewart remembered her driving. Not excessively fast, not like a speed demon, but around ten miles an hour faster than whatever posted speed limit there was. Hubert did not seem to mind, but Stewart was nervous. Speeding tickets, or the possibility of speeding tickets, made him nervous. And his old Nissan, now dead, seldom managed to go fast enough to break any rural speed limit.

Despite her speed, Lisa was also a very good driver, always looking at the road, even when talking, and always keeping her hands in the "nine and three position" on the steering wheel.

"So, how do you know this vet?" Stewart asked.

"A customer at the Rooster talked about her. There's not that many lady vets in the area and when I was little, I wanted to be a vet."

"Why didn't you? You're smart enough."

Stewart winced after he said that, thinking that it may be not only an obtuse compliment, but perhaps some sort of back-handed comment on female intelligence.

But Lisa did not appear to be offended.

"I ran into high school chemistry. None of it made sense. Atomic numbers. And I sort of figured that to be a vet you might have to know something about chemistry. And besides, I liked writing more. I was better at writing. I love animals, but writing is who I am."

Stewart nodded.

He wondered, for the next three miles, why he had chosen political science as his major at Penn State. He wasn't political, didn't really like politics, and had no patience with layers upon layers of bureaucracy and systems organization.

He wished he had a passion, like Lisa.

Maybe it's not too late to find a passion.

"We're almost here," Lisa announced, bringing him out of his reverie.

He stared out his window.

"Not much of a town, is it?"

"It's about the same size as Wellsboro."

Stewart smiled.

"Like I said, not much of a town."

Lisa broke her safe-driving record by letting go of the wheel with her right hand and playfully punching Stewart in the arm, giggling as she did.

"Look for Broad Street."

They drove on for just another minute.

"One of us should get a GPS unit in their car," Lisa said.

"I've got a map thing on my phone, but this place is like two pixels wide."

Stewart was pretty sure Lisa would have punched him again, but she was too intent on finding the address.

"Next street," Stewart said.

"Good eyes."

And they pulled up in front of the large Victorian House with the sign EMMA GRAINGER DVM in front.

"Looks like our house," Lisa remarked.

"But in better repair."

Hubert was up now, sniffing loudly. If Stewart had to guess, he would have said that the sniffs were nervous in nature.

The three of them got out, and Hubert had to be urged to accompany them to the porch. Stewart actually had to grab his collar to get him through the front door. Once inside, the dog huddled behind Stewart's legs as Lisa went to the counter.

"Hi," she said, in a most innocent manner, "I called earlier. Lisa Goodly. We're bringing Hubert in. He's a stray, so we don't know if he's had any shots or not."

The young woman at the counter nodded.

"You can go into examination room number 2. We actually

only have one exam room, but saying we have a number two sounds better, don't you think?"

Stewart hoisted Hubert onto the stainless-steel table in room number 2. The dog was trembling, just a little.

"I know, Hubert. It smells funny in here."

The vet, a most attractive younger woman, came in wearing a white lab coat and carrying a stethoscope. She introduced herself and Lisa gave a quick, though somewhat misleading, history of how Hubert came to be with them.

"He just showed up one day. And he's such a nice dog. We asked all around, but no one seemed to be missing a dog. And we'd like to make sure he's healthy and get all his shots and stuff."

Dr. Grainer nodded and began an examination, listening to his heart and lungs, taking his temperature, which Hubert did not like one bit. She brought out a small unit that looked like a fat magnifying glass without the glass, and slowly ran it over his body, focusing on the shoulder blades and neck. Then she felt that area, carefully and thoroughly.

Hubert did not mind that as much as his temperature check.

"No microchips that I can read or feel."

"Good," Lisa said. "I mean, good that no one thinks he's lost. Well, maybe they do—but you know what I mean."

"I do," the vet said.

She looked very carefully at Hubert's face.

If Stewart had been asked, he might have said that there was an unasked question in her eyes. She checked his eyes and ears and teeth.

"He looks to be in good shape. The scars he has are old—but they healed nicely. There must have been some serious abuse in his past. But besides that, he does need a shot—a combination vaccine."

"Rabies, right?" Lisa said.

"Rabies, yes, and parvovirus, distemper, and hepatitis as well. I like to give all at once. Some vets do one at a time, but his will save you some money. And it's just as effective."

"Good," Stewart said.

She slipped out and returned with a syringe, tapping at it with her finger, just like real doctors do when they give injections. The shot itself took Hubert by surprise, and he yelped and twisted when she injected him.

"Good boy," she said, petting his head.

Hubert did not look like he was buying her pleasantries—not after what she had just done.

The vet turned to write something down on Hubert's chart.

Lisa leaned to Stewart and whispered into his ear.

"She's wearing a cross. I bet she's a Christian."

Stewart was not certain that wearing a cross implied belief, but it seemed to make Lisa very happy and he nodded back at her.

"Well, you're good to go. The young lady at the front desk will have your bill and your rabies tags. And good luck. Hubert seems like a very nice dog."

"He is," Lisa said. "Thanks."

Stewart took out his checkbook and paid for the injections and exam—more than he expected, and more than he usually spent on his own health care. But Lisa was right. He needed to be sure that Hubert was healthy and posed no health risk to them or anyone else.

Above the reception area, Stewart pointed to a framed poster.

I can do all things through Christ who strengthens me. Philippians 4:13.

"You were right. She probably does go to church."

The young woman behind the counter smiled.

"You're right, sort of. I mean, she does go to church. She has to. She's dating a pastor in town."

⟶

As the three of them piled into Lisa's car and drove off, Emma, the veterinarian, sat behind her desk, thinking, and worrying.

This sort of thing used to be easy. Before I met Jake.

She sighed deeply and picked up the phone. On her desk was a faxed copy of Hubert's picture—sent from the Wellsboro Police Department to all veterinarians in the tri-county area.

It's the bandit dog. For certain. A very good-looking animal.

The phone call connected and she heard the buzz of the first ring.

I just can't lie anymore. He's managed to complicate one more aspect of my life.

And just before the police picked up, she looked at Pastor Jake's picture on her desk and smiled.

But he makes it all worth it. He does.

Chapter Twenty-Six

T HE FOLLOWING MORNING, Hubert seemed none the worse for wear. Stewart was careful not to pat the spot of his injection, but it was apparent that the dog had all but forgotten, or perhaps forgiven, Stewart for the indignities he had made Hubert suffer through the day before.

His shift at the Tops Market did not begin until ten that morning, so he woke a little later than normal. He drank his first mandatory cup of coffee in the dark, the outside illumination matching the inside of the apartment. Hubert was up, of course, and sat at the foot of the chair where Stewart sat, waiting patiently until he finished that odd-smelling beverage and put on shoes.

Shoes meant "Walk" to Hubert.

Stewart grabbed a jacket and looked for Hubert's leash.

It was nowhere to be found.

Then Stewart remembered—he had taken it with them on their visit to the vet's office and he must have left in Lisa's car. He made his way quietly down the steps, telling Hubert to walk softly.

Rats. Lisa must be working the early shift today.

Lisa's car was not in the driveway.

Stewart bent down to Hubert just inside the downstairs door.

"Hubert, I don't have your leash today. If we go for a walk, will you promise to stay right next to me and not run off? Promise?"

Hubert looked up at him with wide, innocent eyes, as if attempting to assure him that whatever it was he was requesting, Hubert, being a good dog, would do his best to accommodate him.

"Okay. You stay beside me. We need to do this quick because the sun is coming up and we don't want people to see you—not just yet."

Stewart and Lisa had discussed having Hubert "come out," as it were, once they figured things out. In one of their plans, Stewart would offer complete restitution for the lost merchandise and they would purchase the necessary dog license from the city and make sure pets were allowed in their building.

"But we can't do that now. Not just yet," Stewart said, summing things up. "We have to think this through. Maybe we broke some laws we don't even know about—and neither of us can afford big fines, right?"

"Right," Lisa replied. "We'll figure out something."

Hubert and Stewart walked together on the sidewalk, heading away from town. The sun was higher than Stewart thought it would be, so, in essence, the pair was out in broad daylight. That was something Stewart had avoided most of the time.

Better to be cautious.

But they could be seen—or, more accurately, Hubert could be seen and identified by anyone out walking, or driving slowly. Anyone, that is, who was observant and on the lookout for criminals.

Criminal dogs.

And then it happened. Something Stewart had tried to avoid and shield Hubert from.

A Chevy Cavalier, speeding toward them, slowed down, just a little, then a lot.

Drivers often slowed down for people with dogs, not knowing what that dog might do at the last moment.

The Cavalier appeared vaguely familiar.

Then Stewart recognized it from the parking lot of Tops Market. It was always parked in the farthest row of spots, in order "to make room for the people who pay our salaries."

The Cavalier bucked and squealed to a stop, as best as a decades-old Cavalier could do—a well-used car with mediocre brakes to start with. The sudden stop caused the vehicle to fishtail and the rear end of the car swung farther out into the street, narrowly missing a parked Ford Escape, its back tires actually smoking a little from the stop.

It's Mr. Arden! I knew I recognized that car.

Mr. Arden, already dressed in his standard heavily starched white manager's smock, leaped out of the car, pointing, gesturing wildly, and screeching, "It's the bandit dog. It's the bandit dog!"

Stewart had seldom, if ever, heard such a high-pitched screech, almost as if Mr. Arden had been inhaling helium just before he spoke.

"Stewart! He's right there! Catch him! Noooooow!"

Hubert looked up at Stewart, obviously confused, and Stewart could see a deep anxiety form in the dog's eyes. Hubert's face reflected something nearly overpowering to him, something deep and frightening.

"Hubert!" Stewart said and lurched for his collar.

And that was when Hubert, against his better judgment, took off like a wild animal, racing away, his paws barely touching the ground as he ran. Stewart took off after him, calling his name, running as fast as he could, losing ground with every step.

⟶

I need to get more food. I need more food.

The screaming and the squealing tires and the pounding feet in pursuit spurred Hubert's nearly involuntary, automatic, flee-or-fight, instinctual response. Actually, it was less instinctual and more learned behavior. He had experienced all those actions and sounds and smells before—many times.

The noise and the terror and the anger and the pursuit reminded him of those long-buried memories, the memories that were seared into his mind and scarred onto his body.

Screaming is followed by hitting and hitting is followed by hunger and more hitting. And hunger. A long time of pain and hunger, but mostly hunger.

The terror of those memories drove Hubert faster and faster, and he did not even slow down until he came upon the automatic doors of the Tops Market.

⟶

Mr. Arden, back in his car, followed Stewart as he ran, swerving in and around cars and other obstacles.

"He's your dog? How could you?"

Stewart did not answer, just panted, sucking in as much air as he could. He had not jogged, or run, since high school, probably. His sides already began to ache, after only three blocks.

"He's your dog? I don't believe it."

Stewart turned on Maple and Mr. Arden squealed his Cavalier around the corner, still shouting through the open passenger window.

"Were you holding out for a bigger reward? Is that it? Money is what drove you and your criminal dog friend?"

Stewart grabbed at his left side.

"No."

"That's extortion, isn't it, Stewart? Or maybe blackmail."

Stewart did not answer.

"Whatever it is, you are in serious trouble right now, mister. Serious trouble. Both of you."

And they both came to a gradual stop as they saw Hubert, now just a blaze of black-and-white dog, tear past them on the other side of the street, headed back to his home, to Stewart's home.

Stewart gasped one more time, then turned and ran back toward home.

"Trouble! You're in for it now."

Mr. Arden continued to rant until Stewart could no longer make out the words over his panicked breathing.

⟶

Hubert was inside Stewart's apartment, sitting in the corner of the small living room. He had hung his head down in obvious reaction to the bad thing he had just done and was awaiting, without whimpering or trembling, the punishment that was certain to follow.

But at least he now had food stored, under that flat, soft thing. He had a stack of rawhide bones. They would not be enough to stave off all hunger, but they would be enough to keep him alive. And he was pretty certain that the Stewart person wouldn't take them from him.

Maybe the Stewart person didn't even know where Hubert had hidden them. After all, they had been there for a long time, and the Stewart person did not move them or take them.

Stewart burst into the apartment, panting, gasping for air.

Hubert tried not to whimper, but he did, just a little. He did not like being hit. Stewart was not carrying a strap or a piece of wood, and for that Hubert was grateful.

Stewart walked over to Hubert. Hubert lowered his head even farther, his nose almost touching the ground. He let a soft whimper escape. He didn't want to whimper because that showed weakness and Hubert was not a weak dog, but he couldn't help it—not this time.

Stewart took several more deep breaths.

He knelt down in front of Hubert.

Then he put his arms around Hubert's neck. That surprised Hubert.

No one ever touched him, gently touched him—before they began hitting.

"Hubert, I don't know why you went to the store again. But it's okay. You don't know that it's wrong. It's okay. I'll protect you. I'll make sure nothing bad happens to you. I promise, Hubert. I promise."

Hubert softened when he realized that there would be no hitting today—only nice, calm words. He wasn't sure what they all meant, but his Stewart person seemed to be kind, even when bad things happened.

That's what a person in a pack would do. Maybe Stewart finally sees. Maybe he is tired of being lost. This is the way it all should be. He has to see that. He has to know that now.

Hubert looked up into Stewart's face. He could see worry

and confusion and tiredness and . . . well, he could see peace—
or almost peace.

He must know. Almost.

Then he leaned his head on Stewart's shoulder and pressed
against him and hoped that this moment would never have to
end.

Even though they both knew that it would.

—

Neither Stewart nor Hubert heard the car pull into the driveway. Perhaps Hubert heard it, but he was paying more attention to being hugged by Stewart than monitoring events
outside. Stewart and Hubert both looked up as they heard the
footsteps on the stairs outside.

The knock sounded more official, and more firm, than any
knock Stewart, or Hubert, had yet heard.

Stewart sort of, almost, knew who it was and why he was
here.

*Who else could it be? Much too loud for Lisa and much too
determined to be the landlord.*

Stewart rose and slowly walked to the door. When he
opened it, there stood one of Wellsboro's finest, a portly, older
policeman who wore a LT. QUINN nameplate pinned above his
left pocket.

Hubert did not move, but Stewart heard him whimper.

Stewart stepped back and Lieutenant Quinn took two steps
inside. Then he shook his head, almost as if in disbelief at what
he was being forced to do that morning.

"Listen, son, I don't want to be here, either. Chasing dogs

is way down on my list of police priorities—just under chasing skateboarders and hoodlums off the street by the mayor's house."

"Okay," Stewart replied. "I'm ready to pay any fine that I need to pay."

Lieutenant Quinn shook his head again. Stewart imagined that Lieutenant Quinn shook his head often during the course of a standard police shift.

With bemusement, I bet. Maybe I should become a policeman. They all seem to like their jobs. The ones on the cops shows on TV, anyhow. Lieutenant Quinn —well, I can't tell.

"You're Stewart Coolidge, right?"

"I am. Do you need to see some ID or something?"

"No," the policeman replied. "I think I can trust you on that. I mean, who else would you be?"

Lieutenant Quinn looked over into the living room, where Hubert was. The dog had not moved and his head was still hung down, avoiding all eye contact with humans.

"And that's the bandit dog, right?"

"I guess."

Lieutenant Quinn arched his left eyebrow.

"I mean . . . he is."

"Okay," the policeman answered. "You know, son, this is all so stupid."

Stewart nodded, agreeing with him.

"But I have my orders."

"Orders?"

"All this over a bunch of dog toys."

"Rawhide bones, actually."

"Whatever."

Hubert sank lower, as if trying to hide in the carpet.

"Listen, I have to take the dog with me."

And at that, Stewart stood up straighter, and his eyes widened.

"What? No. Wait. I'll pay the fine. I said I would pay the fine."

"Sorry, son. No can do. There's a special city council order that requires me to take the dog into custody. Like I've got nothing better to do with my time."

"Wait a minute," Stewart said, his voice rising with anxiety. "Taking the rawhide bones is not a felony. It's a misdemeanor at best. That only requires a court appearance and a fine, probably. Not arrest."

Lieutenant Quinn adjusted his belt, the second belt, which held up his holster and pistol and Mace and handcuffs. Stewart later wondered if that was simply a psychological ploy to divert his attention or to draw his attention to who really held the power in this situation.

"He's not dangerous. He's had his shots."

Lieutenant Quinn nodded.

"I know. The vet in Coudersport called me yesterday. Well, left a message for me. Didn't get it until this morning."

Stewart's face must have reflected his dismay and disillusionment.

"Vets don't have doctor–patient confidentiality. Real doctors do, but not vets."

"Oh."

"And besides, Mr. Arden, that weirdo, called the police eight times in the last ten minutes, demanding that we deal with this issue—in light of the special city council order of enforcement."

At that moment Stewart heard a car door slam and a fast rattle of feet on the steps. Lisa burst into the room, as breathless as Stewart had been a few minutes earlier.

"He's come to take Hubert," Stewart said, trying to be calm.

Lisa turned to Lieutenant Quinn, her face hard and set and nearly angry.

"You can't do that. The dog is private property."

Lieutenant Quinn turned to face Lisa full on and Lisa shrank back, just an inch or so.

"Listen, miss, I am and I can. Special city council enforcement order."

Lisa rose back up, as if pushing against an incoming wave. Stewart had never seen her in action before, or at least not action like this.

"That has no legal status. A special order? Come on, now. I don't think that's even a legal . . . law, or legal ordinance."

Lieutenant Quinn shrugged.

"Maybe it is, maybe it isn't. You have money to get a lawyer to debate the issue?"

Lisa shriveled back just a bit, but then stiffened and glared at the policeman.

"Didn't think so. So let's all be nice and civil and don't give me any more heartburn than I already have. Get the dog into my car and we'll take good care of him."

Lisa rose up, and actually seemed to get larger, like a mother bear defending her cub.

"And what if something unfortunate were to happen to Hubert? What about that?"

Lieutenant Quinn seemed to grow older, and slumpier, if that were possible, as they talked.

"The sheriff is up for reelection this year. You think he wants someone to shoot a cute, defenseless dog on his watch? If something were to happen to this dog before the city council votes on it—well, I would be on permanent night patrol at the gravel quarry. And I don't want to work nights looking at rocks."

Lisa had to smile, just a bit.

"You promise to take good care of Hubert?"

"I do."

"I promised him that nothing bad would happen," Stewart said, his voice rattling, plaintive. "I don't want to be a liar. Okay?"

"Okay, son. But just help me get him into the squad car—and if you have a leash, that would be swell."

Lisa got the leash from her car, and Hubert came quietly, slowly climbing into the back of the patrol car, sniffing loudly. As it pulled away, Stewart and Lisa could see Hubert turning around, staring back at them, with imploring eyes, wondering why they were not going with him.

As the car drove away, Stewart put his arm around Lisa and she did the same to him, each trying silently to let the other know that this would all work out for the best, even though they weren't really sure of anything at this moment.

Lisa called "her" lawyer, Nathan George, on retainer, as it were, from the Wired Rooster, when they got back up to Stewart's apartment. To her dismay, he agreed with the policeman's assessment on most major points.

"He's right—you can't afford to pay me to do research on this and there aren't enough free lattes to make it worth my while. And since the dog could be labeled as a public nuisance, it can be taken into custody by the police. At least on a temporary basis. Until the city council meets next week."

So she and Stewart sat in the two chairs in the living room, not really talking, for the rest of the morning, thinking how empty the apartment suddenly felt.

↦

Once Stewart left for work, Lisa dialed a Pittsburgh phone number.

"Heather Orlando, here," came the very chipper reply.

Lisa launched into a recap of the story so far: how the entire town was literally abuzz with the arrest and capture and lockup of Hubert. Lisa came clean on her involvement in the cover-up—and Heather either laughed or commiserated at the right places.

Then she provided Heather with the potential bombshell leads: the two women she couldn't find from the closed animal shelter in Lewisburg. But she was sure that the dog had not come from there and was sure that Bargain Bill had never adopted him.

Lisa could almost see Heather grinning over the phone.

"You take it easy, Lisa. And I'll take it from here. And good work."

Lisa thought she would be happier, but she wasn't.

Chapter Twenty-Seven

WITHIN TWENTY MINUTES of Hubert's capture, Bargain Bill had altered his reward sign to declare loudly CAPTURED! and JAILED! and BUY A CAR AND HELP ME FIGHT CITY HALL! using a super-wide-tipped waterproof marker.

Bargain Bill stood back and admired his handiwork as an old and somewhat battered car rattled onto the lot, the driver's face a mix of excitement and firmness.

My first customer of the day—and it is only eight thirty. I love this dog.

⌐

Mr. Arden, once he was satisfied that the dog was under lock and key with an armed guard, ordered two stock boys to take down the REWARD sign from the front of the store.

"You can leave the posters on the telephone poles. Somebody from the city...or the phone company, will get those. That's what I pay taxes for."

As he watched the two young men drag the sign back toward the store, he allowed himself a self-satisfied grin.

Now I don't have to worry about paying out the reward money. A policeman can't claim it. And actually, I'm the one that found him.

⤚

Perched on his chair at his desk in the *Gazette* offices, Dave Grback pounded away on his keyboard, his old-style corded phone jammed between his shoulder and cheek, getting information first from the police department, then the mayor, then Lisa, and then a few people who called in to say they'd witnessed the last daring daylight robbery that the bandit dog committed—just before being captured, at gunpoint probably, and locked up.

This is wonderful. Hate to see the end of this story, but we do have the city council meeting next week. That should be a real circus. I'll have to have a photographer assigned to that. And I'll go as well.

After he had the rough draft of the story completed, he sent e-mails to several dozen fellow editors, from Pittsburgh to Erie to Philadelphia, alerting them that another installment of the "bandit dog" series was about to be published in this Wednesday's edition.

A little self-serving publicity, that's all. Everybody does it, right?

⤚

That morning, Joe Witt, the current mayor of Wellsboro, busied himself shuffling papers on his desk at his insurance agency. He had already fielded a call from the police chief telling him that the dog had been captured, from Mr. Arden demanding that the dog be captured, and from the editor of the newspaper asking where the captured dog was incarcerated.

Joe did not like these sorts of phone calls. He had run for mayor thinking that it might be good for visibility, and, thus, good for business, but he had not experienced any mayoral bump in insurance customers.

In fact, he thought, there were just as many people angry with him for some civic reason as were happy with him for the same civic reason.

"It's a zero-sum game," he told his wife, although he wasn't sure what a zero-sum game entailed, exactly.

And now the infamous dog bandit of Wellsboro was behind bars and a special meeting of the city council had been called for the following week, two weeks ahead of schedule.

Maybe then the phone calls will stop.

He did have a most troubling thought, and it had actually kept him up most of the night before—something that rarely, if ever, happened.

What if we have to put the dog down? Maybe it has rabies or something. Or mange. If that happens, the animal lovers will be incensed. And they'll want me put down as well.

He reached into his top drawer and, without even looking, found the familiar bottle. He unscrewed the top and spilled out three antacid tablets, popping them into his mouth and carefully and thoroughly chewing them up, hoping that the third tablet would put him over the top and return his stomach to normal.

But I doubt it.

＊

Jerry Mallick slammed his palm against the front fender of his truck and a small dusting of rust and dirt trickled down onto his boots like dirty snow. He scowled and adjusted his camouflage baseball hat, leaving another small streak of dirt on the bill of the cap.

"That dag-blamed dog was right here all along," he snarled, more for impression than because of actual anger.

He had noticed the police car when it had pulled into the driveway and had immediately slipped out the front door. Once he'd figured out that the cop was at the back door and on his way upstairs, he'd hightailed it a few blocks over.

Just in case. I don't know what he's here for, but you never know. Old parking tickets, maybe. I'm pretty sure I have a few.

But now that he had found out that Stewart was hiding his free ticket to a new truck, or a newer truck, he was both relieved that the authorities weren't there for him and badly riled that he was no longer eligible for the rewards.

I wonder if hiding a criminal dog is like . . . grounds for kicking Stewie out of the apartment.

But he quickly changed his mind.

I sort of like the guy. And he pays his rent on time. Not like that old lady who used to live here. Always sayin' her Social Security check was late or stolen or something.

⟶

Lisa moped through her second shift at the Wired Rooster. She begged the manager to let her skip out that morning once she had gotten the news about Hubert, promising that she would take a second shift that afternoon.

Kevin or Kellan or Carl was sitting at the back table complaining to anyone who would listen about the injustice in the world and how a poor working stiff never catches a break.

"That cop who nabbed the dog—now he gits the reward. I tell you, the whole thing wuz rigged from the git-go."

Kevin or Kellan or Carl was wearing a wide-brimmed leather hat indoors—a practice Lisa found most uncivil.

But this is Wellsboro and he's one of those pretend mountain folk, so what do I expect?

To make it more "real," Kevin or Kellan or Carl had attached a real squirrel tail to the back of the hat, so whenever he turned his head, it looked like he was wagging his tail in excitement.

"Listen, the police can't claim rewards for doing their job," Lisa explained as she steamed a pitcher of whole milk. "So nobody gets any reward."

Kevin or Kellan or Carl did not appear to be mollified by that fact, not in the least.

"Well, that's what I mean, then. No one gits nuthin' around here. None of it's fair, I tell you what. The little guy always winds up gittin' the shaft."

⟶

Stewart was stunned as he picked up his phone and saw a text from his grandmother.

When did she learn how to do that? And when did she get a smart phone?

"Stewart," the text read, "I understand they caught that dog. And the newspaper said that you are the owner. Is that true? Were you lying to me all this time? And what else have you lied about? And, by the way, they found someone for the pool job. Don't bother applying. Your Grandmother."

Stewart wanted to delete the text right then but thought better of it.

I'll call her tonight and explain. Maybe.

⌐

"So you talked to that Heather reporter from Pittsburgh?"

"I did, Mom. Just to let her know what's going on. She said she wanted to do a follow-up story."

"Well, that's nice. Are they going to offer you a job, then?"

Lisa closed her eyes and wished her mother was more aware of how things actually worked—or at least how the current process of finding a job worked.

Maybe when she was young it was different.

"No, I don't think so. But she did invite me down to the city and she said she would introduce me around. That's a really good thing."

Lisa was pretty certain her mother didn't really get what that entailed, but she was positive and encouraging nonetheless. "Well, that's so nice. And how is it between you and that young man . . . Stewart, right?"

Lisa had known she would ask and had an answer prepared.

"Yes. Stewart. We're still friends."

She was not about to tell her of the magical kiss they shared or the hugs or the hand-holding.

"Just don't get too serious. No repeats and no more scares, okay?"

"Okay, Mom. Like I've already told you a hundred times."

"I'm just being a mother, okay?"

"Okay. And will do. Or won't do, as the case may be."

Lisa thought that was clever and funny, but her mother didn't laugh.

Too soon. Too close. Maybe never, I imagine.

⟶

Stewart's phone rang again. He seldom logged in more than one call per day, so today was a red-letter day in terms of data usage.

"Hey, Stewie, they caught the dog, didn't they? And it was you all along. You get the reward?"

Stewart slowly explained what had transpired early that morning. His father sounded disappointed.

"You coulda played this one better, Stewie. Made a few bucks off of it."

"I know, Dad. I guess I didn't figure out the right angles."

He would have argued with him, or pointed out that he did not want to profit off the situation, but knew it would be a frustrating proposition to try to do so.

"And I hear you were up in Coudersport getting the dog shots or something. I used to see that lady vet around more. But I ain't seen her in any of the usual spots for a long time. I hear she got religion or something."

"Yeah, the receptionist said she's dating a local pastor."

"A preacher? Don't get me started on preachers. I tell you what, Stewie, they're all just after your money. They're all hucksters, I tell you. But don't get me started."

I will do my best not to get you started, Dad. Really I will.

"And you were right here yesterday. You could have stopped by. I had a six-pack in the fridge and there's a Pizza Hut right around the corner."

"Sorry, Dad. I had to get back to...work."

"Yeah, I know how that is, Stewie. Work night and day and no one cares, you know?"

"I know, Dad. I know."

Later that afternoon, after Stewart had finished work, he realized that simply being at work was awkward, since no one in the store knew exactly how to broach the "dog" subject with him, so they'd left him mostly alone. He was, at the same time, an abettor and a hero. Thankfully, Mr. Arden was in Sunbury all day for managers' training and had had to leave moments after the police arrived to arrest Hubert. After he punched out, Stewart walked to the police station, which shared space in the municipal building with the city council offices and the city clerk, as well as serving as the downtown fire station.

Sitting at the first desk was the dog-arresting officer from this morning, Lieutenant Quinn.

"Sir," Stewart said, a little louder than he wanted, but he wasn't really sure of protocol in this situation.

"You're Stewart, right? The one with the dog."

"Yes sir. I just wondered if you could tell me where they're keeping Hubert?"

Lieutenant Quinn appeared puzzled.

"That's what we called the dog, sir. Hubert."

Lieutenant Quinn tightened up his already tight face.

"Odd name . . . but, whatever, you know."

"Yes sir. So is Hubert at the pound or what?"

Lieutenant Quinn wiped at his face in a soul-weary sort of gesture.

"Son, you're not from around here, are you?"

Stewart shook his head.

"No. I grew up in Lewisburg."

"Well, Lewisburg may have a dog pound or a city animal shelter or whatever, but Wellsboro doesn't. No call for it, really. Until today, that is."

"So . . ."

Lieutenant Quinn stood up and adjusted his belt again. It appeared to Stewart that belt adjustments were a very common occurrence with Lieutenant Quinn.

"We have two holding cells here. Hardly ever use either of them. They're small. If we got prisoners, we take them over to the Tioga County Prison. They're set up for it. You know— meals, showers, beds, all that sort of stuff. And bathrooms. These cells lack certain necessary amenities, if you know what I mean."

"So . . ."

"We have . . . your Hubert in cell number two. It's a little bigger and it has a window."

"Lieutenant Quinn, I know I'm not from around here, and I don't want to sound stupid, but can I visit him? I think he was mistreated by whoever had him before me and I sort of promised I would take care of him. I don't want to lie to a dog. Not to Hubert."

Lieutenant Quinn's gruff expression gradually gave way to a more sympathetic expression.

"I hear you, Stewart. And to tell you the truth, I think you coming in would be a great idea. "

"Really?"

"It would."

Stewart was forming a new opinion of the policeman.

"In fact, Stewart, I would appreciate it if you came in a couple of times a day. You know, to take him for walks and stuff. I don't want to clean up after a dog. And I don't want anyone who works here to clean up after a dog. That's not on anyone's job description, let me tell you."

"Really?"

"All of this, this pain in the behind, is because of that Mr. Arden. And Bargain Bill didn't help matters, either, what with his reward and all."

Lieutenant Quinn stepped closer to Stewart and lowered his voice.

"Stewart, this place is always open, so you can sort of come in whenever you want. Just check in at the desk. Providing the night clerk isn't sleeping, that is. He'll give you the key to the cell. That sound okay to you?"

Stewart felt like singing, at least briefly.

"Sure, that sounds great, sir. I could come in early and maybe once during the day and once more at night. Could I bring a blanket or a cushion so Hubert has something to sleep on?"

"Sure, Stewart. Knock yourself out," Lieutenant Quinn said.

"Listen, I have to run home to get his food and a water bowl. That's okay, right?"

"Sure."

"And is it okay if Lisa—you met her this morning—if Lisa comes with me to visit?"

Lieutenant Quinn rolled his eyes, but then smiled.

"Sure, kid, you can bring your girlfriend with you."

Girlfriend? Is that what she is? Wow.

⤙

Lisa and Stewart hurried back to the municipal building in Lisa's car. Lisa carried a soft pillow and a thick blanket and Stewart carried a plastic Tops bag with Hubert's food and two bowls—one for the kibbles and one for water.

Hubert appeared ecstatic when the two of them walked in, and even more ecstatic when Stewart took the fist-sized key the clerk had given him and unlocked the door. Hubert leaped and licked and offered barks and whimpers of happiness. Eventually he settled down and Lisa and Stewart sat on the concrete platform that must have been intended as a bed for the unfortunate prisoner. Lisa made sure the pillow and blanket were arranged just so on the floor. Hubert sniffed and inspected the bed carefully, circled it a few times, then lay down just for a moment, but rather than be apart from them, he jumped up on the rock-hard bed with his two humans, grinning and smiling and growling.

"I've never been in a jail cell before. Have you?" Lisa asked.

"Nope. I've been in a couple of jails—as a visitor. My dad was locked up a few times. Nothing serious. Disorderly conduct. Public intoxication. That sort of thing. A few days. A week once."

Lisa grew serious.

"Stewart, I'm sorry. I didn't mean to bring up bad memories."

"It's okay, Lisa. He is what he is. And I can't change the past."

"But that's so hard. Seeing a parent in jail. Especially for a kid. How old were you?"

Stewart did not look at her when he answered.

"Maybe ten, the first time. Maybe younger. I'm not totally sure."

Stewart looked away and out the small window. You could not see anything but the dark blue afternoon sky.

"I'm sorry, Stewart," Lisa repeated and hugged his arm tightly.

"Yeah. Well, lots of people have it a lot worse than me."

Hubert was watching them talk and when Lisa hugged Stewart's arm, he began to get excited, a little, whimpering with an odd whimper—not of pain, but some manner of canine celebration, nudging Stewart closer to Lisa, pushing the two of them together, tighter and closer.

They sat, a tight-knit group of three, for a long time.

"We need to take Hubert for a walk. I told you what Lieutenant Quinn said about not wanting any accidents in here to have to clean up."

"Sure."

Lisa was about to make a comment about this being the first time she has been in public with a known criminal, but as soon as the thought entered her mind she glanced at the serious look on Stewart's face and self-censored the remark, chiding herself for being insensitive and unthinking.

But at least I didn't say it.

⟿

The three of them skirted the main streets in Wellsboro—not that there would be that much traffic, but they didn't want to stir things up more than they were already stirred. Seeing them out in public might set Mr. Arden off and force Lieutenant Quinn to take a harder stance on visitation.

When they returned, Stewart poured out kibbles into the dish and filled the water bowl with fresh water from the fountain in the hall outside the cells.

Hubert sniffed at both, but did not taste either. He seemed content simply to know that both were there when he did get hungry or thirsty.

Hubert looked up at them with canine satisfaction, or contentment.

They petted and hugged and petted again, then slipped out of the cell, and while Stewart locked the door, Lisa was on her knees, petting Hubert through the bars.

Stewart knelt down as well.

"Listen, Hubert. You have to stay here tonight. You understand? You have to stay here. It will be okay. I'll come back in the morning and we'll go for a walk then. But you have to stay here alone tonight."

Hubert stepped back and sat down, his face gone serious, almost somber, as if he finally understood that he was under lock and key and would not have Stewart sleeping nearby.

He barked once, a serious bark, a bark of understanding.

"You'll be okay, Hubert," Stewart said as they approached the outside door. "We'll get all this straightened out in a few days. Okay?"

Hubert barked one time, softly, as if saying good night.

As Stewart and Lisa walked to her car, she turned to Stewart and took his hand.

"Stewart, what happens if this all goes bad? What happens if they declare him a public nuisance or a threat to the public health or whatever? What if we lose him? I talked to my attorney friend and he said they could issue a big fine—or even have him put down."

Lisa's voice trembled as she said the final words, as if saying them would somehow give them credence, which she did not want to do.

Stewart did not know where his sudden calm came from. He thought he would be more distraught than Lisa was.

But he wasn't.

There was something about the way Hubert stoically sat there, in jail, waiting for someone to keep his promise, expecting that promises made would be promises kept. And Stewart had little experience with people keeping their promises. But this time would be different. This promise would be kept—or he would sacrifice all to make it happen.

"It will all be okay, Lisa. It will."

He looked deeply into her eyes.

"I promise."

Chapter Twenty-Eight

S TEWART FAITHFULLY came to the police station three times a day: before he went to work, after his shift was done, and later in the evening. Hubert must have timed his arrivals. Every time Stewart walked through the front door of the department, he could hear Hubert barking—not loud or insistent or frantic, but more like calling out, or just saying hello.

On the evening of the third day, Stewart asked the officer on duty if Hubert barked while alone in the cell.

"Nope. Quiet as a church mouse. Only barks when you show up."

"That's good. I would hate to have him be a bother," Stewart added.

The officer, a young patrolman with a shaved head, leaned back in his chair, the chair squawking in complaint, and stretched his arms behind his head.

"He's okay. We all go in to check on him, you know. I think it's pretty stupid to lock a dog up. We all do. Make you pay a fine or whatever. But such are the ways of small-town politics, you know?"

"I guess."

"He's a really nice dog," the officer said. "Reminds me of my dog when I was a kid. Kind of gave me the urge to get another one. Or adopt one from a shelter or something."

Stewart walked into the cell area and unlocked the door.

Hubert, of course, was wiggling with excitement, whimpering, head bobs, and all.

"Must be boring here, all by yourself. Nothing to look at."

Hubert barked in agreement.

"Well, let's go for a walk first. Then I'll feed you. And we can talk. Okay?"

Hubert barked again, again in agreement.

They took their normal, stay-off-the-main-drag route, and twenty minutes later were back at the jail. As they walked through the office, there was a stack of books on an unused desk, right next to the entrance to the very small cell block. A handwritten sign was taped above the stack: HELP YOURSELF. So Stewart took one, thinking that he could read for a while as he sat with Hubert to keep him company.

Stewart filled Hubert's bowl with food and the other with fresh water and returned and sat on the floor with Hubert, drawing his knees up and leaning his back against the concrete bed. It was not the most comfortable place to be, but Stewart thought that if Hubert could endure it twenty-four hours a day, the least Stewart could do was to spend a few more moments with his dog.

My dog. That sounds weird. But I guess that's what he is. Mine.

Hubert sat next to him and leaned against him, and Stewart put his arm around the dog's neck. That caused Hubert to wiggle closer. Stewart grabbed at the book, thinking the station must have some sort of free lending library for people waiting disposition of their arrest, or whatever.

It was not a contemporary book.

It was a copy of the Bible.

"But it's not black. It doesn't have a Bible cover."

He showed it to Hubert, who dutifully sniffed it.

"Is that legal, Hubert? A Bible that doesn't look like a Bible, I mean."

Hubert grinned and sniffed at it again, nudging the book with his snout, nudging it closer to Stewart, as if asking to be read a story from the book.

"Hubert," Stewart chided with a smile, "you don't understand English. Or at least this kind of English. Too many *thee*s and *thou*s for a dog, even a smart dog like you, to understand."

Stewart flipped open the book and read a few sentences. To his surprise, he could actually read it and it actually made sense.

"They must have changed this since I went to church as a kid, Hubert."

Hubert nudged at the book again with his snout, growling happily.

"You really want to hear something?"

Hubert barked, not loudly, but firmly.

Stewart flipped the book open at random and began to read. It was somewhere in the middle of a section marked Daniel and, while Stewart didn't exactly follow the story since he'd started it in the middle, Hubert appeared to like listening to him read aloud. He leaned more and then slowly slid down, until he was on his side and his head was in Stewart's lap. His eyes were half open and there was a faint smile on his dog face.

"Huh. I sort of could figure things out in this. Like it was almost modern."

He closed the Bible for just a moment and looked at the cover again. It did say HOLY BIBLE in small print, and Stewart was pretty sure they couldn't print that if it wasn't true.

He flipped it back open, closer to the end.

"That's the new part of the Bible, Hubert. That much I know."

It was a section marked John.

He scanned the page and his eyes stopped on one particular verse—or sentence. Stewart wasn't positive what they were called in this new version.

Stewart read aloud, "*I am the way, the truth, and the life. No one can come to the Father except through me.*"

"They talk a lot about truth in this book, don't they, Hubert?"

At this, Hubert scrambled to his feet, or paws, and butted his head against Stewart's chest.

"What?"

Hubert looked up and grinned, then butted his head again, as if he wanted to push that thought into Stewart's heart.

"You want me to read more?"

Hubert offered a quiet bark in reply.

Stewart thumbed through a number of pages, ran his fingers down the pages, at random, then stopped and read, "*And you will know the truth, and the truth will set you free.*"

At that, Hubert barked again, and bounced up and down, and offered one last head butt against Stewart's chest.

Stewart closed the Bible and set it on the concrete bed and put his arm on Hubert's shoulder, wanting to settle him down.

"This is what Lisa knows, isn't it, Hubert? This stuff about God and knowing about the truth and peace and stuff."

Hubert growled, agreeing.

"I could ask her what this all means, couldn't I?"

Again, Hubert growled, a truly-happy-at-last sort of growl.

Stewart looked at Hubert, looked into his eyes, and thought he could see something mysterious and otherworldly there, as if Hubert had a secret, had the truth, and was waiting for Stewart to come upon it.

"Lisa knows all about this, right?"

Hubert growled and began to dance and wiggle, excited.

"Hubert, be serious now."

Hubert stopped moving and stared back.

"This is what you knew, right? When we left you here that first night. In jail. You knew . . . something . . . something that gave you peace. Right? I didn't think dogs understood things like this—but I guess if God made people, He made dogs, too, and maybe He made some dogs who know more than others. Right?"

At this Hubert began to dog-dance and bounce and whimper and growl and lick and head-butt with wild abandon.

Stewart let him go on for a long moment, then gathered the wiggling dog in his arms and just held him, held him firm and tight.

And the truth shall set you free.

⟶

Hubert had been in jail for five days.

Stewart continued to show up for work and do his job as best he could, but very few of his fellow employees said much to him, afraid that if they were seen consorting with him, and if Stewart somehow got blamed for everything that had gone on during the dog bandit's run of brazen, daylight thefts, then they might be cojoined with him—and somehow be exiled from favored employee status.

And no one wanted to be exiled and left adrift on Mr. Arden's bad side.

To Stewart's surprise, and to everyone else's, Mr. Arden had hardly said a word to Stewart about anything. Stewart heard a few snatches of gossip—that Mr. Arden had been instructed by the company team of lawyers and attorneys and HR consultants to steer clear of "the offender" until the city council held its hearing on the locked-up canine. Then, once Stewart and the dog were found guilty, in an almost court of law, the corporate hammer could fall on him.

No one wanted to be near that corporate hammer when it fell.

The only person who expressed interest in the situation was Denny King, who worked nights most of the time, and who was said to have a checkered past, and, as some claimed, was working only because of a state program that found jobs for ex-convicts.

"Tough," Denny said the morning after the arrest. "You weren't busted, were you? Like for aiding and abetting or anything?"

"No. Just the dog."

"Good. If you need it, I got a name of a great lawyer in Lewisburg. He's sort of a weasel—but then, aren't they all?"

Stewart nodded, not sure if he actually knew any lawyers personally.

"He can get anyone off on anything. You need him, give him a call and mention my name. Okay? He's a righteous guy, if you know what I mean."

Stewart didn't know what he meant, but thanked him for the information. He was sure he didn't need a criminal lawyer. And even if he did, he couldn't afford one.

And I don't think animals get court-appointed legal representation—like the criminals do on TV.

Now, after five days of Hubert's incarceration, Stewart had made friends with most of the police force of Wellsboro—not that there were that many to befriend. To a man (and two women) they all expressed dismay at having a dog locked up, and even further dismay over the sad state of political affairs— even in a small town like Wellsboro.

And as he got to know them, he became more interested in the paths they had taken to join the police force. To his great surprise, one of the older patrolmen had actually majored in political science at the University of Pittsburgh.

"Waste of my time," he explained to Stewart. "Should have just gone to the academy right out of high school."

"And you like what you do?" Stewart asked.

The patrolman smiled. "It's the best job I ever had, son. I love every day. Always something different. Like dogs who steal, you know?"

Stewart was mostly certain that he was telling the truth and that he did really like what he did.

I wonder what that feels like—to like what you do?

—

The evening of the fifth day of Hubert's incarceration, Lisa and Stewart walked from their house to the police station. It was a warm evening, and Stewart liked walking with her. It extended their time together and it gave them a chance to talk with no interruptions.

Hubert, Stewart stated, seemed to be holding up well. "He looks a little bored, but he's happy every time I come and doesn't whine too much when I have to leave again."

That evening, Stewart and Lisa gathered up a bouncing Hubert and took him out for his nightly constitutional.

The warm air was thick with the scent of real lilacs or some other flower filling the night, and the sky showed dark and clear, holding a canopy made up of the jeweled light of the stars.

A few blocks into their walk, Lisa pulled Stewart's hand close to her. All three of them stopped and Stewart and Hubert looked at her, wondering why.

"Stewart," Lisa said in an almost whisper, earnest, and a little scared, "can we break him out?"

Stewart actually stepped back a half step.

"Break him out? Hubert?"

Hubert listened, then sat, thinking that this conversation might take more than a few moments. His head was tilted to one side, as if trying to follow dialogue being spoken in a foreign language.

Lisa looked both ways, up and down the street, as if checking for eavesdroppers. They were standing next to a vacant building that used to house a video rental store.

"Listen, Stewart, I was thinking. I couldn't live with myself if something happened to Hubert. And I have to think that a lot of this hubbub over the bone stealing and all was because of the stories I wrote for the *Gazette*. If the stories weren't there, no one would care, probably. So...I just couldn't bear to see something bad happen."

Stewart turned to face her directly.

"Nothing bad will happen, Lisa. It won't."

Lisa turned her head, almost as if she were about to run off, or like she was unwilling to make eye contact.

"You can't know that, Stewart. You can't."

"I'm sure. I am."

Lisa snapped back to him. Her eyes flashed, even in the dark, angry, or at least upset.

"My father said he would never leave my mother—and he did," Lisa hissed. "So what's sure and certain in this world, Stewart? We have to take care of Hubert. We have to. I don't want to spend the rest of my life feeling guilty. I've done enough of that already."

Stewart was confused, and a little scared. Even Hubert, all of a sudden, as if feeding on Lisa's emotions, seemed to grow nervous, and anxious, and whimpered a bit—more of a low whine, a noise Stewart had never heard him make.

Stewart dropped the leash. He was sure Hubert would not move anywhere, not without the two of them by his side. Stewart put his hands on Lisa's shoulders—stopping for just a moment, thinking how small and delicate her shoulders were, how precise and how doll-like they felt—and turned her to face him.

"Lisa, I understand what you're asking. I've thought about it. I could just say that he got off his leash and took off. But then what? I would have to hide him upstairs and then we would have to move. I would think even the police here in Wellsboro would consider me as a prime suspect. And Hubert is not a dog I could hide under the bed. And if we had to leave, I would have to leave you. I don't want to do that. Not now. Not ever. Besides that, I don't think lying is something they teach in church. I don't think lying is part of the truth, you know?"

Lisa stared up at Stewart—angry, sad, confused, worried—and then, slowly, all of those feelings began to change and turn into something else, perhaps akin to wonderment, or a sudden, joyful acknowledgment of an unspoken dream, a goal she'd had but had not mentioned yet to Stewart.

"The truth? What do you mean, Stewart? The truth? Like the Bible sort of truth?"

That was when Hubert barked and bounced and placed his front paws on Lisa's shoulder as well. He couldn't quite stretch that far, but he came close, as if he were trying to explain something very important to Lisa, trying his best to see what actually had occurred and that she should be happy.

Stewart knew that what he was about to say would be confusing. He was still a little, or a lot, confused. But he felt something different as well. Confused, to be sure, but also certain that he was on the right path. Often, in the past, Stewart had felt as if he were left alone in the darkness, but now, way off in the distance, within reach, he could now see light. He could now see a way out of that darkness.

And he could see, or sense, a glimpse of that peace.

And truth.

He looked into her eyes and did not look away, even though the words were hard to grab on to.

"I picked up a Bible. There was a stack of free ones in the jail. They probably have them there for like, hardened criminals and deviants and, you know, bad guys. But I started reading it to Hubert. He seemed to like it. I got the feeling that he wanted me to read it. And he would fall asleep with his head in my lap when I did. And to be honest, I sort of like reading it. I like when it talks about looking for the truth, or finding the truth."

Lisa appeared to be near tears.

"Really?"

"Really."

Lisa's broad, happy smile gradually faded and she grew puzzled.

"But I thought you went to church. I thought you knew all about faith."

Stewart shook his head. "After my parents both took off for good, when I was a freshman in high school, my grandmother took up with this...sort of crazy church. I'm not sure it was a real, honest-to-goodness church. You know, like a real church that follows the rules and all that. I guess we went to church when I was real little. But not for years and years. So I didn't know what to expect. But I thought that her new 'group' was pretty nuts. Lots of screaming and shouting. And lots of blame. She blamed everyone but herself for everything that had gone wrong in her life and with her family. And she acted like all of a sudden she knew all about what to do and not do. She was always telling me all the things that I can't do and if I did do them I would go to hell and she would point out people that we knew who were going to hell. And for sure my dad was going to hell, and of course, my mother—after a while, I stopped listening."

Lisa was crying now, very softly, very small, the tears on her cheeks catching the starlight as little jeweled facets.

"I didn't know."

Stewart felt a sudden, and unexplained, sense of boldness.

"And I didn't know that I didn't know. But then I met you. And I watched you, Lisa. That's what I did. It was nothing that you said, really. It was how you acted. Sort of how you lived. I saw right away that you had a sense of peace that I didn't. And I wanted that. So I paid attention. And it's also because Hubert seemed to keep nudging us together."

"You think?" Lisa sniffled. "Hubert?"

"I do. Don't you? Didn't you get the sense that he was the happiest when we were together?"

Lisa sniffled again, louder this time, and almost laughed.

"I thought it was just me. I thought I was imagining it. Or that I wanted it—to get to know you—and that I was projecting onto poor Hubert."

Stewart looked down at the dog.

"No. I think he's had a hand in this from the beginning. Or a paw, as it were. I think he knows what he's doing. He knows about the truth. I see it in his eyes."

Hubert bounced several more times, barking and growling.

Stewart decided then that a very long embrace was just what Hubert would want to see, and apparently it was, because as they hugged, Hubert sat back down, then found the loose end of the leash and picked it up in his mouth and sat, grinning, watching his two humans hold tight to each other and whisper soft things to each other.

Stewart broke the hug after a while.

"We better get back or they will think we've let him go."

Lisa giggled in response.

"And, Stewart, you won't tell anyone about what I asked, will you? About breaking him out and escaping? I don't know what came over me."

Stewart, still feeling bold, bent down and kissed her on the forehead. He kept his eyes open and saw that Hubert almost dropped the leash when he pressed his lips to the top of Lisa's head.

"I won't say a word. And it was nothing that I didn't consider a few hundred times myself."

Stewart reached down and took the leash from Hubert's mouth.

Being together, the three of them, felt like they had been doing it forever, which, of course, they had not, but each one of them, without saying another word, all hoped that this feeling would never end and that the three of them would always be together.

And then Stewart thought that not all things go according to what we want—and he would be okay, no matter what happened.

Stewart guessed he would have no choice but to trust.

～

When the three of them were back in the jail cell, Lisa, in a mouse-small voice, said, "We could pray about this, you know. I sort of forgot to do that. Maybe that was part of my problem."

Stewart locked the cell door and knelt back beside Lisa. They had been kneeling like this all along to be able to say good-bye to Hubert and pet him just before they left. But tonight, Hubert whimpered and growled a little and then put his paw through the bars so Lisa could hold it.

"Could you pray, Lisa? I'd rather hear you pray than me. And I'm still not sure of what words to use, you know?"

And she did, quietly, offering a prayer as soft as a rabbit's fur, as gentle as a morning mist, and as heartfelt as a toddler's request for a hug. It was all perfect and it was all planned and Hubert whimpered along with every word Lisa said to God, as if Hubert were adding his voice to hers, to make it better understood by the Divine Creator, that guiding force of nature that Hubert knew as his protector.

And Stewart, in that most pellucid moment of clarity, was certain that the prayer was heard and that its requests were being considered—by the very Creator of all things bright and beautiful.

⌐

Wellsboro, after dark, grew soft and hushed. There were a few bars open with loud music, and a few late-night businesses, but for the most part once the sun went down Wellsboro relaxed, yawned, and grew still.

Stewart and Lisa said the final good-byes to Hubert, said good-bye to Sergeant Wilson who was at the desk, and stepped out into the darkness again.

But this darkness was different. Stewart, in the past, preferred the daylight hours, where nothing could hide in the shadows. But tonight, that fear—that unconscious, unknowing fear—while not vanished, was less than it ever had been.

Stewart would think back on this night and ponder why.

Maybe it's because I finally admitted to someone the truth about my parents. Like opening a door into a locked cellar. It doesn't change what it was, but it changed me.

He took Lisa's hand in his, this time on his volition, and they walked for several blocks, in silence. The only sound they made was their soft footfalls on the sidewalk.

"Do you really think Hubert had a plan?" Lisa asked as they turned down Maple.

"I don't know," Stewart said. "I mean, no one will ever know. But it sure seems like he knows what he's doing. And he really likes us together. And he got me to think about the Bible and all that. So . . . I guess he did have a plan."

"Good dog, Hubert," Lisa said. "Good dog."

"I think he helped me grow up," Stewart said. "I never had someone in my life who needed protection."

Lisa squeezed his hand.

"I know you mean Hubert," she said, "but when I'm with you, I feel protected, too."

"Good. I meant you, too."

Lisa was silent for a half a block, as if she had something to say but was searching for the right words.

"You've been damaged, Stewart," was what she finally said. Lisa pushed a few strands of hair from her face and turned to look at him as she spoke. "We all have been damaged, I think, in one way or another. The world is broken, Stewart. I used to think that if we tried hard enough, everything would be better. I think trying to be good is a good thing, but the world will stay broken. You know what I mean?"

Stewart said that he did.

"When my parents divorced," Lisa said, "I was hurt. It's still hard to trust. But everyone thought that once the thing that causes the pain is over—like a bad marriage or a divorce—then the pain will be gone."

"And it's not," Stewart added.

"No, it's not gone. It's kind of like an echo that never fully fades away."

Stewart nodded, making sure that she saw him nod. He had read somewhere that if a man wants to show his interest in a woman, he had to be sure that she knew he was listening to her.

I don't remember where I read that. It sounds like it would be true.

"My mother still wants me to be careful with you, Stewart," Lisa said quietly, almost as an admission of guilt.

"Why?"

"She doesn't want me to get hurt. Like she was. But more because I was . . . before. She worries a lot. And to be honest, I gave her reasons to worry. I've done things that I'm not proud of."

Stewart nodded again.

After a moment, he said, "And my grandmother still wants me to be careful with you."

Lisa stopped walking and turned to Stewart.

"But she doesn't know me at all."

It was obvious to Stewart that Lisa's mother's warning went down easier with Stewart than did his grandmother's warning to him about Lisa went down with Lisa.

I read about that, too . . . somewhere. The differences between men and women.

"She thinks you're after my money."

Lisa could not hold her laugh.

"And you have money?" she asked.

"No. I don't. That's what makes it so bizarre."

Neither of them had paid much attention to where they were walking. Across the street was the Wellsboro Park, almost in the center of town. In the center of the park lay a sculpture inside a large fountain. Without needing to ask, they both walked toward the sound of the water. A ring of benches surrounded the fountain. A few other people were in the park that evening, but if asked later, Stewart would not have been able to tell you if there was one or a hundred.

From off in the distance, a few blocks over, perhaps, came the sound of music. It was a live band doing "All the Hits of the 60s, 70s, and 80s." It was like listening to a car radio three or four cars over. It provided a pleasant background, and you could talk over it.

Stewart waved his arm, indicating that Lisa should take her pick of the benches. She chose the one farthest from the other people, the one bench that was more in the nighttime shadows than the others.

She sat and Stewart sat and she sidled up closer to him—not in a pushy way, he thought, not in an aggressive way at all, but out of a desire to be close. He put his arm around her shoulder and she leaned her head against him. She reached out and took his other hand in hers and they sat in silence for a long time, for at least one full set of whatever the band was playing: three Beatles tunes, one from the Jefferson Airplane, the Young Rascals, and two by Creedence Clearwater Revival.

Stewart knew them all.

"I listen to the oldies station a lot. I like that better than the music on the Top Forty."

Lisa voiced her approval and nestled closer to him.

"I like the older stuff, too," she said. "Simpler times."

From the distance an owl called out.

"Barn owl?"

"Screech owl," Stewart said. "I was sort of a nerd back in high school. I watched birds a lot."

Lisa squeezed his hand.

"Maybe you can teach me about them."

"I'd like that."

They sat for a very long time that evening, just being together, just listening to the sounds of the water and the lonely sounds of an owl patrolling the night skies.

Chapter Twenty-Nine

DAY SIX of Hubert's incarceration was noted by more people than just Stewart and Lisa.

Heather Orlando arrived in town, her news crew in tow, and interviewed all the constituents again—from Bargain Bill, who almost broke down on camera, to Mr. Arden, who almost went apoplectic on camera, claiming that the "bandit dog" was being coddled in a luxury cell, being walked three times a day and being fed "on the backs of the poor taxpayers of this town."

＊

Bargain Bill ran into the house nearly breathless. "I'm going to be on TV again."

His wife looked up from her word search book with a puzzled expression.

"For what? You didn't win the lottery, did you?"

"I don't play the lottery. For the dog. My poor, lost, jailed dog. Heather Orlando from Pittsburgh came back to town and interviewed me about my lost pooch."

His wife carefully put her pencil in the book, closed it, making sure that the pencil would stay where she put it, and looked up at her husband, now with a pained expression.

"Bill, he's not your dog."

"Shhh," Bargain Bill replied. "You said you would go along with this. You promised. And business has been fantastic. I sold four cars yesterday. Four. On a Wednesday. In the middle of the month. That has never, ever happened before."

His wife raised her eyebrows, a skeptic's response.

"Listen, if I can sell four cars on a Wednesday, then that dog is mine forever."

She sighed, deeply, theatrically.

"Well, that's nice."

—

Mayor Joe Witt saw the TV News van pull up outside his office and he groaned, reaching for the bottle of antacid tablets he had in the top drawer. After popping just two tablets, he grabbed a small mirror from the second drawer and gave his appearance a quick review.

The tie is okay. I wish it were a brighter color—like red, or even yellow. They say bright colors increase confidence in people. I saw that in a recent Insurance Monthly.

He grabbed his sport coat and quickly put it on, even though his tie clashed a little, according to his wife.

He ran his palm over his thinning hair, making sure there were no errant flyaway strands that the camera would catch.

He took a few deep breaths, hoping that he could sound polished and adept in front of the camera. Then he stepped away from his desk and nearly tripped over the chair leg, catching himself at the last moment, and hearing the disturbing sound of fabric ripping in protest, and immediately feeling a new sense of ventilation toward his backside.

Heavens to Betsy, he thought. *Now I'll have to keep my back to the wall.*

And it was at that moment that Heather Orlando and crew entered his insurance office, almost overwhelming his easily overwhelmed assistant with bright lights and brighter smiles.

The first question: "So tell me, Mr. Mayor, exactly what is a 'special council order of enforcement'?"

And at that moment, Mayor Witt wished he had taken three antacids, instead of just his normal two.

Kevin Connelly and John Stricklin sat at "their" table in the Wired Rooster, speaking in hushed tones. Both of them, independently, had seen the Action News van as it made its way through Wellsboro and they both knew, with a bit of a sinking feeling, just what it was there for.

"They have to be here about the dog and the 'special council order of enforcement,'" John said, his tone nervous and anxious.

"I think so, too," Kevin whispered back. "I never thought it would get this far."

"What are we going to do? It's not a law. You made the whole 'special order' up."

Kevin winced at the thought.

"I know. But we all voted yes on it, so none of us are off the hook."

"Blisters and toes, this stuff doesn't happen in Wellsboro."

"I know," Kevin replied, sipping on his second latte of the morning.

They sat in morose silence for a while—at least a half latte's worth of quiet.

"Well, what's the worst that can happen?" John asked.

"They could fire us," Kevin replied, then laughed. "Or hold a special recall, I guess. Hard to fire a council member. But to tell you the truth, that wouldn't be so bad, would it?"

John nodded. "No. It really wouldn't be."

"But they won't."

"I know. They'll keep us on and make us suffer, won't they?"

"Yep," Kevin agreed, and drained the last of his latte, the lid of the cup making slurpy, siphoning noises as he did.

⌐

"So, Stewart, you have made my return to Pennsylvania an absolute impossibility, do you know that?"

Stewart sat in his living room and, with her every word, he slumped a little closer to being totally horizontal.

"What?"

"You heard me, Stewart. You were harboring a criminal. People who do that go to hell, Stewart."

"Grams, it's a dog, for Pete's sake. He's not a criminal."

"You watch your language, mister. You know what happens to people who swear and curse, don't you?"

They no longer have to talk to their grandmothers?

"Sorry. But Hubert is just a dog. He's not a criminal."

He heard his grandmother sigh, loudly, a loud, deflating sigh of absolute resignation.

"I can't ever show my face anywhere near Wellsboro again.

Not even in Lewisburg. You have made my return impossible. People would point and snicker and gossip and laugh. That is what would happen, Stewart."

He sat up in the chair. He scowled, then let his expression go back to normal.

"Were you planning to come back, Grams? You said when you left you never wanted to see this place again. So when were you planning on coming back? Soon? This summer?"

Stewart's grandmother did not answer. There was only silence.

"Grams, I have to go to work now. Sorry the pool position didn't work out. But I really don't like the water all that much, anyway."

And as Stewart clicked off the call, he suddenly felt better than he had felt in a long, long time.

—

Heather Orlando swept into the Wired Rooster like a small celebrity hurricane.

"Lisa," she called out as she entered, camera crew trailing her. At first every customer and every employee stared at Ms. Orlando and her bright pink suit and toothy smile, but when she uttered Lisa's name, everyone pivoted, almost in unison, to stare at Lisa.

"Your last story was perfect, Lisa," Ms. Orlando gushed. "Absolutely perfect. It was funny and sad and it almost made me cry: the poor dog, locked away in a dark cell—for the sin of being a dog."

Lisa hoped she wasn't blushing, but she could feel the heat in her cheeks.

To get this sort of endorsement from a celebrity newsperson— wow.

"You're why we came back up here today to do a follow-up story. My producers have been bugging me to get the latest scoop on what's happening. You have a minute to sit and chat?"

Lisa's manager of the day shrugged and waved her off.

"Go, Lisa," he said in a whisper. "She's drawing a crowd and it's midafternoon. That never happens. So go and talk. And mention the Wired Rooster a couple of times if you can."

With Heather seated across from her, a bright light shining on her, and camera lenses seemingly inches from her face, Lisa tried to recap the last story she'd written for the *Gazette*, written in Stewart's apartment, as he sat across the kitchen table, smiling at her. It had been hard to make it sad and emotional when she'd felt happy and emotional instead.

In the story, she admitted her involvement in the situation, and that she'd participated in aiding and abetting the nefarious canine criminal—but she insisted she did so out of love for the sweet animal, who had no doubt suffered abuse and deprivation before he arrived in Wellsboro and found safety and solace with Stewart Coolidge.

Even Dave Grback, the crustiest of crusty, curmudgeonly editors, said he had admired her balance between pathos and "well...not pathos."

After a ten-minute conversation with Lisa, Heather wrapped it up with a few comments.

Then she stood and gave Lisa a hug, which everyone in the Wired Rooster took note of—a real-life celebrity coming emotionally, and physically, close to a local person, an unknown, a noncelebrity.

"This was great, Lisa."

Her camera crew began to switch off gear and fold up lights and all the rest.

"I wish we could have talked to this Stewart person. But the number I had didn't work."

Lisa brightened.

"I could call him."

Heather appeared pained. She looked at her watch.

"If I want this on tonight, we have to run. You know, break some speed limits on the way home. The station manager wants it as well. Sweeps week, you know. This will kill. Really."

Lisa walked Heather out to the van.

"Did you find anything out about those two ladies from the animal shelter?"

Heather offered a most curious, enigmatic smile.

"Maybe. I'm still working on it."

Lisa looked down and she shut her eyes in dismay. She had worn a Wired Rooster apron during the entire interview.

I look like a scullery maid.

Well, at least the name of the place was pretty visible.

Just after Lisa left work that day, her mother called.

"I keep hearing all about this dog thing."

Lisa tried to remain calm.

"Mom, I told you like a hundred times all about it. The boy upstairs taking the dog in and all that?'

"Oh, sure. That dog? Okay, then. I thought it might be some other dog."

"No, Mom. There's only one famous dog in Wellsboro at the moment."

Lisa patiently waited for what she knew would be the next question.

"And you and this boy...you're still just friends?"

Lisa wanted very much to tell her all about it, how they had become close and how Stewart had all but found faith—because of her and because of Hubert—but she held back.

It's not the right time. Not yet.

"We're good friends, Mom. He's very nice."

Lisa heard a sharp intake of air on the other end of the call.

"Lisa, you just have to be careful. Promise me that you'll be careful. You can't go through what you went through last time."

Lisa closed her eyes and tried to remain calm and even.

That will never happen again. I promised myself that. And I promised you. And God. And she promised not to bring it up every time I mention dating again.

"Mom, he is a great guy. And, yes, I am careful. But—I have to live life. I can't think every person out there is going to disappoint me or hurt me. I want to fall in love, Mom. And I can't do that always being cautious and scared and unwilling to be open."

Lisa only heard silence.

Then a small cough, as if her mother was simply announcing that she was still on the line but had no idea how to respond to what her daughter had just said—that there was no reason to be careful.

"Mom, I have to go. I'm just getting in the car, and driving and talking on the phone are illegal here."

"Oh. Okay. But—"

"I'll be careful, Mom. But you have to trust somebody sometime. And maybe I'm starting now, okay?"

Her mother responded with a small, and uncertain, "Okay."

↩

Robert Kruel sat in his office in downtown Sunbury, looking out over the smattering of afternoon traffic. Kitty-corner to his office was a Tops Market, its parking lot only half full.

Not a shopping day here in beautiful downtown Sunbury.

Robert "Bob" Kruel had the distinction of being one of the two outside attorneys on retainer for the Tops Market chain. Inside the small corporation, they employed one official attorney who handled all the mundane real estate and tax issues that the small grocery chain incurred. But with situations outside that purview, more well-versed assistance was called in— an attorney acquainted with the "real" world.

Robert had gotten the call involving the dog stealing bones from the Tops store in Wellsboro.

He had talked, at length, to Mr. Arden...

Way too long.

...and had interviewed a few others in the store, then had reviewed the sparse case law about animals and stores and thievery.

He stopped staring out into the distance and shook his head.

"I went to law school at Penn State for this?"

He looked down at the notes he'd made for the Wellsboro City Council meeting tomorrow evening. He had circled and underlined the words "special council order of enforcement."

"And just where did they get that ordinance from? A box of Cracker Jacks?"

Then he began to rub the bridge of his nose in anticipation of the headache that was just beginning to form.

—

"Well, Hubert, tomorrow is the big day," Stewart said as he and Lisa settled into the cell following their evening walk. "Or, I guess, tomorrow evening is the big evening."

Lisa had been silent on their walk over to the jail, as well on their joint walk. In her purse she carried a plastic Ziploc bag that held three cut-up hot dogs—"the good ones and not the store brand," she said as she showed it to Stewart. "Hubert deserves a good meal."

Stewart agreed, but Hubert had shown no discomfort with the kibbles he had been eating. Somewhere, Stewart read that dogs don't mind eating the same thing over and over again. He recalled the article stating that sometimes too much variety can be stressful on a dog.

I have no idea why—but it was printed somewhere, so it must be mostly true.

Finally, Lisa spoke, still holding the closed bag, which Hubert had noticed. He was now sniffing the air intently. "I wanted to do something nice for Hubert, but then I had a thought about convicts and their last meal and..."

She stopped talking and began to cry, a little, and not loudly.

Hubert appeared confused.

Obviously she had some sort of treat for him, but then she started crying, so it was apparent that he did not know what to do next.

Stewart moved closer and put his arm over her shoulder.

"It's not a last meal. Please. You'll upset him if he thinks you're upset."

"But I am upset. A little."

Stewart hugged her from the side.

"I looked stuff up on the Internet. Unless the dog is showing rabies or something dangerous like that, or if he has chewed somebody up, they won't be able to do anything. And all Hubert here has done is steal things. That's not a capital offense in any state of the union. Maybe like over in Arabia or someplace like that. But nothing bad will happen to Hubert. At least not right away. It would require like a real court order and a real judge."

"Are you sure?" she asked.

"The Internet doesn't lie, does it?"

She began to smile.

"I guess not."

So she sniffed once more, then unzipped the baggie and began to dole out the hot dog slices to Hubert, one at a time.

If it was possible for a dog to simply swallow a hot dog slice without chewing, that is what Hubert did. He appeared to truly enjoy them, but did not take a lot of time eating them or savoring their all-beef, no-filler goodness.

"You're just like a man," Lisa chided. "Just give them the

food. No subtlety at all. No noticing the lack of additives and preservatives, no enjoying the authentic Ball Park frank experience."

After the last slice had been swallowed, she reached down and stroked Hubert's head. He whimpered as if he truly enjoyed her touch, and probably the meal as well.

"You're such a good dog, Hubert," she said, and he looked up and climbed up onto the concrete bed beside her. After a few minutes of trying to find the perfect position, he lay down beside her and placed his head in her lap, closing his eyes as she petted him.

"Why don't you read something to us, Stewart? Hubert likes being read to, don't you, Hubert?"

Hubert growled happily without opening his eyes.

"Okay. I read this last night at home. I guess it's famous or something. I probably heard it before, but I liked it. It's short."

Lisa nestled in closer to both Stewart and Hubert.

"It's from the Psalms, although I can't figure out why they don't call them 'songs.' That's the way it's pronounced, right? Songs. Change the spelling. Get with the times."

Lisa nudged him in the ribs, making sure she did not move too much and disturb Hubert.

Stewart flipped through the pages, then stopped, and went to the front of the Bible, and to the index of chapters. He found the page number and flipped to it, then thumbed through a number of chapters, finally stopping.

"You think they could do all this alphabetically. It would make it a lot easier to find stuff."

He smoothed out the page and adjusted the book in his hand and then began to read, in a clear, serious tone:

*"The Lord is my shepherd; I have all that I need. He lets
me rest in green meadows; he leads me beside peaceful
streams. He renews my strength. He guides me along right
paths, bringing honor to his name. Even when I walk
through the darkest valley, I will not be afraid, for you
are close beside me. Your rod and your staff protect and
comfort me. You prepare a feast for me in the presence of
my enemies. You honor me by anointing my head with
oil. My cup overflows with blessings. Surely your goodness
and unfailing love will pursue me all the days of my life,
and I will live in the house of the Lord forever."*

No one spoke for a long moment after he was finished.
Then Hubert raised his head and growled with certain em-
phasis.

"Hubert liked it," Lisa said. "And I thought it was beautiful.
That's one of my most favorite parts of the Bible. When I was
little, and scared or lonely, I would read that."

Stewart didn't say anything, just pulled her close to him.

And they sat there, on the hard concrete bed, in the Wellsboro Jail, for a long, long time. No one wanted to break the
magic of that intimate moment.

⟶

It was Stewart who said "It's time to go. You and I have to be
at work early tomorrow."

"I know. But I wanted this to last."

"Me, too."

They slipped out of the cell, and both knelt again at the

door, giving Hubert one last hug and a pat on the head as a farewell.

Hubert, as he had been doing during his incarceration, whimpered and growled as they left—not a lonely growl, but simply one of acknowledgment, saying he knew they had to leave and he knew they would be back and they would not ever forget about him.

⌒

Hubert watched them leave. He was glad that the Stewart and Lisa humans held hands as they left. He knew that human people do that when they care about each other. That the Stewart human and the Lisa human cared about each other was almost the best thing that Hubert could imagine happening.

The best thing was that the Stewart human had begun to understand what it meant to be part of the pack. And understand what Lisa called God. Hubert did not know that word, but he knew what it was—the power of all nature, the clarity of the world, the need to be loved and warm and fed. To a dog, that was what God was. The best dog of the best pack. To be at peace. And now Stewart had began to understand the meaning of that and to feel it in his heart. Hubert could tell his heart was changing.

That was the best and most wonderful thing Hubert could imagine.

Hubert knew something was going to happen tomorrow and that the something involved him in some way. He could tell this by the urgency with which the humans spoke about something happening. When things were far off in the future, too far off for dogs to be concerned about, humans spoke with a certain tone. When that thing got closer, Hubert noticed, the humans' tone grew different—a little faster, a bit more urgent.

He could tell from what they'd said tonight that something would happen tomorrow that they considered important.

Hubert knew that he did not know all the ways of humans, but he trusted his Stewart human more than he had ever trusted any human in the past. Stewart said that he would take care of Hubert and that was exactly what Hubert chose to believe.

He would not lie to me.

Hubert circled his pillow and blanket, mooshing it down just so, and then he stopped and looked up at the moon through the small window.

Stewart is now found. That's what I needed to see. And now that he is found, it doesn't matter what happens to me. That power that Lisa called God . . . He will be happy that I helped— that I was somehow involved in the process of finding. And if this is the last thing I ever get to do with humans, then the God of all knows best.

And with that, Hubert sat down, and then lay down. He could still see a sliver of the moon as it glistered in the darkness and, deep within his dog soul, he knew that full moons meant safety, since no dangers in the forest could slip into existence from out of the shadows—not with a bright moon above. Moonlight offered safe haven, and Hubert closed his eyes, knowing— hoping—that he was safe and always would be.

I did what I was supposed to do.

He closed his eyes but felt the moon on his face.

It would be enough if that was all I could ever do.

Chapter Thirty

STEWART HAD REQUESTED an early shift that day, which had been approved. He wanted time to get ready for the evening's special city council meeting and jot down a few notes. If he was called on to testify, he wanted to make sure of saying the proper thing.

He had researched city council meeting protocol and practice in Wellsboro and discovered that as a resident of the city, he had a right to be recognized and heard, as long as he was "respectful and civil, and that [his] comments remain germane to the topic at hand."

That was from the city's Web site, and Stewart copied the description down in his notebook—just in case someone tried to prevent him from speaking.

Lieutenant Quinn had already given him the okay to bring Hubert to the meeting.

At first, however, the lieutenant was skeptical.

"Listen, I don't think they allow animals at these meetings," he'd explained, rubbing his temples as he spoke. The whole Hubert-in-jail scenario appeared to have given Lieutenant Quinn a permanent almost-headache.

"But the dog is on trial," Stewart countered. "He has a right to face his accusers."

Lieutenant Quinn's face indicated that he wasn't buying the

argument, despite having no affection, or respect, for the city council process.

"He's not a citizen," Lieutenant Quinn stated. "He's a dog."

"But I think it will be really important to show that Hubert is a good dog, well behaved, and not a threat to anyone."

Lieutenant Quinn raised one eyebrow.

"And you're sure he won't start to get hysterical at the meeting and chew off the mayor's leg?"

"I'm sure. Hubert and I had a long talk about behavior this afternoon."

"So no politically induced mauling?"

"Nope. Not a one," Stewart replied.

"Rats."

After a moment, Lieutenant Quinn relented, smiling.

"Okay. You take the dog. I want to be there to see it. This will be fun."

⌐

Stewart came to the jail to get Hubert at six thirty for the seven o'clock meeting.

They did not have far to go, being in the same building and all, but Stewart wanted to take Hubert for a quick walk before the meeting, just in case it ran long.

The normal city council meetings were held upstairs in a not-so-large meeting room, but due to the larger than normal crowd expected for this special meeting, the council had shifted their location to the fire department section of the building, parked their two fire engines out on the street, brought in chairs from the Methodist church, and borrowed two large coffee urns from the Lutherans down the street. They left the two fire truck doors up, owing to the mild temperatures.

The ten or so city council meeting regular attendees, most of them senior citizens, who always arrived early, were impressed.

"We never got free coffee before," William Hasse remarked, both irked and pleased, which was his normal go-to-meeting attitude.

"Ought to have more light-fingered dogs in town," John Lucas replied. "Or light-pawed."

John paused and his face wizened up like a raisin.

"Do dogs have fingers? I'm sure they don't, but what are they called?"

Joe Cambruzzi waved his hand, dismissing both of them. "Who cares, Lucas? Nobody."

William scowled back at Joe, continuing a feud that began back in the 1970s over parking meters in the downtown business district. "Pads. They're called pads. And lots of people care. Vets, for one."

Joe waved his hand again and walked away, slowly, making sure not to spill coffee on the immaculately clean floor of the fire station.

When Stewart arrived, Hubert calmly, sedately walking right beside him, he created a minor stir among the crowd that now filled nearly half the available seats. Stewart heard the murmurings and saw numerous finger-points. He sat in the front row, thinking that if he did have to speak, or if someone wanted to point out Hubert, that would be the best vantage point.

Since he sat at the end of the row, he could watch people arrive. Mr. Arden came in only a few minutes later, accompanied by another sallow-faced gentleman who appeared as though he would rather be anywhere in the world than in one of the open bays of the Wellsboro Fire Department.

The very bright fluorescent lights did no one's appearance any favors.

Mr. Arden pointed at Hubert and whispered something to the sallow-faced man, then grinned, a grin that was devoid of happiness but saturated with smugness.

Two tables were set up in front with a scattering of nameplates for the council members, all brought downstairs from the regular city council meeting room. But since they were simply flat panels that fit into permanent holders at the real city council tables, the nameplates had to be propped up against white foam coffee cups with little bits of masking tape to hold them almost upright.

"We know who we all are," snapped Larry Ringhofer, council member from the far west side of town. "This looks stupid."

Someone in the middle of the crowd called out, "And for certain you know stupid."

Larry glared at the crowd. He suspected Joe Cambruzzi, but by the time he located him in the fourth row, Joe was sporting an angelic look, a senior citizen angelic look.

Mayor Joe Witt fussed with a stack of papers piled on the table in front of him, checking his watch every three minutes. He liked to start meetings on time.

Councilman Kevin Connelly whispered, "How come the mayor has papers? Did we get a packet for this meeting?

John Stricklin whispered in reply, "Nope. No packet. But think about it. Have you ever seen Witt without a stack of papers in front of him?"

Kevin arched one of his eyebrows, then smiled and nodded. "Maybe he brought them from home."

"Makes him look busy," John added.

⟡

A van door slammed and everyone's heads pivoted to the right,
or left, depending on where they sat, to stare out to the street.

The Action News Alive at Five van had pulled up and its
occupants began to exit, carrying all manner of TV equipment
and cameras and lights and sound-recording apparatus. One
portly news team member hoisted the microwave tower on top
of the van, checking to see if they had the power and reception to do a live remote.

And from the front seat, Heather Orlando descended, in
her trademark pink suit, full-coverage makeup, and impossibly
high heels, carrying an Action News wireless microphone and
a clipboard.

And then Lisa Goodly stepped out of the van, smiling.

"She's that gal from the Rooster who wrote those stories,"
someone in the crowd whispered, loudly enough so that virtually everyone could hear.

Lisa spotted Stewart and Hubert and waved, then subtly
pointed to Heather with a *Can you believe this?* look on her
face.

Mayor Witt appeared dismayed, which was a standard look
for him during many city council meetings. It was obvious that
he wanted to stand up and tell Ms. Orlando and the rest of her
news team that this was a closed meeting that only the resi-
dents of Wellsboro could attend, but that would require a full

vote by the council, debate, and then someone appointed to check everyone's ID so they could prove their residency status. And it was just as obvious that Mayor Witt knew he could not do that, and was trapped into letting a camera crew record every second of this special meeting.

Heather beamed as she walked into the open bay and pointed to a corner of the room where the camera could be set up that would not interfere with anyone's sight lines.

Lisa took a seat next to Stewart and gave him a quick hug.

Heather took a long time walking to the front row and perched in a seat next to Lisa.

And after they were settled, heads pivoted again, as Bargain Bill Hoskins drove up in his trademark firecracker-red convertible and took a seat on the other side of the front row, waving to just about everyone in the audience, and especially to Hubert.

Hubert did not respond to Bargain Bill, but then Stewart had told him to relax, remain calm, and not get antsy.

From the middle of the crowd someone said loud enough for everyone to hear, "They should have charged admission to this one. They could have cleaned up."

⟶

At exactly seven o'clock, Mayor Witt took the official gavel and rapped it on the table. The sound produced was a sort of hollow thump, not nearly the call-to-order sound that his podium upstairs made. He had to hit the table another five times just to get everyone in the large room to shut up.

After nearly a minute, the murmuring slowly ebbed, like water draining out of a very slow-draining tub.

Once it was quiet, Mayor Witt rapped the gavel again and almost shouted, "I hereby call this special session of the Wellsboro City Council to order."

He stood and then declared, "Now we will all stand for our National Anthem."

The council members stood, as did the crowd, slowly and with hesitation, who all looked about and then at each other and then back to the mayor.

"Did the city clerk bring down the official—what da ya call it—the official city boom box?"

The city clerk, Paul Hatch, a rail-thin older man, appeared befuddled.

"Do we have one of those?"

Mayor Witt was growing impatient and more dismayed.

"Whatever it is we play the National Anthem on upstairs, for heaven's sake."

Paul made a vague move with his hands as if trying to catch a slow moth. "But, Mr. Mayor, that's, I think, built into the sound system upstairs. It's not what you might call portable."

"Well, now what are we going to do? We have to start meetings with the National Anthem."

The crowd began murmuring again. Obviously, this was not the way the mayor had planned on starting this special session.

Finally, in the rear row, Miss Hazel Irwin, a high school music teacher and one of the longest tenured teachers at Wellsboro Area High School, stood up and in a very firm I'm-taking-charge-of-this-unruly-class-of-students voice, declared, "Good grief. We all know the song. Let's just sing it and get this meeting started."

She began, "Oh say can you see . . ." in a higher pitch than most people were comfortable with, but the crowd gamely mumbled and sang along, a weak, reedy, off-pitch rendition, but, to the relief of the mayor, they got through the whole song, and it got the meeting started, making it "official."

"All right, then. We are here to discuss the 'special city council enforcement'...area...ordinance..."

Councilman Stricklin interrupted gently, "Special council order of enforcement, Mayor."

"Yes. That. Because of that dog. Over there," he said and pointed directly at Hubert, who was sitting next to Stewart at the end of the row, hardly moving, just turning his head in order to see who was talking. The dog had appeared to enjoy the singing of the National Anthem and looked as if he hoped they would do more of that later on.

The mayor's hard glare dissolved for a moment.

"That is the dog, right?"

Stewart stood up, as did Hubert.

"It is, sir."

The mayor sighed audibly.

"Good."

Hubert would have been a hard dog not to recognize, from the two large signs at the market and at Bargain Bill's used-car lot, from the articles in the *Gazette* and his picture printed twice as large as the picture of the newly crowned Miss Tioga, and from the several hundred posters nailed to telephone poles all over town.

The mayor officiously extracted an envelope from his stack of papers and unfolded the letter that was inside. Obviously it was an official letter since the stationery appeared to be thick, with some sort of embossing on the top.

"I have here an official request from the legal counsel representing the Tops Market, a registered business within the Wellsboro city limits, and a Mr. Robert Kruel, attorney at law and special general counsel for Tops, who has requested to speak before the city council in regards to the complaint against said canine."

Mayor Witt often lapsed into a curious amalgam of legalese and nonsense chatter when he attempted to sound official.

The rest of the council members remained silent, obviously unsure if this needed to be motioned or voted on or approved by voice vote or what.

"Since Tops Market is indeed a legal entity within the city of Wellsboro," the mayor continued, "they have the right of citizens to present petitions and requests seeking redress of complaints and..."

Mayor Witt must have lost his train of thought, because he stopped midsentence.

"Well," he continued, "I guess then Mr. Kruel can state his case. Or whatever."

Mr. Kruel tried to not be obvious in shaking his head in disbelief, but he wasn't good at being subtle.

"Thank you, Mayor Witt," he said and he stood and looked a little confused himself, as if searching for some sort of podium to stand at and place his thick file folder of notes and papers.

One of the firemen seated off to the side stood, hurried into a back room, and returned with a black, well-used music stand. He crouched down, as if to avoid walking through the light of a projector, even though no projector was in use, and placed the music stand near the attorney from Sunbury.

Of course the entire crowd stared at him intently as he did so.

The attorney quietly said, "Thanks," and placed his folder on the music stand and, with a broad sweep of his arm, opened the folder and picked up the first sheet of paper.

If nothing else, Attorney Robert Kruel was adept at speaking in public.

Not good at it, just practiced, and he managed, in the span of fifteen minutes, to recap the entire story of the dog bandit, list the date and time of every crime the dog committed, elucidate every lost man-hour of labor, speculate on the lost prestige of the store in question—and to lull several members of the audience to sleep.

As he spoke, Bargain Bill turned often to the person sitting next to him, who happened to be his nephew, Karl Loughner, a third-year law student at Penn State in need of a new used car, which Bargain Bill promised him a "fantastic" deal on if he would unofficially represent him at the council meeting tonight.

Lisa did not say much to Stewart, but she did take his hand in hers, which made Hubert look up and grin, and made Ms. Orlando raise her eyebrows, just a little, and in a most professional manner.

Lieutenant Quinn stood to the side, his back to the street, trying not to smile or look bemused by the special meeting, but he was not doing a good job of it.

Jerry Mallick sat in the back row, as far away from Lieutenant Quinn as he could get, and slouched down in the chair, almost on a horizontal plane. Apparently he was attending the meeting, according to what Kevin or Kellan or Carl had told Lisa at the Wired Rooster that afternoon, in a fast-fading hope of getting some sort of reward for his unwitting provision of a place for the bandit dog to live for the past few months. "He said to me, he said, 'That oughta be worth something. A couple of bucks, at least,' is what he said."

The store attorney turned over one more page in his file, looked at his watch, perhaps checking on billable hours, and summed up Tops Market's case against Hubert in a single sentence.

"The main element of our complaint against the dog, and owner, if that is to be decided at this meeting, is that the dog," he said, and pointed directly at Hubert, who lowered his head in canine shame, "did, with malice, steal eleven rawhide chew bones valued at thirty dollars and fifty-eight cents, plus tax."

He waited until the full import of that statement sank in.

"We are asking for damages of . . . ten thousand dollars to be levied against whomever is the owner of that dog."

Both Stewart and Bargain Bill stiffened visibly when they heard the words "ten thousand dollars."

Mayor Witt also looked stunned. He turned to the city clerk, who whispered in his ear.

"I am told that the city council cannot levy special, one-off fines. Nor impose financial judgments. That would have to come at a civil trial or maybe after a criminal trial first— because we are talking about a crime here."

The attorney appeared miffed, legally speaking.

"We'll deal with damages after the city council decides on what . . . to do about all of this," he said, and furiously scribbled something on that last sheet of paper in his file folder.

"Well, okay then," Mayor Witt said. He looked up and down at the row of council members on either side of him.

"Do any of you have any dispute with the facts as presented so . . . thoroughly by Mr. Kruel?"

Normally, even in the most sedate cases or situations before the city council, most of them had questions about something: paint color, height of trees, species of bushes, setbacks from lot lines, egress, driveway coating, signage, size of signage; just about anything and everything brought before a city council engendered questions, lots of questions—some spurious, some specious, some serious.

But tonight, in front of the glare of big-city news reporting and publicity, no one said anything. Not a single city council member raised his or her hand or coughed, or even looked back at the mayor. He looked left and right and only saw a series of folded hands on the table.

"So the facts in question are not in dispute in any way?"

A few mumbled "No"s and a few "Okay by me"s rippled from the row of council members.

"So then," Mayor Witt continued, wishing for a moment that he had never run for the mayor position and wishing that he had no script of previous mayoral action to review that might guide his response this evening, "we need a motion or something from the council to proceed to do—take a vote or something." The meeting, as he was certain that it would, was descending into chaos. As he'd described to his wife before he'd left, "This is all virgin territory. No one has ever sued a dog in Wellsboro before."

Larry Ringhofer, often the first council member to speak—and the last—spoke up. "I say we make Bargain Bill pay for the bones and he gets the dog."

Mr. Arden could no longer contain himself and jumped up,

his arms spread out wide, and pointed at the mayor and then the dog.

"No. The dog has to be punished. He stole from my store."

A murmur of boos rose from the crowd, as if people weren't sure if booing was allowed at a special enforcement meeting of the city council.

Mr. Arden spun around and glared at everyone who was sitting behind him and booing, which was a lot of the town's citizenry.

As he sat down, he muttered, loud enough for most everyone to hear, "What do you expect from the yokels in this town?"

Another chorus of polite boos and hisses followed that statement as well.

Attorney Kruel closed his eyes as if hoping that no one was really paying attention to his client for the evening, but he was sure that they were.

Another councilman, Warren Dunlop, who seldom said anything at meetings, spoke up.

"That's a good solution. Make Bill pay for what his dog stole and since he's claimed all along that it's his dog, give it to him and if the dog ever steals again, we know who to come after. Right, Bill?"

Bargain Bill grinned and nodded furiously, obviously thinking that he could put the dog in a big cage at the car lot and he would be a fabulous draw for customers, who would come to pet the "bandit dog" and have their picture taken with the infamous canine.

Lisa appeared not to be the least bit upset by what was apparently happening.

Neither were Stewart or Hubert, but Stewart couldn't imagine why Lisa would be so calm about it. After all, this was Hubert they were talking about—and what the council was suggesting would take the poor dog from them forever.

But Lisa remained implacable and serene.

Hubert looked up at Stewart and grinned his loopy dog smile, as if to say: *Everything will be all right. Don't worry.*

Stewart sat back, squeezed Lisa's hand for assurance, took his cue from Hubert, and relaxed.

The crowd was still bubbling over the last suggestion and Mayor Witt suddenly looked up, brightened, and dug like a groundhog through his stack of papers, which was now a most disheveled pile. He found what he was looking for and held it up, not that anyone farther than five feet away could make out what was written on it.

"Mr. Arden, I almost forgot."

Mr. Arden and Mr. Kruel looked up, a glimmer of hope in their faces.

"Before I forget—oh, I just said that. Anyhow, I looked up the city ordinance about posting signs."

Mr. Kruel spoke for the two of them.

"Signs? What signs?"

"The big poster thing by the store was fine since it was not permanent and was indeed removable. Not that, but the other signs."

"What signs?" Mr. Kruel asked again.

"Mr. Arden nailed signs about the dog on probably ninety percent of the telephone poles in town."

"And?" Mr. Kruel asked.

"That's illegal. You're not allowed to post signs on tele-phone poles. The phone company says the nails make it hard to climb the poles. Or it might have been the electric company. One of them complained once."

Mr. Kruel began to sputter.

"They don't climb poles anymore. They have those trucks with that basket thing."

"Cherry pickers," someone called out.

"Yes. That kind of truck. Nobody climbs poles."

The mayor remained sanguine.

"Still, the law is on the books. The ordinance states that the offender must pay a fifty-dollar fine for each poster placed on a pole within the city limits. You'll have to make sure that they're all taken down. Okay?"

A few people in the crowd offered a smirky laugh and Mr. Arden did not answer, just turned a brighter shade of crimson in response.

The murmurings and the chatter among the audience ebbed and flowed, like waves on the beach. The council members whispered to each other but no one seemed to be up to mak-ing any public pronouncements—especially with the glare of a big-city media star sitting in the front row.

But Bill Hoskins was up for it.

He stood, first faced the crowd, so they all would know who he was, and then faced Mayor Witt.

"If I may, Your Honor, I would like to say a few words."

The normal procedure was to have people sworn in and registered to speak, but since this was a special enforcement meeting, no one on the council thought it necessary to do so. Besides, everyone in town knew who Bargain Bill Hoskins was, and what he did for a living, and what he had claimed to own—the "bandit dog" in question.

"Your Honor. Council Members. Citizens of Wellsboro. Friends. Family."

Bill's wife was in attendance, working on a word search puzzle during the lulls of discussion.

"Guests. Members of the freedom-loving media."

It was apparent that Bargain Bill sought to enumerate every separate group of people in attendance at the meeting.

Dave Grback, who carried an old-fashioned, authentic stenographer's pad, was busy scribbling notes, while on the other end of the media spectrum, Heather Orlando sat quietly and tried to absorb the goings-on without being burdened by taking notes.

"Sirs . . . and Ladies. I will keep it very simple. I want my dog back. We have been separated long enough. The poor pup has suffered enough. It is time he comes back to his loving family and his life can then return to normal."

Bill caught the eye of his wife and nodded, just a little.

"My wife misses him so terribly."

At that, Mrs. Hoskins rolled her eyes, big enough that everyone could tell her true feelings.

"No one should come between a man and his dog, and it appears that circumstance has done just that to me and Rover. He's mine and I miss him."

Bargain Bill stopped talking and pretended to wipe a tear from the corner of his right eye.

"Of course, I will pay for all that the poor dog was forced to steal to stay alive. If there is any—appropriate fine I will also pay that. And I will build the biggest, most luxurious, and most escape-proof kennel on the site of Bargain Bill's Motors so that the poor dog will be safe, warm, fed, and protected forever."

The audience was silent.

Bargain Bill let the words hang out there for a long moment, then added, "And if the dog is returned, I will discount every car on the lot by ten percent for the next thirty days."

Stewart, still holding Lisa's hand and becoming quite comfortable with her small, delicate fingers enmeshed with his, looked at the faces of the individual council members. He began to grow alarmed, though he did his best not to show that alarm to Lisa—and, most of all, to Hubert.

The councilmen, and councilwomen, were nodding, smiling, acting as if what Bargain Bill had just proposed was the most sensible and sane solution that would wrap up the bandit dog situation in a neat and tidy box and then everyone would be happy.

Except Stewart.

And Lisa.

And, most of all, Hubert.

Larry Ringhofer spoke up again, and everyone, almost in surprise, turned to listen.

"Here's what we need to do. Fine him a hundred dollars. Or whatever. Two hundred. Call it a 'special use permit fee' and not a fine. Make him pay for the stupid bones. Make sure he builds a sturdy kennel. And then let's go home."

The crowd seemed pleased. It was not the fireworks and fire and brimstone they had hoped to hear, but it did appear to be a plausible and sensible solution. Everyone would be satisfied—well, everyone except Mr. Arden. And most everyone in the audience had no love lost for the man—even if his store prices were the cheapest in town.

Bill would get his dog, the townsfolk would get a good deal on a used car, and everyone would win.

And that was when Lisa let go of Stewart's hand and jumped to her feet.

Literally jumped, almost a foot in the air, as if she had been primed for this one specific moment in the meeting and had to speak now, or forever hold her peace. Heather Orlando remained seated, but with a very broad, very self-satisfied smile on her face. And as Lisa jumped to her feet, Heather turned around to face her cameraman and mouthed the words: "You are rolling, aren't you?"

Lisa was nearly breathless, without having exerted any physical energy.

"Your Honor . . . Mr. Mayor . . . Council Members . . ."

Everyone in the audience, including Stewart and Hubert, braced themselves for an eloquent, impassioned plea for mercy or justice or something.

Instead, Lisa took one step toward the mayor and said, as sweetly as she could, "May I request a five-minute recess?"

The mayor leaned back, surprised by the request.

"Well, this isn't exactly a trial or anything, Miss . . . Miss . . ."

"Lisa Goodly. I wrote most of the dog stories for the *Gazette*."

"Oh yes, you're the clever writer. A pleasure to meet you. My wife thought your stories were quite funny—and touching."

"Thank you, Your Honor."

"Mayor. I don't think I'm a 'Your Honor.'"

"Thank you, Mayor."

"Well, Miss Goodly, this is not a trial, as I said, but...I could use a cup of coffee."

He picked up his gavel, thumped it against the table, making that hollow sound, and stood. "Everyone take five minutes to stretch your legs. Get some coffee. And don't forget to thank Saint Paul's Lutheran Church for the coffeemakers and the coffee. Most appreciated. Five minutes, people. Then we start again whether you're here or not."

Then he leaned toward Lisa and smiled.

"Will you need more than five minutes?" he asked sweetly.

"No. Five minutes is fine. Thank you."

Chapter Thirty-One

W HEN THE CROWD stood, Stewart and Hubert were immediately surrounded by people wanting to pet Hubert, or to meet him, or to take a picture with their cell phones, or to post a selfie of them and Hubert. Stewart had wanted to ask Lisa what she was doing and why she'd asked for a recess, but the two of them, Stewart and Hubert, were surrounded by people, four and five deep, with no way of ignoring the questions or requests for photos.

Hubert looked up at Stewart and grinned again, as if he had not a care in the world. His two most favorite people were here, and all was right in Hubert's world.

He just doesn't know what might happen. We may be separated forever.

—

Lisa and Heather, now with the Action News cameraman in tow, descended on Bargain Bill. Heather actually grabbed him by the forearm, smiling while she did but not letting him slip away.

"Ms. Orlando," he said, not noticing her hand on her arm, "I am so happy to see you again."

"Mr. Hoskins, we have something you might want to see."

Lisa could not be sure, but she thought he flinched, just a

little. She reminded herself to watch the tape closely and study his reaction.

"But I have a lot of people here to greet. There are a lot of well-wishers and supporters. I need to at least shake some hands."

Heather's smile did not leave her face, but her tone iced up, and even Lisa could see the pressure from Heather's grip on his arm increase.

"No, Mr. Hoskins. What we have to show you is more important that you chumming the waters for customers for your used cars. Much more important."

Bargain Bill's eyes had that deer-in-the-headlights look, as if he knew something semi-monumental was about to happen but he really didn't want to participate in the unveiling.

Heather tapped at her cell phone and a picture popped up of a middle-aged woman in a denim jacket, with hair that would charitably be called flyaway.

"Do you recognize this woman, Mr. Hoskins?" Heather asked, the sweetness in her voice laced with a razor's sharpness. Lisa looked on in obvious admiration of her style.

Bargain Bill bent over the screen and studied it.

"I do not recall this woman. Was she a former customer of Bargain Bill's?"

"No, she is not a disgruntled car buyer," Heather replied, to Bargain Bill's obvious relief. "I didn't think you would know who she was."

"Okay, now can I talk to my friends?" Bill asked.

"No," Heather replied. "You need to hear what she says."

Heather tapped at the screen and the woman started to talk. The woman appeared a bit puzzled, then a voice was heard, just off camera, saying, "Just tell your story, Judy. Like you told me."

"Oh. Okay. Well, like I said, my name is Judy Kubista and I used to run the Rainbow No-Kill Animal Shelter and Dog Rescue organization here in Lewisburg—along with my friend, or should I say former friend, Emily Sillers. We had to close down months ago because 'someone' never paid the electric bills on the place and spent the money on an RV."

Judy Kubista's venomous glare was thick, and very obvious, even on a small three-inch screen.

A piece of paper appeared from off camera, with the question, "Do you recognize this dog?"

It was a photocopy of Hubert, printed in full color.

Judy took only a moment to answer.

"Nope. Handsome dog, but he never came through our shelter."

"Are you sure?"

"We took pride in what we did. Or at least I took pride in what I did. I knew every dog that came through our doors. And this dog was not one of them."

"One last question: Was there, or is there, any other dog rescue or animal shelter adopting out dogs in Lewisburg?"

Judy scowled.

"No. And that's just such a darned shame. We were the only ones doing it. And thanks to somebody spending our money on a crappy RV that I hope breaks down in the middle of the desert, no one is doing what we did in Lewisburg. Now people have to drive over to Sunbury or Reading. Thanks a heap, Emily."

"And did you ever do any business with a man named Bill Hoskins at your shelter?"

"Nope. Never."

"Thank you, Judy. You have been so very helpful."

Judy tried to smile.

"And if you manage to track Emily down, let me know. Or just punch her in the nose for me, okay?"

The screen went black.

Heather slipped the phone into her suit pocket and smiled a sugar-coated smile at Bargain Bill, who looked more than a little nervous.

Actually, he looked a whole lot nervous, as if he were trying to think of some way out of this obvious dilemma.

"It appears, Mr. Hoskins, these dog rescue women never saw Hubert before. And never saw you. And since she never had him, Hubert could never have been adopted out—not by you, not by anyone."

Bargain Bill swallowed hard.

"And it appears that your telling the good citizens of Wellsboro that he was yours is a very elaborate falsehood. In other words, you lied. To the public. That is not a good character trait for a man who sells used cars for a living, now, is it?"

Bargain Bill narrowed his eyes. Then he put on his best car salesman smile.

"Okay. You got me. Now what do you want?"

❧

Mayor Witt banged on the table a dozen times, thinking that the muffled gavel sounds were hard to hear over the general rumbling of the crowd. Slowly, they began to make their way back to their seats, virtually all of them now holding a white foam cup filled with Lutheran coffee.

"Okay, everyone, sit down. We're about to start again."

Hardly anyone paid attention, but eventually, the crowd quieted.

"Okay, now, we're back in session."

He hit the gavel on the table one more time, as if a gavel banging made a meeting official.

Before anyone spoke again, Bargain Bill stood up. He stood slowly, as if he really did not want to stand, but both Heather and Lisa were staring at him. Heather had taken her phone and held it where Bargain Bill could see it—just in case he decided to change directions on them.

Lisa reached over and grabbed Stewart's arm and hugged him close to her, and smiled down at Hubert and gave his head a gentle pat.

She leaned up and whispered something in Stewart's ear and Stewart responded with a most quizzical look.

Bargain Bill paced a few steps.

He started off by saying, solemnly, "Your Honor..."

"Mr. Mayor is fine, Mr. Hoskins. I'm not a judge. I sell insurance, remember?"

Bargain Bill offered a weak smile.

"Mr. Mayor..."

He grew silent for a long moment, and looked as if he were thinking deep thoughts. Then suddenly his eyes opened wide as if a wonderful new thought had entered his consciousness, a liberating, freeing thought.

He turned to the crowd and opened his arms.

"First, I am publicly stating that I, personally, will pay whatever fine, or special fee, the city council deems right to levy against the actions of this poor dog. And I will pay for every piece of merchandise that he took from the Tops Market. As owner and operator of Bargain Bill's Dynamite Used Cars on Route 287 at Charleston Street, I have always tried to do what is best and sometimes I let my heart get in the way of my head."

He looked down at his hands.

Heather leaned over to Lisa and whispered, "He's good."

"I can see that a bond has developed between the dog and Mr. Coolidge, who rescued him from the streets," Bargain Bill continued.

This is when Bargain Bill choked up and put his fist to his mouth as if he were holding back a sob.

"I have to admit to you—to all of you—my friends and family and customers and citizens of Wellsboro...that I have misled you. On purpose. A good purpose, but I have not been honest."

No one expected a loud, collective gasp to ripple across the audience, but that was what happened.

"The poor dog there...he was never my dog."

Another gasp, this one a little less gaspy.

"I lied to you. And do you know why I lied?"

He let the audience hang there for a long moment.

Heather leaned over again to Lisa and whispered, "I take that back. This guy is really good."

"I lied to try and save this poor American dog from death. I thought I could make a difference in a poor dog's life. When Mr. Arden began offering a reward, I was terrified that they would catch the dog and put him to sleep."

He paused, theatrically.

"And I could not live with myself if that happened."

He sniffed loudly.

"So, I made up the story that the dog was mine. To save his life. To make sure he had a home. And now that he has found a loving home..."

Bargain Bill's voice cracked.

"I am happy. He has found what he was looking for. A home."

The audience had been on the edge of their seats. Normally, to find this sort of emotion, people would have to pay twelve dollars for a ticket at the Arcadia Community Theater.

"We have saved this poor animal from death. And that alone is my reward."

And then the audience stood, a few at first, then most everyone, and applauded. Some even cheered.

And Bargain Bill raised his head and looked skyward.

This time Lisa leaned over to Heather and whispered, "This is great publicity for him, isn't it?"

Heather nodded. "He is very, very good. And this will make a dynamite segment. Absolute dynamite."

⟶

The mayor tried to bring the meeting back under control, but after everyone rose in their seats and began swarming over Bill and Stewart and Heather Orlando and Hubert, he decided that it was no longer necessary.

He turned to Paul Hatch, the city clerk, and nearly shouted over the noise.

"Issue a fine—or a fee, for one hundred dollars. Make sure

he pays for the stolen merchandise. And make sure the young man with the dog buys a dog license, okay?"

"Will do."

"And we can call this meeting closed, okay?"

"We can."

Stewart and Lisa hugged in the midst of the crowd while Hubert bounced and barked in happiness. Heather was busy signing autographs and having pictures taken with the mayor and every member of the city council. Even the Tops attorney, Robert Kruel, asked for a picture and an autograph. The Action News camera crew was busy getting all sorts of feel-good images of the dog and the citizens lined up to pet him and Bill Hoskins beaming and shaking everyone's hand—while passing out business cards, of course.

The only person who immediately left the meeting was Mr. Arden.

Once he saw that there would be no justice served, he stormed out in a huff, mumbling to himself about backwoods kangaroo courts and pea-brained elected officials, wondering if he could force a stock boy to remove all the posters and how he might mark that on the official time sheets that were turned in weekly to the central office.

Chapter Thirty-Two

STEWART ROSE exceptionally early the next morning, still excited and happy over the outcome of the previous night's meeting. He actually had had to go to the mayor, after he was done taking pictures with Ms. Orlando, and ask him what the council decided.

"That means I get to keep Hubert?"

The mayor, who looked as relieved as anyone at the meeting, grinned. "It means you keep the dog, Mr. Coolidge. But stop by city hall tomorrow and buy a dog license. It's eight dollars and forty-five cents. But two dollars less if the dog is—you know—fixed."

"Thank you, Mr. Mayor, thanks so much."

This morning, both Stewart and Hubert had been up well before sunrise. Stewart had his necessary cup of instant coffee while Hubert sat next to the kitchen table, grinning and watching him.

"Looks like we're a team now, Hubert. Officially."

Hubert started to wiggle, just a bit, and that wiggling backside had always preceded his full-bounce dance of happiness.

"You should be happy, Hubert. You don't know how close you came to being given to Mr. Hoskins. Or worse. Really. That could have happened."

Hubert was having none of that. His eyes indicated that he

never had any doubt that he and Stewart were somehow meant to be together.

"I bet you think it's all part of God's master plan for my life, don't you?"

At this, Hubert did bounce, and dance, and growl with happy growls, his backside almost overtaking his front paws as he maneuvered about the kitchen, his nails making small tap-dancing sounds on the smooth linoleum floor.

"How could you be so sure, Hubert?" Stewart asked. "I mean, you're a dog, and dogs don't understand faith and God and all that."

Hubert abruptly stopped all movement. He actually appeared hurt.

Stewart saw his eyes. He thought he could see a reflection of disappointment.

"You do understand?"

Hubert bounced and growled.

"And you know about God and faith and stuff?"

Hubert looked hard at Stewart, then began to bounce again, smiling.

Then the dog stopped.

"And this was part of the plan all along? Your plan?"

And Hubert danced and growled his way around the kitchen and did not stop until Stewart, laughing, got out his leash and put on his shoes.

Spring had turned to summer during the dog's thievery streak and the mornings grew warmer and the walks longer. Hubert trotted along, smiling, looking back over his shoulder every so often, as if to make sure Stewart was following him. When

Hubert saw that his walking companion was still with him, he smiled, and turned back to sniffing and exploring as they walked.

They walked along the nearly empty streets of town, and when the dawn colored the sky red, Stewart made a left turn and headed back home.

"Time for breakfast, Hubert. You hungry?"

Hubert bounced up and down, indicating that he might be nearly famished, even with the two celebrative real hot dogs he ate last night.

Stewart added a cup and a half of kibbles to Hubert's dish and Hubert looked back at him as if to ask, "Where are the hot dogs this morning?"

"Hot dogs are only for special events, Hubert, not a steady diet."

Hubert waited another moment, just to make sure Stewart was absolutely serious about that new dietary restriction that Hubert had not agreed to.

Obviously.

Stewart did appear totally serious, and Hubert methodically nibbled on his food, taking a long time to eat.

Stewart made himself another cup of coffee and was about to sit down in the living room and watch the sky brighten when he heard a very faint, very soft, tapping at his door.

Lisa stood there, in shorts and an oversized man's shirt, appearing as if she might have slept in those last night.

"Do you have any tea?"

Stewart heated water and Lisa greeted Hubert with a long hug of celebration, which Hubert appeared to expect that morning.

When the tea was ready, Stewart added twenty seconds of microwave to his coffee, so his coffee and her tea would be at the same temperature.

They sat in the two chairs in the living room.

Lisa sipped her tea and remained silent, appearing to be deep in thought. Stewart didn't mind. He just liked having her near.

"I have some big news," she said, almost with a hint of fear, or perhaps regret, in her words.

Stewart waited. He had a good idea what that news might be. His heart hurt, just a little, but he had steeled himself for every eventuality.

People leave. I have to accept that.

"Heather Orlando...she offered me a job. As her assistant producer."

"In Pittsburgh?"

Lisa thought Stewart was being funny and smiled, then realized he considered the question legitimate.

"Yes. In Pittsburgh. On the Action News team."

Stewart maintained a calm exterior, but his interior was suddenly in turmoil.

How do I respond?

"That sounds like your dream job."

"It is. It's not reporting, but I'll be working on a news show. This is huge, Stewart. Huge."

"That sounds great," he said, hoping he sounded truthful.

Hubert arrived in the living room, his chin still dripping water from his after-kibble drink. He looked at Stewart and tilted his head as if not understanding something. Then he looked at Lisa, stared for a moment, and whimpered. Then he lay down between them, a little bit away, so that he could see both of them without turning his head.

After a long period of silence, Lisa said, in a mouse-small voice, "Come with me."

Stewart had not expected those words, nor that request. None of it matched his daydreams of the past several months.

"But I don't have a job. I mean, I don't have a job in Pittsburgh."

Lisa leaned forward in her chair, suddenly very earnest. "You could work at a Giant Eagle store if you had to. Or you could go back to school at Pitt. They offer a degree in law enforcement. I looked it up last night. I couldn't sleep."

Stewart listened, totally unsure what to say next.

I guess they need bag boys in Pittsburgh, too.

Hubert whimpered and looked at Stewart with deep, serious eyes.

"But... what about us?"

Lisa's bottom lip trembled, just a quiver or two.

"We are a couple, aren't we?" Stewart added. "I mean... we're us, now. Right?"

Lisa smiled and nodded.

"We are, Stewart, we are. Us. Me and you. I love you, Stewart."

Hubert stood up and growled and whimpered and looked for all the world as if he were trying to tell Stewart something important. He walked over to Stewart and butted his thigh with his head, like he was trying to impart some wisdom to Stewart—or like he was simply telling Stewart to "wake up and smell the coffee."

Even if it was instant.

"Well..." Stewart began, then he paused.

Hubert barked, twice, very seriously, very firmly, and stared at Stewart, then at Lisa, and then back at Stewart.

"Well, I love you. So we should get married," Stewart finally said.

Lisa smiled. She more than smiled, but that was all her face could do that early in the morning.

"Stewart, that's what I was thinking, too."

Epilogue

LISA CLIMBED the steps to the apartment, on the third floor of a grand old Victorian—this one well maintained and freshly painted, in Shadyside, just to the east of the campus of the University of Pittsburgh, and only a fifteen-minute bus ride from the Action News studio. She walked softly, almost on tiptoe, and carefully inserted the key into the door, hoping it would not click too loudly.

She nudged the door open and peered inside.

Lying in a pool of afternoon sunlight, on the couch they'd bought at the resale shop in Wilkinsburg, was Hubert, his paws hanging over the edge of the cushions, his head resting on the thickly padded arm of the sofa.

He was snoring.

She crept up to the couch and sat down beside him. He snorked once, and raised his head, and when he saw it was Lisa, he smiled and growled a happy greeting, his tail wagging.

"Don't get up, Hubert."

He didn't.

She sat, quiet, next to the dog, stroking his side. Hubert's eyes closed. In a moment, Lisa was asleep as well, a quick afternoon catnap for the both of them.

Ten minutes later, the door opened again. This time it was not opened silently. Stewart walked in, wearing a gray police academy sweatshirt.

Lisa jumped up and hugged her husband and he hugged her back and Hubert stretched, allowing them to have their private greeting, which they apparently enjoyed, and then he slowly made his way off the couch, grinning and growling and dancing about the living room, surrounded by the two people who loved him and the two people whom he loved in return.

And at that most perfect of moments, at that most clear and wondrous of moments, the two most important humans in Hubert's world stood together, his world now complete—and he basked in the smile of his Creator in the warm afternoon sunshine on the third floor of a house just east of Pittsburgh.

Reading Group Guide

1. Hubert, the good dog, did not really have a human understanding of God—yet helped Stewart find his way to faith. Do you think God would use an animal—like Hubert—to draw people closer to Him?

2. It seemed as if all the main characters in the story had a painful past—Lisa, Stewart, and Hubert. Do you think that pain prevented them from finding the truth—or helped them find the truth?

3. Lisa assumed that Stewart had a faith in God simply because he had a Verse-a-Day calendar in his apartment. Was she simply fooling herself or did she truly believe that was all it took to indicate a belief in God? Does that say something about Lisa's spiritual maturity?

4. When Stewart "finds" Hubert and takes him in, he seems to realize that he is skirting the law, if not breaking it outright. Is breaking the law, or staying silent about a "crime," ever the proper thing for a believer to do?

5. Obviously, Stewart had some unpleasant experiences and

memories of the church that his mother attended after leaving the family. With that in his background, were you surprised at his willingness to go to church with Lisa? Or do you think it was simply an attempt to get closer to her without having any intention of paying attention to what was preached in her church?

6. Stewart's grandmother is an obviously controlling, negative person. How was Stewart finally able to stand up to her and establish his own independence? Was it his relationship with Lisa—or Hubert—that helped him most?

7. Lisa obviously had issues in her past that she was ashamed of and had promised not to let happen again. Do you think her mother was justified in reminding her so often of her past failures—and reminding her so often of the need to be careful? Do you think such reminders could have had negative, and unintended, implications for Lisa's behavior?

8. Hubert had a very painful and traumatic past—as evidenced by the scars on his head and back. But in his innocent and simple way, he simply chose not to think about those memories. Is that something we should strive for as well—saying no to unpleasant memories? Or do we have to deal with every unpleasant memory in some fashion?

9. When Stewart heard the sermon about the lost sheep, he didn't really understand it, nor did he think he was one of the lost. But yet the sermon helped him draw closer to the truth. Obviously, he didn't get exactly what the

preacher meant—and Lisa did not really push him to ac-
knowledge what that pastor meant. Was that wrong on
her part? Should she have been more "confrontational"
about Stewart's grasp of the true meaning? Would that have
helped him—drawn him closer—or pushed him farther
away? How much should we insist on "proper orthodoxy"
for those who are outside the church but are seeking to
come inside?

10. At the end, Stewart and Lisa decide to get married—almost
    as a spur-of-the-moment decision. Do you think that was
    wise? Should they have waited longer? Did Lisa truly know
    that Stewart had found faith?

Look for

THE DOG THAT WHISPERED

by Jim Kraus

Available from Center Street in Summer 2016 wherever books
are sold.

A preview follows.

Chapter One

GRETNA STEELE SHUFFLED past the television. She kept the set muted, but it stayed on for the entire day.

"Nobody in this 'retirement village' can hear worth beans. Why should I turn up the volume? I'm already being forced to listen to six other programs from every apartment on this floor."

What was being shown on the screen caught her eye. She shuffled to a stop and pulled the remote out of the pocket of her pastel housedress. She stabbed at the yellow button while pushing the remote toward the TV, to help push the electronic beam toward the set's electric eye.

She knew the extra push made the television respond faster.

The older analog TV, the size of a small refrigerator, barked into full voice.

Sad music was playing.

"No. Not sad. Plaintive. Manipulative."

Gretna often self-narrated the small events in her daily routine.

She leaned forward and narrowed her eyes. She had glasses somewhere, but seldom wore them.

"They make me look old. I may be eighty-five, but I don't have to dress the part," she often said.

The commercial continued. A series of dogs with sad faces appeared on the screen.

"Adopt one of these," the announcer said, with just the right amount of gravitas, "and you'll be making the world a better place for one lucky dog or cat. And yourself."

And then Gretna noticed something. The commercial was not the finely tuned, slick presentation of a national campaign. It was not a video done by some corporate animal rescue organization. This had to have been locally made and produced— perhaps by some volunteer at the shelter who happened to have a decent video camera.

In the foreground were two sad dogs, each apparently selected because they could emote maximum pathos. In the background stood another dog. This dog was black and active and bouncing and grinning and looking directly at Gretna, almost as if he was daring her to look away, to not be affected by the announcer's plea, smirking and wiggling and grinning cheek to jowl.

"That dog has guts," she said to herself. "He's not buying into their propaganda."

Then the black dog in the background stopped and simply stared, but his grin remained at half power. Gretna was sure the semi-happy beast was staring directly at her.

She thought for a moment.

"So where is this place, anyhow?"

And in a few seconds, the announcer gave the address. Twice. And asked for donations three times.

It took less than an hour for the taxi to arrive. Gretna climbed in, pulled out a small pocket-sized notepad, and made a most deliberate show of writing down the cabbie's name and cab number. She made sure the cabdriver saw what she was doing.

"Mizz Steele, you don't scare me. I drive you six times in a month," the driver said with a thick accent. Gretna thought it was perhaps Caribbean, perhaps Middle Eastern. Even African. He was from somewhere else and not here—of that Gretna was certain.

Gretna leaned closer to the Plexiglas partition, narrowing her eyes, determined.

"Maybe."

"I did, Mizz Steele. Last time, we go to de Giant Eagle. Remember? You paid in quarters."

"Maybe."

The driver, one Sharif Moses Yusry, sighed and put the cab into gear.

"Where to, Mizz Steele?" he asked. "De Giant Eagle again?"

Gretna scowled at the rearview mirror.

"No. I don't eat that much. Or spend that much. Who do you think I am? A drunken sailor?"

The cabdriver sighed, signaling that he knew arguing, or even adding a comment, was futile, but stopped when he reached the end of the circular driveway.

"So . . . where to, Mizz Steele?"

Gretna flipped the page on her notepad.

"Sixty-six twenty Hamilton Avenue."

Sharif did not pull out.

"What's there?"

Gretna scowled again, then responded with a more agreeable tone.

"You're a cabdriver, for heaven's sake. If you don't know

where it's at, then let me call for another cabdriver who does know."

Sharif slumped in the front seat.

"Mizz Steele, I know address. I know street. What will I look for? A house? A store? What?"

"And that's none of your business, actually. But if it helps you find the place without taking me on a wild-goose chase, then it's the Animal Rescue League of Western Pennsylvania."

Sharif remained still, even though his surprised expression was reflected in the rearview mirror.

"You adopt a kittycat?"

Gretna leaned back in the seat.

"Again, none of your business. But, no. I'm adopting Thurman."

⤙

Professor Wilson Steele set his cup of coffee down on the round kitchen table with precision—the very same table that had been in the kitchen since Wilson was a child: chrome legs and Formica top, the table surface mainly gray with a squiggling pattern of red and gray lines, which Wilson always thought looked like snakes, or some sort of 1950s virus, worn almost colorless in a couple of spots by several thousand meals eaten at those very places.

Wilson had rotated the table one-half turn fifteen years ago and now sat at a relatively unworn location, his chair still facing the same direction as it had when he was younger— the same direction he had always faced, since birth, the truth be told.

Or at least since being able to sit in a high chair.